D0247736

Bob Langley was born in Newcastle-upon-Tyne
and started his career as an insurance clerk.
After a period of National Service and three years
travelling round North America, he joined Tyne
Tees Television, first as a scriptwriter and later as
a presenter and roving news reporter. In 1969 he
moved to the BBC, becoming first a national TV
newsreader, and then going on to work on
24 Hours and *Nationwide*. He is now best known
as the popular presenter of BBC 1's lunchtime
magazine show, *Pebble Mill at One*, and of the
late-night chat show *Saturday Night at the Mill*.
Bob Langley is married and lives in the
Lake District, the setting of his second thriller,
THE WAR OF THE RUNNING FOX. He is
also the author of the highly successful novel,
DEATH STALK.

Also by Bob Langley in Sphere Books:

THE WAR OF THE RUNNING FOX
DEATH STALK

Warlords
BOB LANGLEY

SPHERE BOOKS LIMITED
30–32 Gray's Inn Road, London WC1X 8JL

First published in Great Britain by Michael Joseph Ltd 1979
Copyright © Bob Langley 1979
Published by Sphere Books Ltd 1981

TRADE
MARK

This book is sold subject to the condition that
it shall not, by way of trade or otherwise, be lent,
re-sold, hired out or otherwise circulated without
the publisher's prior consent in any form of
binding or cover other than that in which it is
published and without a similar condition
including this condition being imposed on the
subsequent purchaser.

Printed and bound in Great Britain by
Collins, Glasgow

Excerpt from Feasibility Study on the Invasion of the British Isles, carried out for the President of the United States by the Operations Special Research Board of the Central Intelligence Agency:

"In conclusion, the British, though by nature phlegmatic, do have a tendency, as the last war demonstrated, to unite strongly against a common enemy. In view of this, and bearing in mind the special relationship between our two countries which could well make overt hostility unacceptable to the American people, it is considered that an armed invasion along conventional lines would prove self-defeating. The recommendation of this Board is that the British system be subverted by Covert-Action Operations carried out by agents of mainly British Origin."

It's a strange sensation being hit by a bullet. For Farran, there was no pain, only a permeating numbness in his left shoulder like the effects of a dental injection. For some reason he couldn't immediately explain, he was on the ground and rolling fast, one hand groping instinctively for the Starfire .380 in his waistband holster. The wet pavements were shiny as fresh tar, reflecting the flames billowing over the rooftops of Notting Hill Gate. Sparks danced everywhere, transforming the night into glorious day.

Farran took a deep breath, catching the scent of burning rubber and timber. Footsteps clattered on the concrete. People were charging headlong in all directions. There was no purpose to their movements, just an aimless desire to escape the holocaust, and they paid no attention to Farran or to the desperate duel being fought on the pavement. Must think straight, he told himself, get the bastard who fired that shot before he gets me. He spotted the man facing him, half-crouched by the edge of the kerb, fumes whirling about his legs and chest as he perched in the classic firing position, both arms outstretched, carefully taking fresh aim. Farran felt his throat constrict. It was Toby. Jesus Christ, Toby. Nothing was making sense any more. Toby was supposed to be his friend. They'd trained together, gone through the miseries of Camp Fremont together, and now here was Toby getting ready to blast him into oblivion. He'd do it too unless he, Farran, got in first.

Farran fired once, quickly, not bothering to aim, and watched the gunman hit the ground in a tangle of arms and legs. He was on his feet in an instant, hurt but clearly not immobilised, scrambling along the kerb for his weapon.

This time Farran took his time, holding his breath as he squeezed the trigger. Toby seemed to jump into the air as if some hidden spring beneath his shoes had just been activated. He slammed hard across the bonnet of an abandoned car, his jacket open, his shirtfront an ugly blotch of blood. For a moment he hung there, face slack, mouth open, spittle glistening on his lips and chin, then with an almost reluctant grace he slid down the metal bodywork, leaving a smear of scarlet in his wake. Oh Toby.

Farran staggered to his feet. He felt sick, partly from fear, partly from a sense of betrayal. He touched his shoulder. Blood stained his fingertips, but not much. Was that a good sign or a bad sign? He shuddered, leaning against a shop window. People passed him in a rush, their faces bright with panic. Got to think, Farran told himself. Got to sort this out. Everything out of context. What the hell was Toby thinking of, trying to take him out like that, unless of course he was following orders. Was that possible? He swallowed hard at the thought. Jesus, he had to find somewhere to hide, somewhere to burrow. He had to get out. The game was over and he was through for good.

He turned awkwardly and began to shuffle back the way he had come, making for Shepherd's Bush. A convoy of fire engines went clattering by, their bells shrill and discordant on the smoky air. Fire engines, he thought, and grinned wryly to himself. There was something comforting in that. Something reliable, familiar. The world had not come to a total halt after all.

He was still grinning when he saw the second man moving towards him from across the street. This man was a stranger, small and dapper in a summerweight suit and brightly polished shoes. When he realised Farran had spotted him, his arm came up in a dizzy blur and Farran saw the .38 Special Colt Cobra glinting in the firelight, saw the burst of flame emerge from its nozzle and heard the bullet zip above his head with a sound like tearing silk. Farran tried to fire back, but nothing happened. The bloody Starfire had jammed. Christ. His nerves seemed paralysed, unable to move. The man was already

8

picking his way through the line of crashed cars at the kerb-side. Another second and he'd be close enough to blast again, and at this range it would be impossible to miss.

Farran turned and began to run, his shoulder jolting spasmodically with every step he took. He tried to merge into the crowd, hiding himself in the masses of terrified people. He would present less of a target there. Not that that would stop them, he thought. One death or a hundred deaths, it made no difference. They would wipe out the entire street to bring him down if they thought it was necessary.

Farran's breath choked in his throat. There was a sharp metallic taste in his mouth, and sweat oozed down his face into the grimy collar of his cotton shirt. He was trembling with fear and exhaustion.

He heard someone call his name and spotted a grey Fiat cruising close to the pavement's edge. The door was open, and Myriam was waving to him from behind the driving wheel. He frowned. Myriam? What the hell was she doing here?

Two negroes, their eyes rolling with fright, tried to leap into the car but Farran bundled them aside and slid into the passenger seat, slamming the door behind him. Myriam engaged the gear, rammed her foot on the accelerator and they shot out into the middle of the road. Farran sat gasping for breath as she glanced at him anxiously.

"You're hurt," she hissed.

His voice was barely a croak as he answered. "It's a set-up. We've got to get out."

"Hold on," she uttered grimly.

They ploughed along the Bayswater Road, picking a clumsy route between crashed automobiles and throngs of running, wheeling, desperate people. Farran thought he had never seen such terror and confusion. A man, his face shiny with rain, leapt into their path, frantically waving his arms. Myriam drove straight at him, forcing him to jump for safety.

Above the trees of Hyde Park, the orange reflection of flames, dancing wildly, spread across the skyline. Ahead, the Royal Lancaster Hotel blazed like a beacon. Farran could hear the distant clang of fire engines and the thin whine of a police siren.

"The city's a war zone," he muttered. "It's burning from end to end."

"You knew it would," she snapped. "Don't pretend."

"I didn't think . . . I didn't realise . . ." He gave up. It was the truth, but she would never believe the truth. Why should she? She was in it as much as he, except of course that unlike himself she didn't belong here, so in that respect at least, her responsibility was lessened.

They reached Marble Arch and found their route jammed with wrecked cars. Myriam picked her way through with delicate skill. Terrified people were crouching under the fountains as if afraid they would be engulfed by the flames which raged through the city. A group of students joined hands across their path, trying to force Myriam to a halt, but with her fist on the horn she kept on driving until they were obliged to break ranks.

An army landrover came streaking out of the Edgware Road and skidded in front of them. At the last minute, the driver spun the wheel and shot across the island, crashing headlong into the line of battered cars which blocked the road on the other side. One hubcap went spinning wildly across the concrete.

Farran, his sickness spreading, peered fascinated at the twisting columns of smoke. Above the rooftops, flames billowed between the street openings, setting chimneys and towers in stark relief. The entire sky had turned into a solid wall of flame.

Along Oxford Street the looters were out, smashing store windows, surging through the shopfronts like a swarm of vermin, hauling out furs, fistfuls of jewellery, furniture, vast quantities of spoils wrapped in curtains, rugs, polythene bags. As Farran watched, a police constable, his helmet gone, his tunic unbuttoned to the waist, tumbled out of Selfridge's doorway clutching a television set. Farran shook his head in disbelief.

"It's madness," he whispered, "madness."

"It's war," Myriam snapped, her face set with pale determination. "Revolution. It's what you've been trained for."

Farran let his head fall back on the head-rest. The numbness was fading in his left shoulder and now sharp jabs of pain were lancing into his rib cage.

"My God," he croaked hoarsely, "my God, how did it ever begin?"

ONE

The break-up of the British social system was not nearly so dramatic as some historians later tried to suggest, for the warning signs had been apparent from as far back as the early eighties. There was no reason – that is, no clear logical reason – why the economy followed such a hiccupping road to disaster though many people believed at the time the rot set in when the North Sea oilfields unexpectedly ran dry. This was untrue. The damage was done long before that, during the wave of elation which followed the inflationary crisis of the late seventies when public expenditure was pushed to unprecedented heights in a kind of amendatory reaction. The people had had enough of austerity and no one felt prepared, not even the politicians, to hold rising wage packets in check until someone could evaluate how true or false the new prosperity wave actually was. What it amounted to was a nation living on credit and, as any economist in this right mind should have foreseen, the crunch was bound to come. As the balance of payments deficit grew wider and wider, the government continued to lash out money with the compulsive frenzy of a boatload of Mississippi gamblers. The freeing of import curbs meant the shops were bulging with an avalanche of imported consumer goods. While a favoured minority were able to indulge themselves in this new tide of luxury, millions were pushed over the poverty line. Progressive income tax, the confiscation of lands and property, the legal occupation of teetering businesses wiped out an entire strata of British society, the middle classes. In Britain, as in so many other countries, there were soon only the rich and the poor.

New banknotes were introduced, though the pound itself began losing value at the rate of sixty pence a year. As the ensuing poverty began to bite, the workers reacted in the only way they understood, by going on strike, and this set up a chain reaction which plunged Britain on a spiralling descent into turmoil and confusion. The government's attempts to curb the trade unions only succeeded in escalating industrial chaos. Payments to the unemployed not only failed to alleviate their distress but brought about the collapse of the Treasury. The rationing of food, clothes, petrol and other commodities reached a lower-than-wartime level. The inflation rate rose to fifty-eight per cent, the highest in Europe. Unemployment reached a staggering thirty-two per cent, and violent crime trebled in the space of only eight months. Many basic services ceased to exist. London, for example, became the only city still maintaining a public transport system. Food was unobtainable without queuing for hours on end, and though the people did not actually starve, they seldom had enough to eat either.

The disintegration of the health and social security network caused large sections of the community to lose faith in the fabric of their own society, leaving them baffled, bewildered and filled with despair.

Of course, this despair was felt not only in Britain but throughout Europe and across the Atlantic too. On Monday, May 9th of that year, in Washington DC., the President of the United States called an emergency meeting of the Foreign Intelligence Advisory Group. Among those present were the Secretary of State, the Secretary of Defense, the Chairman of the Joint Chiefs of Staff, the Directors of Central Intelligence and the National Security Council, and the Deputy Director of the Foreign Operations Co-ordination Board.

It was a warm morning, but inside the Oval Room on the second floor, discreet air-conditioners kept the temperature cool and pleasant. The chamber had once been a study for Presidents Roosevelt, Truman and Eisenhower. During the Kennedy administration, it had been transformed into a Louis XVI drawing-room, and later still converted into an emergency Cabinet Room. Ship prints and early photographs of the White House lined the walls. Above the mantelpiece

13

hung Rembrandt Peale's famous portrait of George Washington.

The President was trying to appear calm, but the men who sat in front of him recognised the tell-tale signs of stress, the faint flush above the cheekbones, the drumming of fingertips on the desktop, an almost imperceptible muscle reflex in the right cheek.

"You know why we're here," he said, "so I'll try and keep this as brief as possible. I've had further disturbing news from Britain. They're calling for another General Election, the fourth in two months. The government looks like collapsing on its feet. We must reach a decision and reach it now. Do we go ahead as discussed, or pull out altogether?"

For a moment, the office was silent. The news from Britain had reached them all independently through their separate channels, and each of them knew, as the President knew, that the action they had argued over for more than five months had now to be either discarded or irrevocably set in motion. They sat without speaking, listening to the hum of the air-conditioner, the muffled ringing of distant telephones, the clatter of coffee cups in the corridor outside.

"If the British government does collapse . . ." the President began. He left the sentence unfinished, staring at each of them as if expecting a solution hitherto unthought of.

The Secretary of Defense finished for him. "They'll be one step nearer anarchy," he said, "and we'll be one step nearer the brink."

The President sat back in his chair. "When I spoke to the British Prime Minister by phone this morning, he sounded very depressed. The mood of the country is one of desperation. Everyone's looking for a way out, but nobody will accept the stringent methods needed to find it. They can't form another coalition, so the chances are they'll vote in some lunatic who claims he's found an answer, then vote him out again a week later when they find he hasn't. It's democracy gone wild."

"How the hell did they get themselves into such a godawfu

14

mess?" the Secretary of State grunted. "Britain's always been one of the world's most stable nations."

"Maybe they were too stable," put in Joseph Spengler, Deputy Director of the Foreign Operations Co-ordination Board. "Maybe they grew complacent, lost their sense of perspective."

"Joe's just back from London," the President explained. "He's seen conditions over there at first hand."

They stared at Spengler with sudden interest. Airports in Britain had been strike-bound for over two months, which meant that either Spengler had travelled by sea, or had flown by special plane to a US air base. If so, his mission had probably been on the direct instructions of the President himself.

"How was it?" the Secretary of State asked.

"Not pleasant," Spengler admitted, "but no worse than some South American countries I've been to. The trouble is, there's nothing you can rely on any more. Taxi cabs don't exist because gasoline's too expensive, so unless you live in London, just getting from one place to another is one hell of a headache. Most restaurants have closed down, and those which haven't maintain only the most meagre menus – you need a special visitor's ration card to eat there anyhow. The streets are filled with the unemployed. There's nothing for them to do, nowhere they can go. They sit about on street-corners or play soccer on waste ground. Like everyone else, they're baffled and bewildered."

He knew they were all thinking the same thing. What had happened so dramatically in Britain could easily happen elsewhere.

"Sounds frightening," the President whispered.

"It frightens the hell out of me, sir."

The Chairman of the Joint Chiefs of Staff noisily shifted his feet. He was an impatient man with a reputation for excitability. He too had watched the collapse of the British economy with alarm, but unlike the others he wanted no part of the thing they had come to discuss. He could still remember the ravages of the Vietnam war, and the quiet, almost casual way it had begun.

"Well, I don't see what we're going to achieve by dragging out past history. I mean, Christ, Warren, we're faced with a yes or no decision. Either we go ahead or we don't. Only let's keep this in perspective. What we're talking about is an ally – probably our closest, but still just an ally. Britain is not part of the United States. Jesus, we've poured aid into the British economy until it should be running out of their ears. I say we've had enough. Let's cut out before it gets too late."

The President sighed and drummed his fingertips on the desk. His face looked strained, the eyes overly-bright like those of a man in the grip of fever.

"It's not that simple, Sam, and you know it. We can't afford to sacrifice our military and strategic installations in the British Isles. We've been carefully monitoring and evaluating the Soviet military build-up of the past few years, and by any rational criteria, since it far exceeds what is needed for defence power, it must be seen as offensive in character. The American doctrinal position has always been based on its ability to counter-strike in the event of attack, but to do that we need reliable data on the Soviet missile movements. It's only through Britain for example, that we're able to monitor the Soviet submarine convoys sailing out of Murmansk. Analysis confirms that in the event of a Soviet strike, we still continue to have a cushion of warning time. That cushion is being compressed, but it still exists, and as a result our strategy is still viable. If we pull out and leave the British to their fate, the Soviets would soon gain total dominance in Europe. They'd be in a position to hit us any time they had a mind to."

The Chairman of the Joint Chiefs of Staff looked tense and determined. "Let's just understand what we're talking about here," he growled. "Let's get it out in the open. Revolution. The armed takeover of a country that's not only considered one of the most civilised, but has been our friend for close on two hundred years."

"I know, I know," the President muttered. "I don't like it any more than you do, Sam. For God's sake, my own great-grandmother was British."

"That's not what I'm talking about, Mr. President. I'm wondering whether the kind of operation we're considering here will actually work. Revolution in Britain? The British are by nature the most law-abiding people in the world. I'd call this the long shot to end all long shots."

"Well, we've done it before," the Director of Central Intelligence put in. "Back in the sixties, with less than a dozen agents, we instituted a friendly government in a country on the brink of communism."

"This is different, dammit. We're talking about armed insurrection. I don't want American troops drawn into a full-scale war."

The Director of Central Intelligence glared at him angrily. "Well, Christ, give me some credit for common sense, for Christ's sake. We're not planning to plant American agents over there. We'd be using British operatives only, trained in the US to our specifications."

"How long do you expect to keep a thing like that secret?"

"As long as it takes. If our estimates are correct, we can conclude this entire operation inside seven months."

"Well, I say it's insane. Jesus Christ, Warren, we could get our fingers really burned."

"It's either that, or get our asses blown off," snapped the Director of Central Intelligence. "Come on, Sam, don't give me that non-intervention crap. Without those monitoring systems, the Soviets would possess a first-strike capability against the United States, and that's something we can't, under any circumstances, afford."

He paused, breathing heavily, his face pale with anger. He hated losing his temper in public, but sometimes the inability of his colleagues to face the truth exasperated him beyond measure.

The President looked at his desk and then at the ceiling. "Why don't we ask Joe Spengler," he murmured. "After all, if we vote to go ahead with this thing, it'll be his baby."

Joseph Spengler sat back in his chair. He was a small man, but so slender that he looked almost elongated, as if his frame had been moulded in wet clay, then carefully stretched before it had had a chance to set. His face was long and sombre, with pointed features and a jutting chin. His clothes were neat and expensively cut, his fingers slender as a woman's and beautifully manicured. He displayed an economy of style and movement that seemed almost unnatural. People said he was like a computer, cold, efficient, and heartless.

"I think we've taken our non-involvement policy as far as it can go," he said. "The greatest danger to the British people at this moment comes from themselves. They've lost their sense of direction. The way I see it, there's only one route left open. We must take direct action. If you want an assessment of our success potential – well, I can't give a guarantee but personally I'd call it excellent. Nevertheless, when the shouting's over, the decision really, Mr. President, rests with you." He stared hard across the desk. "What do you say?"

The President sighed. He swivelled his chair to peer through the window. The water sprinklers on the lawn outside cast hazy rainbows in the sunshine. A gardener in dungarees was sweeping out leaves among the shrubbery. A solitary jet traced a lazy vapour trail between clumps of fleecy white cloud. The President turned back, his eyes weary and lined. He looked at them, folding his hands on the desktop.

"I say let's go for broke," he grunted.

Newcastle, England. Thursday, May 12th.

The skies above the river Tyne looked soggy with rain. On the opposite bank, the streets climbed in orderly rows, their roof slates black and shiny under the curtain of cloud. The river's slimy surface reflected the high arch of the bridge above it. Warehouses lined the waterfront, empty and still.

Farran stopped the truck and sat sweatily studying the road ahead. Nothing moved down there, not a car, not a van, not a cat. It was like a madman's dream of the future, a world without people where even the birds seemed muted by the ominous silence.

Massive cranes stood abandoned and unused like elongated skeletons. The dock strike was into its seventh week, but no pickets thronged the quayside. Merchant ships had long since given up bringing in their cargoes, for lack of payment and industrial unrest had discouraged even the most fervent ship-owners. Now the docks were a wasteland where no one wandered, a perfect spot for what Farran had to do.

He re-started the engine, and the noise was like an artillery bombardment on the still air. He bit his lip. If the scuffers were around, they'd nab him in a flash. Anyone with petrol to burn was suspect nowadays.

Farran nudged the accelerator and eased down between the warehouses to the quayside proper. A line of metal capstans prevented him going further. On his right, the river slid silently by, its surface muddy with sewerage. On his left, the huge sliding doors of an empty warehouse stared down implacably. Farran switched off the engine and lit a cigarette. At least he still had plenty of those, he thought. Tobacco, any kind of tobacco, was worth its weight in gold on the black market. People were smoking dried nettle leaves, carrot stumps, even shredded paper when they got desperate enough. Lucky for him, he was a survivor. Knew what he needed and how to get it. When things got rough it was the survivors who flourished every time. History proved that.

Farran did not think of himself as a criminal. In fact, most of his illegal activities were wrought by necessity rather than desire, and there was nothing in the world he wanted more than to be respectable. He had tried to make a success of his life through an assortment of ill-inspired business ventures but they had all crumbled into disaster. Partly as a result of that, and partly through his impassioned need for survival, he had spent seven of his thirty-two years in prison, two in the United States, five in Britain.

Farran was medium-sized, deep-chested, slim-waisted. His face was all angles and corners, as if it had been chipped out of the bone by a mad sculptor after a hard night out. His eyes were brown and moody. He seldom laughed. He gave the impression of an explosive temperament coupled with a sturdy strength which tended to discourage the irascible and querulous.

Farran sat where he was, listening to the hiss of the river and smoking his cigarette until he heard the roar of an engine and spotted a truck approaching through his driving mirror. He took note of the pale faces behind its windscreen, three altogether, and an extra special note of the registration number which tallied with the one he'd been given by telephone. Farran switched on his rear lights and switched them off again. The truck trundled to a halt. He sat where he was and waited. The doors opened and the three occupants clambered out. They were an oddly assorted trio, the first two short and stocky, dressed in heavy brown overcoats and white silk scarfs, the third lean as a beanpole with hair to his shoulders and a short waist-length jacket of sueded lambskin. He carried a haversack slung casually over his left arm. Farran stayed where he was until he was satisfied there was no one else, then opened the door and leapt to the ground.

"Jack Farran?" the first man grunted.

"That's right."

"I'm Walter, this is Ian." He made no attempt to introduce the man with the haversack.

"Hello, Walter," said Farran.

"Got the stuff?"

"Fourteen drums. The best."

"We've got to check that."

"Sod off," said Farran.

"Now, Jack, you don't expect us to take it on trust, do you?"

"I don't give a damn what you do," Farran grunted. "I'm not sitting around this craphouse one second longer than I have to."

"You could be ripping us off."

"You're a mate of Frank's," said Farran. "I wouldn't rip off a mate of Frank's."

The man called Walter took out a handkerchief and mopped his face. He was sweating heavily, but Farran did not know whether it was tension or the effort of walking from the truck.

"We'll take one at random," the man said. "That's fair."

Farran considered for a moment. 'Okay," he agreed. "Take

20

your pick. Only let's have a look at your end first. That's fair too."

The man called Walter turned to the thin one and nodded curtly. The thin man slipped the haversack from his shoulder and passed it across to Farran. Farran checked its contents. There were one hundred ration books, brand new, the printer's ink sharply defined in the pale grey afternoon light. Farran opened one up.

"Good forgery," he said.

"Good? It's a work of art."

"I could maybe use some more of these."

"That's all right. See Frank. He'll get in touch when he wants us."

Meanwhile, the thin man had clambered on to the back of the truck and was moving among its cargo. He selected a heavy dark drum and unscrewed its lid.

"Got a handkerchief?" he said to the man called Walter.

Walter glared at him. "Use your bloody tie, for Christ's sake."

The thin man hesitated, then carefully undid his tie. He looked at it for a moment, then back at Walter, then slowly and deliberately dipped it into the contents of the metal drum. It came out black and shiny. The thin man sniffed.

"Smells okay," he murmured.

"Diesel?"

"Yeah."

"What the hell did you think it was?" snapped Farran, "Champagne?"

"Now, Jack," said Walter. "We had to find out, didn't we? I mean, it's not as though we're old dear friends, is it? You've got what you wanted and we've got what we wanted. Now everybody's happy."

Farran didn't smile. "Get your truck over here," he growled, "and let's get this stuff unloaded. I'm getting jumpier by the minute."

They began to stroll back towards their vehicle and Farran stood watching, his nerves jangling and raw. I'm getting too bloody old for this game, he thought.

21

Suddenly, there was a screech of tyres and a black car came skidding across the open dockfront, the roar of its engine splitting the air like a siren. As it slid to a halt, all four doors burst open simultaneously and men spilled on to the quayside. Walter and his two compatriots stood in stunned amazement as they were quickly surrounded and thrust against the warehouse wall. Farran felt his stomach lurch. Scuffers, he thought.

He ducked fast through a narrow alleyway, running like a maniac, his heart hammering in his chest, his knees wobbly from the shock of discovery. He had to get out. Another minute and they'd have him, and that meant going back inside, only this time there'd be no home comforts. Once in there, survival would be ten times harder.

He paused at the alley opening and glanced quickly around. Metal rails criss-crossed the cobbled waterfront. Directly opposite, a narrow flight of steps led upwards between two tall buildings. Beyond it lay the street. If he could reach the street, they'd never catch him. He could mingle with the crowds, vanish into the background.

Breathing heavily, he scrambled over the rails and reached the foot of the stairway before anyone emerged from the alley behind. His feet clattered in the confined space as he took the steps three at a time. Fourteen tubs of diesel oil down the drain. What a bloody waste. It was miserable bloody luck for the scuffers to turn up like that, so unexpectedly, unless of course he'd been shopped, but that was hardly likely. Frank wouldn't give him away like that. Not Frank. There had to be some other explanation and after he got out of this, he'd bloody well find it.

A shadow fell across his path. Farran felt fear jolt him. Four men were standing at the top of the steps, big men, heavy-shouldered with battered faces.

"Hello, Jack," one of them said.

He tried to turn back, but his retreat was already blocked. The men at the bottom of the steps were almost identical copies of the ones at the top, hard-faced, solidly built, dressed uniformly in raincoats of either blue or brown. Farran felt his heart sink. They had him cold.

"Coming up, were you?" the first man said.

Farran climbed the steps. They made him lean against the wall while they ran through his clothing. Their hands were rough, thorough, expert.

"Let's go, Jack," the first man said. "We've got somebody who'd like to have a chat with you."

"I'm not in a talkative mood," growled Farran.

Someone jabbed him hard in the base of the spine, sending a jagged arc of paint through his vitals. He straightened, sucking in his breath.

The first man smiled. "That's better, Jack," he said. "No need for us to fall out, is there? I mean, you'll like this bloke. He's nicer than you're used to."

Farran stared at him as a slow realisation entered his brain.

"You're not police?" he muttered.

The man went on grinning. "Police? Don't be bloody silly. Do we look like scuffers?"

Farran didn't answer. He was desperately trying to think. If not the police, then who? Had he trodden on somebody's toes with that illegal fuel? He didn't think so. No one was that organised yet. The market was wide open.

"Come on, Jack," the man smiled. "Our party's waiting."

They walked out on to the street and along the pavement past the television building until they came to a pub with a big notice hanging outside which read: 'NO BEER. NO SOFT DRINKS'.

Inside, it was almost empty. A solitary customer sat at a table against the far wall. The barman looked at them with a baleful glare.

"Gin?" he asked sharply.

The big man gave Farran a nudge. "Come on, Jack. It's our shout."

"Whisky," said Farran.

The barman shook his head. "You'll drink gin or nothing. It's all we've got."

"Gin then," said Farran, and added: "No wonder this bloody place is empty."

The barman poured a measure and placed it on the counter. Farran picked it up.

"Go on then, Jack," the big man said, nodding toward the customer sitting by the wall. "He's been waiting for hours."

"Aren't you coming?"

"Two's company, Jack. We're only the delivery boys, aren't we?"

Farran crossed the floor and the man stood up to greet him. He was medium-sized, thirty-five or thirty-six years old, with neatly trimmed greyish hair and a skin that looked as if it had been tanned under a sunlamp. He was wearing a pigskin coat and gaberdine slacks. He smiled as he held out his hand.

"Mr. Farran?" he said in a voice that was unmistakably American. "Jack Farran?"

"Right first time," said Farran.

"Please sit down, Mr. Farran. I'm sorry about the little show of dramatics, but you're not an easy man to run to earth and my time is short."

Farran sat. Now that the first shock of surprise was past, some of his composure had returned.

"Who are you?" he demanded.

The man smiled again. "My name's Theymour, Horace B. Theymour. Here's my card."

The card said: 'Industrial Consultant', and gave an address in New York.

Farran drank his gin. "You've gone to a lot of trouble," he murmured. "I hope it turns out to be worth it."

The man went on smiling in an aimless sort of way. Farran had the uncomfortable feeling that the smile was fixed there for ever and would remain even when the man went to sleep.

Horace B. Theymour folded his arms and sat back, crossing his legs. "Mr. Farran," he said, "I have a little proposition I think might interest you."

From CIA psychiatric file on John Matthew Farran.

"Subject born Newcastle, England. Joined British army as boy entrant at sixteen. Served with Royal Marines, later with SAS Regiment in Aden, Borneo, Oman and Ulster. Emigrated to United States March 1972. Deported after two-year sentence for armed robbery Huntsville, Alabama. In 1974 was considered by Agency as possible inductee, but subsequently dropped."

From psychiatric report dated April 25th, 1974.

"Quote: 'Subject shows marked criminal tendencies which would, in the opinion of this department, make him a high risk factor in covert-action operations.' Unquote."

TWO

Washington DC. Tuesday, May 17th.

Myriam Coldman, twenty-eight years old, slim, blonde, long-haired and virginally innocent-looking sat in the anteroom of Joseph Spengler's office and stared at the posters on the opposite wall. They were travel posters bought at some souvenir store, one showing a gaucho roping a bull at full gallop, the other a group of snow-crested mountain peaks. Both blurbs read: 'Come to Sunny Argentina', and underneath the lettering, some wit had scribbled, 'Meet interesting people and kill them'.

Myriam Coldman worked as an assistant personnel officer in the Western Hemisphere Division of the CIA. Her job was an administrative one, largely office routine, though there were times, she had to admit, when she came into contact with sundry clandestine activities like the bugging of hotel rooms or the selection of agents for surveillance exercises. However, most of this was carried out on paper, which was just the way she liked it, for Myriam Coldman did not consider herself, by any stretch of the imagination, "suitable agent material". She was too innocent, for one thing. She even felt innocent. Devious people had little trouble in deceiving her for the simple reason that she approached all her relationships in life in the same manner, honestly and straightforwardly, and it never occurred to her that others might not do likewise.

She did not even possess the basic cunning most girls develop for the purpose of survival in the mating stakes, and her private life had been a long history of broken love affairs brought about by that fundamental innocence which somehow never tarnished and from which she was never able to escape. When a man said he could not live without her,

Myriam implicitly believed him because she would never dream of saying such a thing unless it were absolutely true. If the man happened to be married, it still did not occur to Myriam that the things he told her at night might be nothing more than a strategy, until of course the man went back to his wife leaving Myriam bruised and bewildered, which was what had happened on exactly four occasions. Still, Myriam's innocence remained unshaken. She did not intend to change just because the world and the people in it did not always live up to her expectations, which of course made her just too artless to be true. And that was why she was surprised to be summoned to the office of Joseph Spengler of all people, Deputy Director of the Foreign Operations Co-ordination Board, a division which specialised in infiltration, subversion and dirty tricks.

She heard Spengler's receiver click as he replaced the telephone and, getting up, she crossed the room, feeling a sour pall of apprehension spreading through her chest.

"I'm Myriam Coldman, Mr. Spengler," she said. "John Simons said you wanted to see me."

He was much smaller than she'd imagined, but very thin, so thin that his face looked as if it had been crushed between two metal plates. He was immaculately dressed, and the hands which rested on the blotting pad were small and delicate with slender fingers. Everything on the desk itself, and everything in the office seemed to fit neatly into place as if tidiness was his basic obsession. He waved her in.

"Sit down, Miss Coldman, this won't take long. Do you smoke?"

She shook her head. Spengler sat studying her for a moment, his eyes shrewd and thoughtful. He went over her from top to toe, not in the usual masculine way which she was used to and understood but with the cold appraisal of an X-ray machine. Suddenly, he smiled. It was meant, she realised, to be an amiable smile, but the eyes never changed and somehow the effect was ghastly.

"How are things in W.H.?" he asked.

"Peaceful, at the moment," she said.

"You've been with them now, let's see . . . three years, isn't it?"

"Three in September."

"Are you happy there?"

"Happy enough. I don't see it as my life's work, if that's what you mean."

He chuckled. "I'll bet. Sifting through personnel reports is hardly the most stimulating way to keep body and soul together."

He sat back in his chair. "How did you come to join the Company, Miss Coldman?"

She hesitated. "The Company" was how most employees referred to the CIA. Spengler was showing a disconcerting interest in her background.

"The usual," she murmured cautiously. "I was recruited at university. A man came out from Washington to see us about a junior executive training programme. It sounded exciting at the time. About thirteen or fourteen of my classmates put in for it, but I was the only one lucky enough to get through the course. That's if you can call it luck."

"You did, however, spend a good deal of your life – early life, that is – in London, England."

"Well, my father worked at the embassy there. We lived in London from about the time I was five until my father was transferred to Washington, which was on my fourteenth birthday."

"Is that why you speak with a British accent?"

"I imagine so."

Spengler nodded, looking down at his blotting pad. He seldom moved, she noticed, unless there was a specific reason for doing so, as if wasted energy was distasteful to him.

"Miss Coldman," he said, "I would like you to leave WH Division for a short while, and come and work for me."

"For you?" she echoed, startled.

"We are in the process of an important operation here," he went on crisply. "Correction. A critical operation, one which could have a direct effect on the world's power balance. I can tell you little more than that, I'm afraid. Because of the extreme sensitivity of this operation we must employ the 'need-to-know' principle and no operative can be informed of the activities of other members of his group unless it's absolutely necessary."

"But . . . I don't understand. Why me?"

"We need you, Miss Coldman. You could pass quite easily for an Englishwoman, and that makes you invaluable to us at this present time."

She felt dazed. She was Myriam Coldman from Personnel. This was something beyond her experience, the other side of the Company's business. Espionage. A wave of panic rose in her chest.

"Well, I . . . I'd love to join you, of course," she stammered, "but Mr. Simons is overworked already as it is. If I left the office now without a replacement, the situation could become chaotic."

"I've already talked to Mr. Simons. He's agreed to let you go if you give the word."

Myriam felt her confusion growing. There was something chillingly direct about this man. He clearly did not expect her to refuse and his assuredness only increased her own uncertainty.

"Would it be impertinent," she said, "if I asked what I'm expected to do?"

He shrugged. "Initially, very little. We're running a training camp for agents of British origin in the Adirondack Mountains. I want you to go there and take part in the course with the others. Most of it should come easy to you. It was included in your basic training. You'll be expected to get involved with everything except the indoctrination procedures. To all intents and purposes you'll be as British as they are. We'll arrange suitable cover. You'll keep your eyes and ears open, watch for dissidents, troublemakers, anyone who appears not to be responding to conditioning. It's as simple as that to begin with. There'll be other tasks later, but I'll brief you on those as they arise. The operation should take approximately seven months."

Myriam felt her heart drop. "Seven months," she echoed.

"Will I be away from Washington the entire time?"

"Probably. I may call you back on occasion, but only for briefing."

"It's just that . . . well, to tell the truth, Mr. Spengler, it's a little awkward at the moment."

He looked at her coolly. "You're thinking of your boyfriend, right?"

She felt her confusion disappear as a wave of indignation rose to take its place. What right did this man have to pry into her personal affairs?

"Is that a hypothetical question," she demanded, "or have you already checked me out?"

Spengler's expresssion never changed. "Don't get sore, Miss Coldman. I wouldn't involve my own brother in an operation like this unless I'd gone through his background like a shredding machine. Your young man works for the Company, doesn't he? Records Integration Division."

She nodded.

"In which case," Spengler said smoothly, "he must understand Company policy. It's in all our interests that you cooperate with us, Miss Coldman. His too. Seven months may seem like a long time now, but believe me, once you get started they'll whip by so fast you'll wonder where they've gone."

There was something unnerving in Spengler's confidence. She had the feeling he would sweep all objections aside in the same unfeeling manner. He was like a battering ram. She felt her resistance melt.

"Very well, Mr. Spengler," she whispered.

"You'll accept?"

She nodded. "If that's what the Company wants," she said.

"Seven months," Dillon shouted. "Jesus Christ."

Myriam looked at him helplessly as he stamped across the room. He had outbursts like this about a dozen times a night, though to be fair they were seldom so extreme. Dillon was volatile and explosive, a lumbering bear of a man with a passion for floppy pullover sweaters, ragged jeans and battered sandals, who had never really matured beyond high school and who would, she felt sure, burst a blood vessel one of these days if he didn't learn to control that mercurial temper. He was also unmarried, affectionate, loyal and kind and she thought she loved him. If not 'loved', she was certainly very fond of him, and love would come in time, she was certain. That was if Dillon didn't give himself a stroke or some other dire consequence of his over-heated nervous system.

"It's not so bad, darling," she murmured, "Look at that time you had to go down to Equador. You thought that was the end of the world but when you came back, it seemed like nothing at all."

"That was only three weeks, for Christ's sake," he yelled. "Seven months? What the hell are they playing at? You know I get nightmares when I sleep alone."

"You could move in with Foley."

"Foley snores."

"Well, you lived with him before you lived with me."

Dillon sniffed. "I didn't know any better then," he admitted. "I thought the whole goddamn world snored."

Myriam slipped her arms around his neck and kissed him lightly on the nose. "Come on, darling, seven months isn't so long. And I might be able to sneak back from time to time when things are quiet."

He stared down at her gloomily. He hadn't shaved for two days, she noticed, and the beard stubble on his chin and throat made him seem more than ever like a lumbering bear.

"Why you, for Christ's sake?" he muttered. "You're only a personnel clerk. This undercover stuff belongs to the field force."

"They need my British accent," she said.

He shook his head in wonder. "British agents training in the Adirondacks, on a course that includes indoctrination procedures. Christ, Myriam, what are those bastards up to?"

She smiled gently, pulling back to undo her bathrobe. Underneath, she was naked. Dillon stared at her, feeling desire surge within him. She laughed, taking his hands and placing them on her breasts.

31

"I've got seven months of celibacy ahead of me," she whispered, "and I absolutely refuse to spend the next few hours talking about the Company."

The plane took off from Bankshill US air base in Lancashire at 1500 hours on Monday, May 23rd. Besides Farran, there were twenty-five men on board and two officers in USAF uniform who were acting as stewards for the duration of the journey. Farran had no idea what their destination would be, for his discussion with Horace B. Theymour had been hampered by vagueness and evasion. In fact, he did not even know what he had been hired to do, beyond the fact that it involved soldiering, but Horace B. Theymour's offer for only seven months' work with no questions asked had been so sensational there was no question of turning him down. Theymour had been honest enough to admit that it involved a certain amount of physical danger, but that was all right with Farran, for anything which got him away from the austerities of Britain was a godsend, and he felt sure the other passengers on board felt pretty much the same way. They were a hard bunch to look at, untalkative for the most part, men accustomed to maintaining their own counsel and (though he couldn't be certain) he felt he had seen two of them before, during his second term of imprisonment at Brixton.

The plane levelled out at twenty-seven thousand feet above a blanket of cloud which effectively shut off Farran's view and made any attempt at guessing their direction, speed or terminating point utterly worthless, so after idling through his paperback Len Deighton, he settled down in his chair and went to sleep. On two occasions during the flight, the air force officers brought round food on plastic trays. They were friendly but uncommunicative, and when Farran asked one of them where they were heading, he smiled and tapped the side of his nose with one finger.

"We're only the hired help around here," he said. "They tell us even less than you."

Seven hours later, they were ordered to fasten seatbelts. Farran peered through the window. It was still daylight, though the pointers on his watch stood at ten p.m. The pilot circled twice then came in to land, cruising bumpily through heavy layers of cloud before bringing them down on an airstrip surrounded by softly wooded hills. Farran caught a glimpse of Nissen huts and what looked like a prefabricated aircraft hangar. An American flag fluttered from a nearby mast.

He joined the queue with the others, and shuffled thankfully out of the heat and smoke of the plane's interior into the air outside. A group of men in American army uniform stood waiting on the tarmac. One, a major, carried a clipboard under his arm. He was smiling.

"Welcome to the United States, gentlemen," he said. "I hope your visit will be a pleasant one. May I take this opportunity of informing you that the time here is precisely 4.10 p.m., and suggest you readjust your wristwatches accordingly. I realise you'll be tired after your journey, but if I may just check your names off my list here, we'll get you on your way with as little fuss as possible."

Farran stood in line with the others and waited for his name to be called. He wondered if Horace B. Theymour, or any of these other men realised he had once been deported from the United States and was officially listed in immigration records as 'undesirable'. Who'd have thought their destination would be America? He'd expected Africa, south-east Asia, or even some South American republic, but not this. Not that Farran really cared. A generous cash advance and the promise of more when the job was done had been enough to stall any misgivings he might have had about the future. Seven months. All he had to do was survive, and Farran considered himself an expert at survival.

One thing puzzled him. Apart from the two men he thought he had seen in prison, Farran felt certain, though he couldn't explain why, that the others were all ex-convicts too. They carried that air about them, that indefinable aura that only an experienced lag could discern. He wondered why.

When the name-calling was over, their luggage was unloaded and they were herded on to a bus with USAF printed on its side. For the next two hours they drove along deserted country roads, winding in and out of high tree-covered mountains.

Farran watched the countryside for a while, then lit a cigarette and offered one to the man sitting next to him. He was taller than Farran, bonily built with a hard hatchet face and closely cropped hair.

"Where the hell are they taking us," he muttered. "Siberia?"

Farran smiled thinly. "Christ knows," he said. "They don't seem in a hurry to get us there."

The man smoked his cigarette and peered gloomily at the hills outside. "It's like the end of the bloody world. I haven't seen a village or town since we got off the plane."

Farran shrugged. "Flight only took seven hours so we must be near the eastern seaboard. Those mountains look like part of the Appalachian Chain. It's too cool for Georgia. We're probably somewhere up north like Vermont or New York State."

"I thought we were bound for Africa," the man said. "They told me this was a soldiering job."

"Me too," Farran agreed.

He hesitated. "Mind if I ask you something personal? Were you ever in the nick?"

The man chuckled. "Half my bloody life," he grunted. "Durham, Wakefield, you name it. Once spent four years on the Moor. Why?"

Farran thought for a moment, then shrugged. "Nothing," he said, "probably just coincidence. I'm Jack Farran, by the way."

The man shook his hand. "Toby Wexler," he grunted.

They drove for nearly an hour more before turning up a narrow track which followed a switch-back trail into the mountains proper. Farran felt the air grow cooler as they climbed steadily. There was nothing to see but rolling hills and pine forests, an unbroken carpet of pine forest which stretched from one horizon to the other. Rivers twisted and gurgled among the trees. Tiny lakes lay like panels of snow under the slate-grey sky. Farran spotted a group of deer grazing by the roadside. They sprang up in alarm at the sound of the engine and went scampering off through the woods, their bunny-white tails bobbing cheekily.

Toward dusk, the ground levelled off and Farran saw ahead a collection of timbered cabins arranged in orderly rows around four central two-storey structures which looked like large warehouses with porthole windows. The central buildings were numbered one to four. A high wire surrounded the outside perimeter, and a sign above the gate said: "CAMP FREMONT".

The bus shuddered to a halt on a small parade ground. A tall clean-limbed young man in ski-pants and padded duvet jacket smiled affably as they filed into the mountain air.

"Good evening, gentlemen," he said. "Welcome to Camp Fremont. My name's Mac. I'd like you to call me that. Although officially we're part of the American army, we wear civvies and like to keep on first-name terms here. It helps to dispense with formalities and we seldom have time for those. I suggest you leave your baggage where it is and follow me to the chow hut. Our other recruits have already eaten, but the cooks knew you'd be arriving late so they're standing by to feed you. I'll try and fill in the blanks as we go along."

In the mess hall, they were served charcoal-broiled steaks with baked potatoes and tossed salad. For dessert, there was deep-cut cherry pie or ice cream with hot chocolate sauce. Machines at each end of the room offered iced water or chilled milk. After the deprivation of their last few months in Britain, the men stared at the food in disbelief.

Farran discovered he was starving. He sat with the others at one of the long tables and tucked in furiously while the man called Mac went through their daily routine for the next few weeks.

"Basically, you're here to learn," he said. "Try to think of it as going back to school. You're all ex-army men, so some of the things you'll study will be familiar to you: the use of weapons, explosives, ground combat training, general soldiering. Some of them will be new and strange. The first three days will be spent in Building 3. In Building 3, your thought pat-

terns will reach new dimensions, your prejudices and emotional hang-ups will lose their importance. It will seem as if a
curtain has been lifted to reveal a world many of you have
never dreamed of. Thereafter, you will attend Building 3 one
day a week for follow-up therapy. We rise at six-thirty here,
breakfast at seven sharp. Lights-out ten p.m. It's not our
policy to enforce a rigid code of discipline, but we do impose
rules, and our recruits generally stick to them. I'd appreciate it
if you all did the same."

He hesitated. "One other thing," he added. "We have a
small female contingent training here, and while we have no
objection to fraternisation, I would ask you to remember what
you came for. Mingle by all means, enjoy physical relations if
you must, but please, no serious involvements until our job is
over. Is that clear?"

Everyone nodded, and the man called Mac rose from his
chair.

"Okay," he said, "leave your dishes where they are and the
canteen staff will take care of the washing-up. We'll collect
your baggage and I'll take you to your bunkhouse."

The barrack hut looked no different from a dozen others
Farran had lived in at one time or another. The floor was pine,
highly-polished, with beds lining both walls. Beside each bed
stood a wardrobe and a small waist-high locker. Metal stoves
cast a blessed glow of warmth from each end of the room.
There was a smell of leather, floor polish, wood smoke and
tar.

"Choose your beds, gentlemen," the man called Mac said.
"When the bell goes in the morning, I expect to see you all on
the parade ground ready for action. In the meantime, sleep
tight."

Farran found a bunk near one of the stoves and dropped his
suitcase on the floor. He took off his shoes, lay down and
stretched himself wearily, his head on the pillow. He felt
whacked, his muscles aching from the long hours in the bus
and plane.

The man called Toby Wexler squatted on the next bed and
looked at him. "Did you hear what he said about Building 3?"

36

he muttered. "What the hell are they running here, a bloody torture chamber?"

Farran shrugged; a deep languor was seeping through his body. "At least they don't intend to starve us to death," he said sleepily. "At this moment, that's all I bloody care about."

Farran came out of a deeply satisfying dream to the sound of a bell crashing in his ears. Around him, men tumbled sleepily out of bed, gasping as the chill mountain air touched their naked skins.

"Jesus, it's still dark out there," somebody moaned.

Farran threw back the bedclothes and reached for his trousers. His brain felt soggy with sleep and the lingering effects of his journey the day before. He rooted through his bedside locker till he found his towel and shaving gear, then joined the throng of men dancing across the polished floor to the washroom.

The air was so cold it seemed to slide in under their ribs, chilling their vitals as they jostled each other to dip their razors into the washbasins or sluice icy water over faces and chests. Their breathing left clouds of steam on the frozen air.

"Why the hell can't those bastards get central heating in here?" Toby Wexler moaned, his pale face almost sick with cold.

Farran didn't answer. He was trying to cope with the discomfort of shaving in icy water, and blood slid down his cheeks where the razor nicked the frigid skin.

After bathing, they made up their beds and tumbled out to the parade ground under a sky filled with stars. Around the camp perimeter, the trees stood bathed in silvery moonlight. Frost coated the grass. The smell of hot coffee drifted in their nostrils from the direction of the cookhouse.

Farran peered about him with surprise. He had imagined the camp held no more than a handful of trainees, but the parade square was surging with people. Almost two hundred recruits bustled and scuttled as they lined up in ranks, their faces flushed in the early morning, their boots scraping the

37

concrete in a crescendo of sound. Orders barked harshly on the chill pre-dawn air.

Farran stood with the others and waited until the man called Mac came to collect them. He checked off their names on a clipboard, then led them to the mess-hut where they had eaten the night before. This time however, it was crammed with people. They lined the tables or queued at the hotplate, waiting to be served. Plates clattered, feet scraped. The room was filled with the buzz of conversation and a sense of muggy warmth.

For breakfast, they ate pancakes with maple syrup, steak and eggs with buttered toast and hot coffee. Bowls of fresh fruit stood at each end of the long tables. Farran gobbled his down hungrily, glad to be out of the stultifying cold. Through the windows the sky was rapidly paling, sending fingers of light across a world streaked with grey. He drank three cups of coffee and lit a cigarette, enjoying the novelty of being able to devour as much as he desired. After months of rationing, such a wealth of plenty seemed almost sinful.

With breakfast over, the other recruits made their way to the various training areas, and Mac reappeared to lead the new contingent across the brightening parade square to Building 3. To Farran's relief, Building 3, unlike their dormitory hut, was warm and pleasant inside. The air held a faint hospital smell, and throbbed with a low monotonous drumming as though some machine or other was ticking steadily close by. They sat on benches in an assembly area while a matronly woman in nurse's uniform called them one by one in alphabetical order. When it was Farran's turn, he followed her down a narrow corridor and into a changing room where cubicles lined both walls. She smiled at him encouragingly.

"Please step in here and remove all your clothes," she said, indicating one of the narrow compartments. "You'll find a coat hanging on the peg. Put that on and wait till I come back."

Farran slowly undressed. He felt no sense of trepidation at what lay ahead. The warmth and the rythmic throbbing in his ears had a strangely hypnotic effect. He was totally relaxed.

Naked, he slipped on the white coat and waited for the

nurse to return. She smiled approvingly when she saw he was ready, and led him into what appeared to be a doctor's surgery. The walls were white and scrupulously scrubbed. Shelves of bottles covered three walls, the fourth was taken up by a large plastic screen. A medical chart depicting a human skull with various parts of the brain displayed hung on the back of the door. The throbbing sound was stronger here, and seemed to reverberate gently up and down his spine.

Two men in white coats stood by a chrome-and-leather bench. One of them was small and elderly with a puckered skin and tiny button-like eyes which glittered when he smiled.

"Mr. Farran," he said, "I'm Dr. Forbes and this is my assistant, Dr. Smithson. We're going to put you to sleep for a while. Not a deep sleep, just a pleasantly relaxing state of inertia from which you'll awaken both refreshed and invigorated. Please don't feel alarmed. It's quite harmless, I assure you. May I ask you to lie on this bench and roll up your left sleeve."

Farran watched Dr. Forbes inject something into his arm. The doctor's wrinkled face and pleasant smile mingled with the persistent throbbing on the warm regulated air and made Farran feel dreamy, disorientated. He lay back, staring at the ceiling, waiting for the drug to take effect. There were thin cracks in the plaster, an intricate network of cracks which stretched from one wall to the other like a vast spider's web. As Farran watched, the lines blurred, lost their sharpness and finally disappeared altogether. He felt his body melting, his brain sinking.

Dr. Forbes leaned over him, peering into his face." Try not to resist, Mr. Farran," his voice crooned. "Let yourself go. Let every nerve and every sinew in your body relax. Leave everything to us. You're in good hands, believe me."

In Farran's brain, the world seemed lit by a splendrous sheen. It danced around him, growing brighter, filling his mind and vision with glorious reflections. It was so peaceful to lie here, to feel the bench beneath him melting away. Numbness crept along his thighs and forearms. He was dying. Passively, helplessly, happily. The blood was draining out of his veins, chilling his nerve responses, shutting off sensation, thought-processes, even existence. Nothing was real except the patterns in his head, and the soothing oblivion rising steadily to engulf him.

For the next eight hours, and again for eight hours the next two days, Farran, though he didn't know it, was put through a process which had found its roots in Pavlov's experiments in conditioned response in pre-communist and early-communist Russia. It had been developed slowly and painstakingly through the fumbling explorations of men like Zeller, Sarkisov and Wu Chuan-ching and finally perfected by the Chinese who used it with devastating effect in reshaping the thought-patterns of American prisoners captured during the Korean War.

The first stage of Farran's indoctrination was drug-induced. He was sunk into a state of high suggestibility in which the critical part of his brain, the subconscious censor which, in Freudian terms, stands guard over the id to prevent repressed feelings overwhelming the ego, could be effectively by-passed. When he was in a suitable trance, he was carefully wired-up with two electrodes attached to separate fingers on the same hand. The electrodes were connected to a device called a Galvanic Nerve Response Meter, a GNR, which gave readings on Farran's suggestibility levels, his body temperature and his pulse rate. Further drugs were administered throughout the day until Dr. Forbes was satisfied Farran's critical censor had been rendered totally inactive. Then the long hours of suggestion and ideo-motor confirmation began. The process was carried out both audibly and optically using vision-graphic impression films. Farran was first taken back to childhood, his fears, desires, sexual drives gradually exposed as his brain was made malleable like soft clay. Then bit by bit, his thought-patterns were gently refashioned with new stimulatory reflex points sunk deep into his defenceless subconscious.

By the end of three days, Farran and his companions had lost any semblance of morality they might have had. Their capacity for discerning right from wrong, good from bad, friend from foe, never particularly strong at the best of times, had been scrupulously destroyed, so that earlier allegiances toward country, government or ideology now ceased to exist. In three days, they had become the perfect revolutionary instruments, devoid of conscience or loyalty to any cause save the one they felt called upon, by some magical inner conviction, to support.

Needless to say, this major intrusion into the workings of their minds had a stupefying effect. They became dull and disorganised, almost zombie-like, sunk in a state of deferred shock. Out of the twenty-five recruits, only two failed to respond to treatment, and both were removed from the camp at the end of the second day. The others, while they slowly recovered from their ordeal, were put through a programme of physical conditioning, running, mountain-walking, callisthenics, weight-training and unarmed combat. At the end of the first week, they were taken once again to Building 3 where this time the quantity and severity of the drugs was reduced, and the use of vision-graphic impression techniques substantially increased. By the time the session was over, Farran had become an implement more deadly than any weapon. He lived for one thing only, to obey orders. Strategically aimed, expertly triggered, he would, without question or compromise, give his life to overthrow his former friends and country, and destroy what he saw as the corrupt, outmoded and opportunist elements who thrived on injustice and oppression.

THREE

The room was dark as Myriam Coldman closed the door behind her. She made no attempt to reach for the light switch. The gun in her fist felt ludicrously heavy as if it belonged on the back of some artillery wagon, instead of clutched sweatily in her tiny palm. She could almost hear the beating of her heart, the place was so silent. Almost. There was something just ahead, a scuffling, a sense of movement, some unidentified sound. Myriam's hand tightened on the pistol. Her nerves strained as she moved tentatively forward, trailing her left hand along the wall as a guide. The floor creaked beneath her foot, a loose board. She paused, swallowing. Nothing. No sound, no sign of life, only her frightened intake of breath and the dull throb of her own pulse.

Eeeyyyoooooowwwwww. The noise sent a spasm of shock along her spine. Directly in her path, a man reared like a pouncing tiger, his coarse face brilliantly illuminated in a flash of orange light. His eyes glittered evilly, the knife in his fist shining as its tip pointed at her jugular. She fired once, a reflex action. The gun almost jerked itself loose from her grip. She saw the spurt of flame. For an instant, the room's interior was lit by the blast and then, with a suddenness that was as startling as his appearance, the man vanished and she was plunged again into dark clammy silence. Weakly, knees wobbling, she leaned against the wall for support, gulping in breath. The abruptness of the attack had made her feel unstable. Breathing hard, she eased away from the wall and shuffled forward, eyes straining into the gloom. The noise came again, startlingly close, its high-pitched shriek resounding in her eardrums. She spun on her heel. Through the window behind her head, she dimly saw a man lean forward, shoulders hunched, face pressed against his chest as he carefully took aim at her stomach along the barrel of an Armalite rifle. There was no time for preliminaries. She fired from the hip, feeling the pistol buck hard against her waist, the heat scorching the skin beneath her denim jacket. Missed. Her heart pounded wildly. Without pausing for breath, she fired again and with a sense of deep relief watched the man and the rifle vanish into blackness. Two down, one to go. She was breathing more easily now, nerves still tense but with some of the apprehension gone. It was only a question of keeping her head. Simple as that. Play it cool, don't get hassled and, when the moment comes, shoot fast and make it count.

She eased away from the wall this time, moving into the centre of the room, and inched forward with one hand swaying in front of her like an insect feeler. Sweat beaded her face and throat. She could feel it trickling beneath her shirt, sliding down the valley between her breasts.

Eeeyyyoooooowwwwww. The noise jarred her senses, vibrating inside her skull. She spun wildly. Nothing there, only darkness. Panic engulfed her. It was a trick, a cold deliberate trick. The noise reached a crescendo, numbing her senses, stunning her brain. She wanted to fall to the floor, block her ears and scream for it to stop, and then in that instant she realised where the din was coming from. The ceiling. My God, he was up above.

She stumbled back, her spine icy. Crouched on the crossbeam, one hand holding on for support while the other aimed a Smith and Wesson .38 at the centre of her forehead, the figure looked breathtakingly huge. It seemed to fill her entire vision, blotting out the apex of the pointed ceiling. In a desperate effort, she swung her pistol in a rapid arc. Too late. The .38 barked once, twice, three times. She saw the little spurts of flame, then the screeching sound disintegrated into a low mechanical buzz, and as she stood gasping with anger and fright, the light switched on.

Without the darkness, the room lost its sense of menace. The figure that had just killed her dangled from the crossbeam like a tattered scarecrow. It was made out of some kind of sacking material, stuffed with straw. Its surface was punctured by ancient bullet holes. The door opened and the woman Myriam knew only as Julia came in shaking her head remonstratively.

'If this was for real, you'd be carrion meat by now. What did I teach you? Never rely on conventional attacks. The enemy can be anywhere and everywhere, and probably will. Like driving a car, think ahead, try to anticipate what he's got in mind. Your reactions on the first two were excellent. A little more concentration and I'd say you've little to fear.''

Myriam nodded, still breathing heavily with shock, and handed over her pistol. She stepped outside and joined the class of fourteen girls who had been watching her progress on a TV screen fed by short-circuit infra-red cameras. They burst out laughing as she came through the door, and she grinned with them. The Close Quarter Combat Hut, the CQC, had become a monumental stumbling block for them all, and so far no one had managed to pass through without being blasted by the electronic enemy.

"I hate that thing," Myriam grunted. "One of these nights I'm going to creep down here with a can of kerosene and set it on fire."

The woman called Julia stepped into the classroom. Like the others, she was dressed in blue denim overalls, her hair tied at the neck with a ribbon. She was smiling.

"Well," she said, "you may be interested to know that in the space of one hour, our entire strike force has been eliminated. I trust that when we return tomorrow, you ladies will be a little less governed by panic. I don't mind a casualty here or there, but to lose my entire Company in the first wave is a little high for any commander. Use your heads in future and don't be stampeded into rash reactions."

She peered at her watch. "Well, it's just on twelve-thirty, so you're free for the rest of the day. I'll expect you on the parade ground at six forty-five in the morning, and I want some cold-headed thinking tomorrow, understand? Meanwhile, have fun, y'hear?"

Sunday afternoons at Camp Fremont were devoted to

recreation. Recruits could choose for themselves from a list of activities which included football, basketball, badminton, squash, canoeing, orienteering, rock-climbing or hockey. Alternatively, they could choose to do nothing, which most of them did. The girls as a rule spent the time preparing for the weekly socials at the mess hall which, since there were nearly two hundred males to only thirty females were, from the ladies' point of view, a spectacular success.

Myriam strolled back to the bunkhouse and changed from her overalls into a pair of ski pants and a woollen jumper. She felt better now, relieved that the ordeal of the CQC Hut was over, and looking forward to the prospect of several hours' freedom. For some weeks she had followed instructions implicitly, taking part in all activities save those in Building 3. Then, she would be quietly spirited out through the side door and left to twiddle her thumbs alone in the barrack room for the rest of the day. She was always shocked when the girls returned in the evening. They looked so dazed and disorientated, like a group of walking corpses.

Sometimes, what was happening here frightened her. She couldn't understand why all her classmates had prison records, or what they were being trained for, or how long the course would continue. It had started with weapon training and field intelligence operations (including the recruitment and disposal of agents, the arrangement of cover and security requirements, room-bugging, telephone-tapping and penetration of liaison services). Later, they were instructed in sabotage, bomb-making, the distribution of propaganda, the disruption of basic services (such as food administration and water and electricity supplies) and the demolition of bridges, railways, airports and canals. It was clear to Myriam that sooner or later the schoolroom theories of Camp Fremont would turn into grim reality. But where and why? And what was the British connection? Spying disturbed her. She hated deceit of any kind, always had, and most of all she hated and feared the things they were being asked to do. If only it was over, so she could return to the peaceful security of her office in Washington.

The sun was warm and pleasant when Myriam stepped outside again. The morning frostiness had given way to a superb afternoon. Balls of fleecy cloud went scudding across a faultless sky. On the hill-slopes, the pines looked lush and green. There was the feel of early summer, a sense of the world renewing itself.

She found Jack Farran waiting for her by the main gate. She had met Farran during her first week, a strange man, moody, introverted, a curious combination of the sensitive and the profane, Farran was not at all like Dillon. He seldom lost his temper, though he carried an air of pugnaciousness that made you feel if he ever did it would cause an explosion that would carry on reverberating long after the initial blast had died away. She could never, she thought, call him handsome, not in any sense of the word. His features were coarse, almost vulgar. His face had the bony chipped look of a man who had spent his life fighting the vagaries of existence, and who would carry on fighting until he died, or collapsed from exhaustion.

In spite of herself, Myriam was strongly attracted to Farran. It wasn't simply physical, though she had to admit there was a good deal of that as well, but it was something she couldn't explain, not even to herself. Farran was unlike any of the men she had fallen in love with in the past, and he was the exact opposite to Dillon. Where Dillon was kind, Farran displayed a hint of subtle cruelty, particularly when he smiled. Where Dillon was voluble, Farran remained laconic, hiding himself somewhere deep inside that embattled skin. Where Dillon could explode at the drop of a hat, Farran simply smouldered, conveying an air of menace so acute that everyone within striking distance felt it and moved instinctively away. And yet, she had been drawn to him from the very beginning. None of which was good management of course. She had thought the complexities of her life already sorted out, and was waiting for her fondness for Dillon to turn into love. Now, in spite of her best intentions, Jack Farran had appeared on the scene to complicate things all over again, and she felt guilty each time they saw each other. Not that anything had happened, she told herself. Nothing physical anyhow. But she couldn't help thinking of Dillon back in Washington waiting for her return – patient, loyal, devoted Dillon. A man you could entrust your life to. Dillon would never betray her, and she knew the value of that, having been betrayed four times in the past. But then Dillon had never aroused the strength of feeling she experienced with Farran either, and somehow the two desires had moved into constant combat inside her, the need for stability and the need for excitement.

Farran was smiling as she approached. His smile always made her uncomfortable for it looked out of place on his blunt bloodless face.

"Got your swimsuit?" he asked.

She nodded.

"Then let's go."

They showed their passes at the gate and set off up a narrow winding trail that picked its way steadily into the hills. Trees crowded in around them, filling the air with the scent of pine sap. Sunlight played across the grass, sliding between the branches in golden shafts. Chipmunks danced warily from their path. Myriam felt good, felt glad to be out on this sun-warmed afternoon with Farran striding along beside her, his hand fastened on hers so that she could feel the strength in him, the dark pulsing power that seemed to generate through her fingertips. He moved like an athlete, with grace, never tiring, his long legs eating up distance as though his body required it for nourishment. He seldom bothered with small talk. Sometimes he could go for hours without saying a word and yet, the surprising thing was, his silences never made her feel uncomfortable. She'd always felt uncomfortable in the past when people didn't communicate. She was by nature a garrulous person, she liked to make contact, and if others withdrew her nervousness caused her to gabble inanely as if the prospect of silence would be too much to bear. But with Farran, it was different. She felt secure in his presence. Whether he spoke or didn't speak was immaterial. He was simply there, a fact you couldn't ignore.

Suddenly he stopped, pulling her to a halt. "Look," he whispered.

47

She stared. "What is it?"

"Bear."

She saw the dark shadow drifting between the trees, and in another second the animal shuffled into the sunlight, round and fat as butter, its black hair strewn with dried grass and broken twigs. She could see its eyes, yellow and small and cautious. She watched, fascinated.

"Think he'll attack?"

"Naw," said Farran, "he's harmless. Just looking for food."

"Can't we give him something?"

"Best not. Feed him and he'll follow you around all over the place. They get to be a nuisance in the end.".

The bear was rooting in the dust, scraping the earth with short staccato movements.

"He's beautiful," said Myriam. "Don't you think so?"

Farran laughed. "He's dirty and flea-ridden, and when he gets mad he can run faster than a horse and climb easier than a cat. Let's keep out of his way."

They moved on along the trail, following a zig-zag path through the trees until, after five or six minutes, they heard the tinkling murmur of the river just ahead. It was Farran who had discovered the rock pool two weeks before, an exquisite place where the river came tumbling out of the mountain into a perfectly shaped bowl, fifteen feet deep at its centre and so clear you could look down through the greenish water and see boulders gleaming sharp and white on the bottom. In the sunlight, it looked cool and inviting. Farran began to unbutton his shirt.

"Last one in's a cissy," he said.

Myriam slipped into her bikini behind the cover of some bushes. Farran never bothered to screen himself. He undressed where he stood, and she heard the splash of his body hitting the water as she tugged the woollen jumper over her head. When she stepped out into the sunlight, he was laughing at her from the pool's centre, his dark hair plastered wetly across his forehead.

She dipped one foot into the water, then took a deep breath and jumped. The pool closed over her head in an icy shroud, driving the breath from her lungs, numbing her skin and stupefying her brain. She rose to the surface gasping and spluttering. Farran was treading water, laughing out loud.

"Oh my God, it's freezing," she hissed.

"It's like chilled wine," he yelled, rolling on his back and kicking his feet in the air.

"Chilled is right. I can't feel my toes any more."

He swam forward and seized her from behind, thrusting his body against hers. "Let me bring a little warmth into your life," he murmured, clutching her breasts.

She laughed. "Unhand me, you raunchy beast."

She broke free, thrusting him away with her feet, and for several minutes swam up and down the length of the pool as the chill seeped steadily into her bloodstream. When she decided she'd had enough, she clambered on to the bank, shaking her hair, and stretching languidly in the warmth of the sun. Farran watched her from the water, his face creased with amusement. She listened to him splashing, the sound mingling with the flutter of birds and the almost imperceptible drone of a far-off plane. She let her body relax as the sun's rays washed over her skin like a warm shower. The scent of pine hung in her nostrils. For the first time in weeks, she forgot her troubles, her worries about Dillon, her uneasiness about Camp Fremont, and felt wildly, gloriously happy.

After a while, Farran climbed out of the pool and stretched himself at her side, breathing hard. His wrist, touching her own, felt like ice. "That's better," he gasped.

She opened her eyes and stared at the water. Sunlight rippled in its depths, picking out the shale and boulders, sending rainbows of colour along the glassy surface.

"I love this country," she whispered. "It's like . . . I don't know, it's just so different from Washington, so empty."

Farran grunted. "Empty's right."

"Everyone needs somewhere like this once in a while, to escape to."

He did not answer. His eyes were closed and he lay still as a corpse, the drops of water which beaded his skin sparkling in the sunlight like tiny diamonds. She stared at his face. In

49

repose, it looked less hard, less pugnacious – almost gentle, she thought.

"Jack?"

"What?"

"How long do you think we'll be here?"

He shrugged. "Long as they foot the bill, I ask no questions."

"You must wonder though."

"Yeah, from time to time."

"I mean, about what we're up to, you must wonder that."

"Obvious, isn't it? We're learning to fight."

She stared at him. "Who, Jack? Who are we learning to fight?"

He shrugged again. "They'll tell us when the time comes."

"I want to know now," she hissed. "I don't like being a cog in a wheel. I'm a human being, like you, and we've a right to know what we're being trained for."

He opened his eyes and peered at her. "Listen," he grunted, "stop worrying, will you?"

"I would, but . . ."

She hesitated. "We were in the CQC Hut today. Can you imagine it, fourteen girls in the CQC Hut? We're not a bunch of hairy marines, for God's sake. In any army in the world, women are used as nurses, ambulance drivers, orderlies, that sort of thing. Why are we learning to kill?"

Farran wiped drops of water from his nose. "When men die," he said, "it doesn't much matter who pulls the trigger."

"But don't you want to know what it's all about?"

"Why should I? At Camp Fremont I get three good meals a day, and a bonus when the job's over. I learned a long time ago never to let curiosity stand in the way of personal welfare."

She looked at him with exasperation. He wasn't a stupid man, she knew that, and yet how could any intelligent being allow himself to be manipulated with such disregard for the motives behind it? Wasn't Farran inquisitive at all, or had they taken care of that too, along with any moral sense he might once have had?

She sat up, hugging her knees. In the pool a fish, catching her reflection, darted for cover.

"Do you like me, Jack?" she whispered.

He stared at her.

"I don't mean sex. I mean . . . like me, care about me?"

"For Christ's sake . . ."

"What if I said . . . what if I told you I'm not who you think I am? All that about me growing up in Manchester, what if I said it was a pack of lies?"

"Huh?"

She looked down at him. "I'm American," she stated. "I was born in Billings, Montana. My parents still live there, in fact. The reason I speak this way is because I lived in London until I was fourteen. My father worked at the embassy there."

"You're not making sense."

"Can't you see? Everything I told you was a lie. I'm a plant, an agent. I'm from the CIA."

He frowned, propping himself on both elbows to look at her. Then suddenly he laughed. She stared at him angrily.

"You think it's funny?"

"Not funny. Common sense, that's all. They're not going to run a camp like Fremont without the odd informer here and there. They've got to think of security, haven't they?"

She felt her exasperation grow. Farran was falling over backwards to fit in with their design. He seemed to have no mind of his own.

"You're not angry?" she asked.

"Why should I be?"

"Because I lied."

"Christ, no."

"Jack Farran, doesn't anything get through that impenetrable hide?"

He chuckled and rolled over, catching her unexpectedly around the waist. "Now that you mention it . . ." he murmured, kissing her hard on the lips and tracing the outline of her breasts with one hand.

"Hey, cut that out," she ordered, crinkling her eyes at him.

"Crowding you, am I?" he whispered.

A wave of desire swept through her. This is crazy, she thought, the whole damned thing is crazy. The minute Dillon's back is turned, I behave like a bitch on heat.

Farran's hand slipped over the steep curve of her belly. Her breath quickened, her heart fluttering with the pressures surging inside her. Her throat felt congested. The world seemed to tilt, losing clarity and focus. His fingers moving between her thighs sent a warning light flashing inside her skull.

"Stop," she gasped.

"Come on," he whispered fiercely.

"Jack, no!"

She thrust his hand away and tugged herself free. Gasping for breath, she sat up, her whole body trembling. Farran stared at her in anger.

"What the hell's wrong?" he snapped. "The minute I put a hand on you, all hell breaks loose. You've got me so I don't even know where I am any more."

"You're too pushy, Jack, you take too much for granted."

She struggled to regain her composure. "I need time to think," she whispered.

He flopped back in the grass, anger tightening inside him. "Jesus," he hissed.

She looked at him, feeling his anger igniting her own. "You think that's all it is?" she snapped. "A quick scuffle in the alley, a hasty possession behind the bushes?"

"Don't start moralising, for Christ's sake."

"Moralising doesn't come into it."

She hesitated, and her voice softened. "I like you, you know perfectly well I like you, but there's someone else involved, someone who could be very deeply hurt. Until I'm sure in my own mind, we keep things as they are. In other words, look but don't touch. Okay?"

Farran didn't answer. He was lying on his back staring at the sky. Myriam sighed and climbed to her feet.

"Let's go back," she said, "I'm feeling cold."

They dressed in silence and walked down the trail, the hostility standing between them like an intruder. Even the sunlight sliding through the leaves failed to penetrate

Myriam's gloom. The happiness of the past hour was shattered. She was back to where she'd started, back with the inevitable tangle, the questions that plagued and tormented and demanded to be answered.

When they reached the camp Farran asked gruffly, "Will I see you tonight?"

Myriam shook her head. "Not tonight, Jack. I have to think. I need to sort things out. I'll see you tomorrow, in the mess."

She left him standing there and strode off without looking back, aware of his hurt, feeling the force of it through the back of her skull as his eyes followed her across the parade ground. But she didn't turn.

Why couldn't things have continued as they were? For the first time in her life, the world had seemed so marvellously uncomplicated. She'd known where she stood, the future had held no unexpected surprises. Now she was back to the same old mess.

As she approached the bunkhouse, she spotted the woman she knew only as Julia waiting for her by the door. Myriam felt her pulses quicken.

"Where have you been?" Julia demanded.

"Swimming," Myriam answered. "Why?"

"There's a flap on. You're wanted in Washington right away."

Myriam caught her breath. "What's up?" she whispered.

Julia shrugged and shook her head. "You know those bastards from FOCB. They don't tell us their little secrets. They've got a plane waiting for you down at the airstrip. You're to report to Spengler first thing in the morning."

FOUR

It was close on midnight when Myriam got back to Washington. She went straight to her apartment. Dillon was undressing for bed and peered up in astonishment as she walked through the door.

"Don't look so startled," she smiled, "I'm not a ghost."

She kissed him longingly, despairingly, moving her mouth harder and softer against his as though experimenting. He was panting when she let him go.

"Things must be pretty damn lean up in the Adirondacks," he grunted.

"Let's go to bed, darling," she whispered. She wanted Dillon to possess her, to drive out all thoughts of Farran, to set her back on an even keel by restoring the comfortable and familiar. But somehow it was all a mess. Even in the sweaty heat of sex, she could not drive Farran from her mind. The hard body clasped between her thighs became somehow Farran's body, and the longing which needed to be assuaged came not from Dillon but from Farran. At the moment of ecstasy, she almost called out his name but just stopped herself in time. Afterwards, as she lay in Dillon's arms staring at the ceiling, a sense of futility filled her, a feeling of remorse, for she had been unfair to them both.

All of this eluded Dillon who chattered happily away in his usual manner, glad to have her back no matter how temporarily, reassured by the energy and extent of her need, as if her body in bed was some kind of temperature gauge measuring the level of her love.

Myriam told him about Camp Fremont and about what was happening there. Like herself, Dillon was puzzled.

"Sounds like they're planning some kind of coup," he said.

"But why train solely British agents?"

"I dunno. Maybe the target's one of those small African countries where they want to restore a sense of the colonial past."

"With ex-criminals?"

Dillon shook his head in defeat. "Jesus," he grunted, "don't ask me. Whatever they've got in mind, you can bet you're only a tiny part of it. Just do your job and get back here as fast as you can. I'm starting to get my nightmares again."

He leaned over and kissed her, and tears sprang suddenly into her eyes. She pressed her cheek against his, feeling the warmth of his body, and the surge of fresh desire rising already within him. They made love for a second time, tenderly and sleepily, but the frenzies of the past had deserted her. She felt defenceless, her vulnerability growing with each second. Though Dillon didn't know it, she had to turn her face into the pillow to hide the tears rolling steadily down her cheeks.

Next morning, she re-packed her things and made her way to Spengler's office. She arrived at eight-thirty, expecting to find the place deserted, but Spengler was there already, sleek and groomed like a photographer's model, his thin face devoid of surprise or emotion. She had the feeling he never came out from behind his desk, that he lived there like some monstrous plant, fed and watered by his subordinates, performing even his bodily functions without removing himself from the swivel chair. His nasal voice made her skin crawl.

"How are things at Camp Fremont?"

"Fine," she told him, "although I have to admit I sometimes wonder what I'm doing there."

Spengler looked at her sourly. "Obedience is all we ask, Miss Coldman, but we require it without query or compromise."

She didn't answer. His smugness irritated her.

"I'm sending you to England," he said. "There's a plane standing by at the airport now. I want you to leave right away."

She looked at him in surprise. "For what purpose?" she asked.

He opened his drawer, took out a photograph and slid it

across the desk. It showed a man in his early sixties, pale-cheeked, silver-haired, with sharp features and a thin haughty nose.

"Ever seen him before?" Spengler wondered.

She shook her head.

"His name is Colonel Richard Savage, now retired. He achieved some notoriety in England a few months ago when he formed what he called the '300 Brigade', an organisation made up of professional sympathisers, doctors, accountants, businessmen and the like, who believe Britain's malaise lies in the inertia of its people. Savage wants the population galvanised back into what he calls the old standards, he wants to introduce a new sense of order and discipline. The British authorities regard him as a crank, but he does have the tacit support of some sections of the community."

Myriam felt her wrists turn cold. "Let me get this straight," she whispered. "You're sending me to England to see Savage?"

Spengler nodded. "He's expecting you at his country home tomorrow at noon."

She hesitated, staring at him in silence for a moment as the implications of what he was saying became clear. A terrible possibility had entered her mind.

"And this Savage wants to overthrow the British government, right?"

Spengler's face hardened. "I didn't quite say that, Miss Coldman."

"Is it true?"

"That's what you have to find out. You're going as the representative of Horace B. Theymour, a Texas billionaire who's desperately concerned about the deterioration of life in Britain, and who wishes to make a substantial financial contribution to any scheme the colonel may have for putting things right. Talk to this man Savage. See if you can discover how far he's prepared to go to establish this new order of his."

Myriam felt sick. It was not, she realised, that she hadn't suspected the truth. It was simply that for weeks she'd been putting the possibility out of her mind. The idea was so inconceivable that even now, hearing him say it, her brain wanted to reject his words. She took a deep breath.

"Mr. Spengler, are you telling me that all this, Savage, Camp Fremont, everything we're working for, is aimed at taking over the British Isles?"

Spengler sighed. He looked like a man in the presence of an idiot child, exasperated, waspish. Sitting back in his chair, he placed his fingertips together and studied her thoughtfully, as if trying to decide how far he should go.

"Miss Coldman," he said, "I told you in the beginning that the only safe security is compartmentation. We've tried to ensure that no one person realises the implications of the tasks he's assigned. However, you're now moving into activities which are difficult to carry out without knowing something of the background. The answer to your question is yes. For reasons of national security, we've decided this country can no longer stand back and watch Britain come apart at the seams."

"But the British are our oldest friends."

Spengler rubbed the bridge of his nose between thumb and forefinger. "I don't like this any more than you do, Miss Coldman. It's a dirty game, and none of us enjoy playing it. Without going into details, all I can say is, it's a question of survival. Ours as well as theirs. Now please sit back and listen to what I tell you, because above all you musn't foul this up."

Myriam sat in stunned disbelief as Spengler briefed her, going over the details of her meeting in England, explaining exactly what she had to do, outlining methods of persuasion, and the hoped-for aim of his department. Even when the lecture was over, Myriam still couldn't accept it. She felt as though something had got out of alignment, a small but terribly essential part of reality, so that she was existing not in the true world any more, but in a distortion of her own past and present. She thought about her childhood in London. She was American, not British, and yet this thing she was being asked to do was like betraying an integral part of her own being.

All through the long flight across the Atlantic, she sat mulling over Spengler's instructions, feeling trapped, smothered, an unwilling pawn in the dirtiest game of all. There were some things you needed to believe in, she thought, some things which must, above all else, remain inviolate, all the stabilising reassuring comforting things which had been drilled into her from childhood and around which she had structured her life. Now she felt soiled, contaminated. And what about Farran? Did Farran know? Did he realise what he was being prepared for?

She sighed, and sank back in her seat. There was nothing she could do, at least for the moment. She needed time, she had to think this out. Later, she might come up with an answer, but right now it was best just to get on with the job.

It was dark when they landed at Fleetcliffe US Air Base in northern Yorkshire. Waiting for her on the tarmac stood a man in the uniform of a full colonel. He touched his cap as she disembarked.

"Welcome to England, Miss Coldman," he smiled. "We have a room for you in one of our barrack huts. It's a little primitive I'm afraid, but it's only for one night."

He led her between the aircraft hangars and down a concrete path toward a maze of barrack blocks, Nissen huts and red-brick office buildings.

"We used to live in married quarters in the town," he explained, "but we've had to more or less barricade ourselves in up here. Since the food shortages began to bite, some of the locals resent the fact that we're getting provisions flown in direct from the US. Can't blame them, I guess, but it sure makes security one hell of a headache."

Myriam looked around. It was the first time she'd been in England for almost fourteen years. The air smelled fresh and clean with a hint of the sea. Strange, nearly-forgotten emotions rose inside her.

"Does Colonel Savage live nearby?" she asked.

"About ninety miles north or so. He has a house near the Scottish border, I understand. My driver will pick you up at my office at nine tomorrow if that's okay."

"Thank you, Colonel," she smiled. "That'll be fine."

Next morning, she was up bright and early. Despite her dilemma, she had slept like a log for almost eight hours, worn out mentally and physically by the events of the past two days. She breakfasted at the Officers' Mess, then made her way to the HQ Block. The colonel's driver turned out to be a curly-haired ex-cowboy from Caspar, Wyoming, who apologised for the fact that the station wagon was cluttered with cans of gasoline.

"We have to carry our own fuel, ma'am," he explained with a grin. "Filling stations dried up weeks ago."

They drove north, following a narrow country road between flat fields and stretches of open moorland. Rivers slid silently through lush rolling meadows. Farmhouses clustered the pastures, caught in the stillness of the early morning. Myriam felt glad to be back. It was like returning to childhood. Though she had never been this far north, the landscape looked reassuringly familiar, clearly and unmistakably British.

Thirty minutes later they turned on to the A.1, and Myriam peered in astonishment at the empty carriageways and lines of abandoned vehicles which cluttered the grassy verge. Their car seemed to be the only moving thing in sight. It was like careering through a world in which life itself had been eliminated.

"Is it always so deserted?" she whispered.

The driver shrugged. "Depends," he said. "Sometimes when the oil tankers come in from the Persian Gulf, you see a few automobiles on the road. Mostly army stuff though."

"The oil still gets in then?"

"Well, only in dribs and drabs. They have to unload offshore because of the dock strike. The Royal Navy ferries the stuff into port. It's a slow business."

They passed a nearby village, and Myriam caught sight of men and women watching them through dull sickly eyes. She shuddered.

"How do the people stand it?" she asked.

"Well, they're scared all right. Or maybe 'scared' is too strong a word. 'Confused' is more like it. They don't understand what's happening, and the more they try to protest, the worse things get. Strikes, demonstrations, they're going on every day of the week, but only among the politically orientated. The ordinary people just get on with the business of living. It's not as bad as it looks at first glance. Food supplies are low, but nobody's starving yet. They've got coal and electricity, and the newspapers are still being printed. You get the feeling society's crumbling, but it hasn't gone altogether, know what I mean?"

They left the motorway shortly before noon and the nature of the countryside began to change. The flatness of the earlier stretches gave way to rolling hills littered with straggling strips of pine. Myriam was filled with an overpowering sense of space.

"Where are we?" she asked.

"Cheviot Hills," the driver said. "Just south of the Scottish border. Sir Walter Scott country."

She peered through the windscreen at softly inviting slopes and steep grassy passes. A solitary horseman wound his way around the flank of a distant summit, a shepherd bringing in his flock. He seemed timeless, untouched by the seasons or the deprivations of the nearby towns. They turned off along a narrow road, the hills crowding in tight and close. Sparkling streams trickled down slopes of heather and gorse. Sheep grazed among the grass. They passed few houses and fewer people.

"It's so green," she whispered, "and so empty. I never realised such an overcrowded little island could be so deserted."

The driver grinned. "It's one of the most sparsely populated sections of the country," he told her. "Yessir, just like back home in Wyoming. I get nostalgic every time I come up here."

They bounced and jostled along for almost twenty minutes, and then, just ahead, perched on a bluff overlooking a small level plain, its gaunt walls silhouetted against the sky, Myriam spotted a massive grey stone house. Stark, grim and cheerless, it reared from the hillside like a spectral skeleton, sixty feet high at least, with walls that looked about nine feet thick.

"That's Colonel Savage's place, ma'am," the driver said.
They drove through the main entrance into a small central

courtyard where a butler with carefully groomed hair led Myriam along a maze of corridors to the colonel's study, a huge oak-panelled room lined with books, suits of armour, weapons, medallions and curios of every size and description.

"The colonel will be down in a moment," the butler told her.

Myriam felt overwhelmed by the solidity of the place. It looked as if it had been standing here since the beginning of time, and would go on standing long after Camp Fremont, Washington DC, the CIA and everyone in it was dead and gone.

She strolled along the wall, peering at the relics which hung there, swords from the field of Culloden, a silver urn from the Jacobite Rebellion, medallions from the Battle of Waterloo, a Spanish double-barrelled flintlock, a jewelled cloak clasp. Above the mantelpiece dangled an ancient sabre, its heavy blade almost worn away with age. Despite attempts to clean it, the metal had rusted in sections, and the handguard was beginning to split around the edges. It looked oddly out of place among the better-kept ornaments, and she leaned forward to peer at it more closely, wondering why it commanded such a prominent position.

"The Savage Sabre," exclaimed a voice behind her, making her jump. A man strolled into the room, tall, slimly-built, dressed in hacking jacket and heavy tweed trousers. She recognised him immediately from the photograph in Spengler's office. The lean face, the haughty tilt of the chin, the gleam of utter self-righteousness which shone in his small beady eyes, there was no doubt this was the man she had come to see. He stood by her shoulder, staring up at the sabre.

"Tradition has it that the ladies of our family used to serve it up at the dinner table when the larder was running low," he told her. "It was a signal for the menfolk to start their pillaging again. That was how we made our living in those days, Miss Coldman, by raiding over the border into Scotland. Blackmail, rape, looting, arson, kidnapping and murder were all considered an essential part of the social graces. And we had the nerve to call ourselves civilised."

He smiled as he held out his hand, and to her relief some of the haughtiness seemed to fade from his features. "I'm Colonel Savage," he said.

FIVE

"The Savages have lived in this house for generations," the Colonel said. "It was built at the end of the thirteenth century on the site of an ancient monastery. In those days, this whole area was a kind of 'badman's territory', rather like the American wild west. There was no law, or none to speak of, and the inhabitants were free to jump the border any time they felt like it and rob, burn, plunder and kill to their heart's content."

He moved, tall and dapper, to the window and pointed across the courtyard. "You see that stone cradle on the tower roof? They used to light a beacon up there to warn the valley when marauders were approaching from the north."

"Was this a castle then?" Myriam asked.

"Not quite. It was a fortified manor house, a pele tower as they were called. When raiders were coming, the locals used to bring their cattle and possessions into the central courtyard. Once inside, with the gates firmly locked, they were impervious to fire or anything else the enemy hurled at them." He smiled. "These walls were built to last, Miss Coldman."

"I can see that," she said, peering through the window at the great sandstone blocks, their surfaces rutted by a thousand years of wind and weather.

"Even if the gates got smashed," the colonel said, "all the defenders had to do was withdraw to the next floor and use that as a second front. The staircases are built in such a manner that should the inhabitants be forced to fight their way upwards floor by floor, their sword-arms will be to the outside, whereas the attackers will be obliged to fence against the restrictive proximity of the wall."

She smiled up at him. "That makes me feel so much more secure," she said.

She got to her feet, sipping her sherry, and joined him at the window. She felt pleasantly relaxed, lulled by her surroundings and the presence of the man beside her. He seemed so sure of himself, so unruffled and reliable. He was not a handsome man, but there was something appealing in the way he moved and the way he smiled. Despite his grey hair, he looked younger than his sixty years, and his cheeks were tanned and healthy. His body was thin, almost painfully so, but there was no weakness there, she felt sure of that. Only his features, proud and hawk-like, and the arrogant tilt of his head spoiled the impression of total amiability.

"Your glass is empty," he said.

"One's enough, Colonel, thank you. I'm not really a midday drinker."

"Good girl. Never touch it myself as a rule, not before four p.m. Sends me to sleep."

Myriam peered through the window again, staring across the gullies of wet peat at the rolling hills and the valleys bursting with woodland. There was no sign of human habitation. Despite its beauty, the land looked bleak and menacing. Distance and perspective seemed to thrust themselves upon her, bringing a new kind of remoteness.

"Do you never get . . . isn't it lonely, stuck out here day after day?" she asked.

The colonel chuckled. "Loneliness is an old friend of mine, Miss Coldman. There's nothing to beat the loneliness of command. I know that sounds banal, but it's perfectly true. You see, I never married. The army was my whole life. In the beginning it was lively enough – I was a bright young officer filled with ambition and hope, but after they promoted me to the higher echelons things were never the same again."

He leaned his shoulder against the window, one hand thrust casually into his jacket pocket, a man of such easy grace that everything he did seemed exactly right. It occurred to Myriam that he would make a perfect politician, or even better, an ideal front for some powerful business consortium. He looked so completely at home with his surroundings. She had the feeling he could never do anything that would jar.

"Besides," he smiled, looking at her, "these hills are never really empty to me. They're swarming with people; the old moss troopers, the marauders, Bothwell, Mary Queen of Scots, the bold Buccleuch who crossed the Esk with eighty men to rescue Kinmont Willie from Carlisle Castle. I'm a romantic at heart, Miss Coldman. I see these hills the way Scott saw them. He once said, 'I like the very nakedness of this land. It has something bold and stern and solitary about it. If I did not see the heather at least once a year, I think I should die.' "

Luncheon was a pleasant meal. They dined in a huge cavern of a room with polished stone floors and a massive fireplace where logs spat and crackled their lives out in showers of cascading sparks. The butler served venison in red wine, with roasted potatoes, stuffed vegetable marrow, poached leeks and shredded walnuts.

"You seem untouched by the ravages of the rest of the country, Colonel," Myriam observed.

He smiled as he poured her more claret. "I'm practically self-sufficient here, Miss Coldman. We keep cattle, sheep, geese and pigs. We grow our own vegetables. Even the electricity comes from my own private generator. On top of that, the forests are swarming with deer and the streams with salmon. In spite of the crisis, I continue to live like an English country gentleman, the finest life in the world."

He frowned suddenly, and without the smile his face looked older, leaner, more determined. She caught a hint of the strength which lay there, the tenacity that came from the belief, nurtured in him since childhood, that he was a member of a chosen race.

"You musn't think I'm unmoved by what's happening," he said. "The politicians have betrayed us, Miss Coldman. They've bungled the administration of this country in a manner that's nothing short of criminal. I've made my views public enough."

Myriam hesitated. It was time to make her approach, or at least to break the ice. First, she had to sound the man out, see if she could discover whether his beliefs could be channelled into an effective policy, or whether he was simply 'sounding off'. She would have to move gently.

"My employer, Mr. Horace B. Theymour," she said, "is deeply concerned about what's happening in England. You see, Colonel, Mr. Theymour's parents came from the west country. Although he is, himself, a Texan, he feels a strong communion with the British people."

Colonel Savage held up his hand. "Miss Coldman," he said, "it is extremely generous of Mr. Theymour to send you here, and to offer to fund any venture I may launch to improve the situation in Britain, but before you go any further, I think it only fair to tell you I am not, in any way, an admirer of the United States. In my view, much of the rot presently destroying this country found its origins on the other side of the Atlantic. It was the influx of American films and other insidious American influences which first perverted our traditional values. Pop music, sloppy manners, vulgarisation of language, peanut butter."

She stared at him, uncertain if he was serious or not. There was no sign of humour in his face. He was watching her closely, his bright eyes glittering. She said cautiously, "I don't believe Mr. Theymour would altogether disagree with you, sir."

Savage leaned forward, his cheeks flushed. "What we're witnessing now," he exclaimed, "this dreadful sickness eating our society is the result of years of conditioning. Our only hope is to remember who we really are, to return to the old truths, the old convictions. This country is being systematically destroyed by shirkers, communists and homosexuals. Unless we wake up to reality damned quick, we'll lose our last hope of salvation."

My God, he's a raving lunatic, she thought. Her earlier impression of grace and breeding vanished. It was as if the colonel had suddenly removed a mask. Nevertheless, she pressed on, choosing her words with care.

"With respect, Colonel, it seems to me that in the present circumstances, any solution would have to be pretty drastic."

"Absolutely," Savage agreed. "The Russians have always

been aware of that. When you have a cancer in your system, it's not enough to try and will it away, you have to cut the damned thing out, no matter how painful the operation. There are times, Miss Coldman, when democracy can be self-defeating. Freedom is admirable, but only when it's earned by blood and sweat. The British people have lost their backbone. They're floundering in the quagmire of past indulgences. The real trouble is, things aren't quite bad enough yet. They haven't really begun to suffer. When they do, hopefully they'll find their spunk again. If not . . ." He shrugged, leaving the sentence unfinished.

"What about this organisation of yours?" she asked. "The '300 Brigade'. Can't they help?"

The colonel shrugged again. "They're only a group of people who feel, as I do, that we've lost direction. We give each other solace, but little more."

"Still, three hundred sympathisers could create quite a pressure group."

The colonel looked embarrassed. "Ah well, that's only a figure of speech, Miss Coldman. The '300 Brigade' doesn't necessarily contain three hundred supporters."

"How many then? Two hundred? A hundred and fifty?"

Savage looked down at his plate, his face colouring. "There are fourteen of us actually."

"Oh!"

Myriam was filled with a desire to laugh. This whole thing was too absurd for words. Spengler had sent her four thousand miles to meet a man clearly in the throes of some mental illness. Damn Spengler. He needed to be taught a lesson.

"If you had unlimited means, Colonel, how would you set about putting things right?"

"There's only one way, Miss Coldman, and that's to take over the government. Not by democratic means either. The people are no longer capable of distinguishing sensible policies from madness. We need a new order installed in Westminster, a strong order."

"Colonel, are you saying what I think you're saying?"

He smiled thinly. "Revolution, Miss Coldman. Armed

revolution. This country must be taken by the scruff of its neck and shaken back to its senses."

"But revolution in Britain would be unthinkable."

"Why? It doesn't have to be a protracted war. Handled correctly, and launched at the right psychological moment, it could be over in a matter of weeks."

Myriam sat back and stared at him. "How?" she murmured.

"I'll tell you," said Savage. "Most insurgents would make the mistake of launching their attack in the cities, notably London. The key to the conquest of Britain lies here, Miss Coldman, in the north. As the leader of a revolution, my first move would be to establish control of the Cheviot Hills. It could be easily done. There are few roads and even fewer villages. A relatively small force could seal off all the vital approach routes. Of course, the army might drop paratroops, but as long as we controlled the roads, their effectiveness would be limited. Once the Cheviots were secured, I'd then do what the Romans did and drive a front straight across the narrowest neck of England to the Irish Sea. It's over barely inhabited countryside so there'd be little or no resistance, and once it was over I'd have sliced the country in two, shutting off Scotland from the rest of England and Wales."

"What good would that do?" Myriam asked, struggling desperately to keep a straight face. The colonel leaned forward, resting his elbows on the table.

"Since the collapse of North Sea oil, Miss Coldman, the Scots have suffered more than anyone. It would take very little to secure their support. With that established, I would then begin my drive to the south."

"Sounds like a long and bloody campaign, Colonel Savage."

Savage shook his head. "The government has already lost the confidence of the people. They remain in power only as long as they have the armed forces at their disposal. If a strong offensive was launched along the lines I've just described, I guarantee the British army would capitulate and join forces with the rebels. There'd be no question of fighting all the way to London."

Myriam sat in silence for a moment, studying the colonel thoughtfully. There was not the slightest doubt in her mind that he was mad, but her instructions had been implicit. Sound him out, and if he seemed committed enough, press ahead with her proposition. Spengler hadn't offered an alternative, and it hadn't occurred to her to say 'supposing he's a nut?' She couldn't help feeling Spengler and Savage deserved each other.

She said softly, "You've obviously given the subject considerable thought, Colonel."

Savage got up from his chair and walked to the fire. He stood with his back to the flames, legs parted, staring down at her like some ageing Heathcliffe. Crimson patterns rippled across his face and throat.

"Miss Coldman," he said, "you asked me earlier if I ever get lonely here. The truth is, I regard this as nothing more than an interlude in my life. I've always known where my true destiny lay. I was born, Miss Coldman, to restore this country to its former greatness. I remain here as a recluse, biding my time, waiting for the call, but I've never doubted, Miss Coldman – not for an instant have I doubted – that the call will come."

Myriam made her decision. To hell with it, she thought. This is Spengler's baby. Let him sort it out.

"Colonel Savage," she said softly, "please listen carefully to what I have to say. I think you'll find your call has come a little earlier than you anticipated."

When Myriam got back to Washington she went straight to see Spengler. He sat in silence, his pale thin face displaying no sign of emotion as she went throught the details of her visit piece by piece, describing her journey, her initial impressions of Savage and ending with his plan for dividing the country in two and overthrowing the government in London. "He's quite mad," she added.

Spengler's expression was inscrutable. "Oh, I don't know, Miss Coldman. Colonel Savage would give the people a focal point, something to cling to."

Myriam stared at him in surprise. She had expected Spengler to throw the idea out of the window. She had expected to be reprimanded for pressing ahead with negotiations with a man so plainly unbalanced.

"You don't seriously believe his crazy idea will work?" she muttered.

"With the right support, why not?"

"He's a screwball," Myriam uttered helplessly. "Even I can see that and I'm no student of military tactics. Colonel Richard Savage is suffering from manic-depressive insanity, an occupational hazard of his profession."

Spengler's eyes were cold and direct. He allowed no sign of what he was thinking to show on his face. "Leave the decisions to me, Miss Coldman," he said. "You've done an excellent job, and now that Colonel Savage's intentions have been established, we can set up our own liaison. Meanwhile, I'd like you to return to Camp Fremont right away. There's a car waiting to take you to the airport."

Myriam felt a stab of disappointment. She hadn't as yet seen Dillon. "Is that necessary?" she murmured. "I mean, couldn't I stay in Washington for just one night?"

Spengler picked up his pen. It was clear he considered the discussion closed. "Miss Coldman, you've been away from the camp long enough. The other trainees might start asking questions. Please leave your report with my secretary on your way out."

On the flight north, Myriam's brain was in a turmoil. She needed to sort things out, decide on what she ought to do, the *right* thing to do because this wasn't a nightmare she was involved in, but hard reality. It was crazy, too crazy to accept if she didn't know it for a fact, and that made it even tougher for God's sake, because who in the world would ever believe her, unless she could furnish proof? She'd become an unwilling instrument in the subversion of a country she regarded as her second home. What would the American people say if they knew what was going on? Surely they would never stand for such a flagrant intrusion into the affairs of a friendly nation. Did the President know? Impossible. Spengler had to be acting on his own initiative, there was no other explanation.

Unless she, Myriam Coldman, did something damned quick, got the news into the open, this whole godawful scheme would go ahead with chilling finality.

When they landed at the airstrip, Myriam made an excuse to go to the ladies' room. She found a telephone booth and dialled Dillon's number in Washington. There was a crackling sound on the line, then a voice answered, hoarse and unfamiliar.

"Dillon Harris, please?" she said.

"This is Dillon Harris speaking."

"Oh Dillon, this is Myriam."

The joy in his voice dismayed her. It brought back all the old pangs of guilt.

"Myriam? Where are you, for Christ's sake?"

"I'm heading for Camp Fremont," she said hastily. "Please listen, Dillon, I haven't much time."

Swiftly, and with as little hesitation as possible, she went through the events of the past three days, telling him everything, from her meeting with Spengler to her trip across the Atlantic and her discussion with Colonel Savage. Dillon remained silent throughout, but when she finished she heard him whistle softly at the end of the line. "You're crazy," he hissed.

"It's the truth, Dillon, I swear it."

"Even the Company wouldn't do that," he told her. "We've always had a special relationship with D16. Goddamnit, there's a signed agreement that no penetration programme will be carried out inside the UK without the knowledge of the British authorities."

Myriam felt hysteria threatening to engulf her. "Don't talk to me about agreements, Dillon," she shouted. "I'm telling you what's happening. I was there, for God's sake. I don't want to argue with you about what's true or untrue, I just want to know what's right and what's wrong. I'm going out of my mind, Dillon."

Dillon's voice was soothing, gentle. "Listen," he murmured, "don't worry about a thing, y'hear? Leave this to me. I'll check it out."

"Check it out?" she bellowed down the phone. "Check what out? For God's sake, what I'm telling you is *fact*, it doesn't need checking out. I want advice. Is the Company doing this on its own authority? Does the President know? What ought I to do, Dillon, tell me what to do?"

"Myriam, listen, calm down, d'you hear me? Just relax and take it easy. Go back to Camp Fremont and carry on with your training, and I'll see what kind of reaction I can dig up in Washington."

Myriam glanced through the glass panel of the telephone booth. She could see a man in blue denims tapping gently on the door of the ladies' room. She thought he looked familiar, one of the staff from Camp Fremont probably sent to collect her from the plane. She lowered her voice.

"Dillon, the driver's looking for me, I'll have to go now. I'll call you at the weekend."

His voice sounded anxious, concerned. "Okay, darling. And listen, just quit worrying, okay?"

SIX

Dillon had to admit he was disturbed. It would be easy to dismiss Myriam's story as the ramblings of an emotional over-wrought female hundreds of miles from home who might, just might, be starting to crack under the strain up there, for if there was one thing Dillon was sure of, it was that no one was less suited to covert-operation work than Myriam Coldman. She had never consciously deceived anyone in her entire life, which was what made Dillon wonder if the pressures of playing such an uncharacteristic role had finally unhinged her. She was not the most realistic of women. It was her artlessness that had attracted him in the first place. Was it possible, could she have gone crazy? But Dillon realised he was avoiding the truth. What he was really doing was looking for a chance to crap out. Myriam hadn't cracked. No one dreamed up a story like that unless it was either eighty per cent true or they were some kind of goddamned genius who ought to be making a fortune writing scripts in Hollywood.

The question was, what ought he to do? He was not, after all, a significant member of his own department. In fact, Dillon could not remember a time in his life when he had been significant at anything. Even his high school teacher had failed to recognise him when they'd met in the street last August. Dillon, despite his size, was an incredible nonentity, which he knew and was painfully sensitive about. He could hardly stroll up the steps of the White House and declare 'Dillon Harris to see the President'. On the other hand, Myriam had placed the ball firmly in his court and Dillon began to realise it was a terrible knowledge to be saddled with.

His first impulse was to share it. A problem shared is a problem halved, he thought, so he went to see his boss Bradford Gordon, Head of Records Integration Division. Gordon was a mild pleasant man in his early fifties who looked like a college professor and who had never, not in Dillon's experience, lost his temper or uttered an ill word about anyone, except perhaps Joseph Spengler. Gordon was sitting at his desk when Dillon peered around the door.

"You busy, Mr. Gordon?"

Gordon smiled. "Never too busy for you, Dillon, come on in."

He frowned when he saw Dillon's face. "You okay? You look kind of sick around the gills."

"I'm fine."

"Sit down. Get you some coffee?"

"No, I been drinking that stuff till it's running out of my ears."

Gordon put down his pipe, his plump face filled with concern.

"Dillon, if you don't feel so good, maybe you ought to go home, y'hear me?"

Dillon shook his head. "Listen, Mr. Gordon, I've got something important I have to talk about. I wouldn't do this normally, I mean I wouldn't put you on a spot like this, but you're the only person I can turn to."

Gordon sat back in his chair, folding his hands across his stomach. "Well, go ahead, Dillon. I've told you before, you got something on your mind, let's talk it out."

"Mr. Gordon, do you know anything about a plan to start a revolution in the British Isles?"

Gordon stared at him in silence for a moment. "Are you serious?"

"Absolutely, Mr. Gordon."

"No, Dillon, I don't know anything about such a plan, and I don't imagine anyone else does either."

Jesus Christ, thought Dillon. Sensing Gordon's disbelief, he began to talk faster, blurting out his words like a dying man trying to make his last confession before oblivion claimed him.

"Mr. Gordon, the source from which I received this information is indisputable. I mean I would trust this person with

74

my life, you understand. It was not just a rumour, but a statement of fact."

Gordon pursed his lips. "Well, Dillon, I suggest that this friend of yours, this 'source' is mistaken."

"That's not possible, Mr. Gordon. This person I am talking about is closely involved with the operation which is already under way, and which is being run by FOCB."

Gordon frowned. "Spengler?"

"Yes, sir. What's more, it may interest you to know that at this moment a team of British subversives is being trained for sabotage and guerrilla warfare in the Adirondack Mountains."

Gordon did not answer for a moment. He made a great show of cleaning out his pipe. He dropped the tobacco into the wastebasket and peered at Dillon worriedly. "I hope you realise what you're saying," he murmured at last.

"I realise it, Mr. Gordon. Jesus, I wish I'd never heard of the goddamn thing, but I'm stuck with it and I've got to see it through."

"Dillon, listen to me carefully now. This is some bag of tricks you're handing me. I've got to know who your informant is."

"I can't tell you that, Mr. Gordon."

"Then you'd better get your ass out of my office. If you're asking me to put my head in a noose, then I want to know where the story came from. Maybe the guy who gave it to you is some kind of nut."

Dillon hesitated only for a moment. "It's Myriam," he breathed.

Gordon stared at him in surprise. "Myriam told you that?"

"Yeah."

"I thought you said she'd gone home to Montana?"

"I know what I said, Mr. Gordon, but I was lying. Myriam's training in the Adirondacks for the takeover of the British Isles."

"That's fantastic," Gordon breathed.

"I know that, sir."

"I mean it's too absurd for words, Dillon. You know one of

the basic Company policies is no clandestine activities in the British Isles without the knowledge of D16."

"Mr. Gordon," Dillon cried, "this is not some little piece of scandal somebody cooked up in the washroom. It is taking place *now*, right under our noses."

"Okay, Dillon, take it easy. Nobody's calling you a liar."

"The thing is, Mr. Gordon, the reason I came here is, what do I do? I mean, the British are our friends, right?"

"Sure, Dillon."

"Is it possible FOCB are carrying out this programme without the Company's knowledge?"

Gordon pulled a face. "As far as the Company's concerned, anything's possible. I learned that a long time ago."

"Does the President know, Mr. Gordon?"

Gordon frowned. "Well, even Spengler, jumped-up little plutocrat though he is, wouldn't dare embark on an operation of such magnitude without the direct approval of the White House."

He hesitated, and Dillon saw the first hint of uncertainty enter his eyes. "Or would he?" he breathed.

Gordon tapped his fingertips on the blotter. All kinds of emotions were tumbling around inside his skull, and Dillon could seem them clearly. The changing expressions on Gordon's face were like a string of diverse TV commercials. He was, always had been, painfully transparent, which was one of the reasons Dillon trusted him. Gordon could never afford to be devious for his face was a mirror, betraying every thought that went through his brain. Dillon waited until he was sure Gordon was convinced, then he said, "See what I mean, sir?"

Gordon leaned forward, his cheeks suddenly pale. "Dillon, we've got to move carefully on this thing. We could be letting ourselves in for a good deal of ridicule. Don't misunderstand me, I'm not questioning the validity of what Myriam told you, it's just that . . . well, supposing she didn't get it exactly right, supposing there's more to this than she even suspects? We could end up looking pretty damned stupid."

Dillon stared at him coolly. "Mr. Gordon, we're talking about the subjugation of a friendly nation. I don't know about you, but if looking stupid is all I've got to lose, I think I know where my duty lies."

Gordon signed. "Okay, Dillon, don't make an asshole out of me. Listen, go back to work. I'll wander around and talk to Spengler, sound him out. Maybe he'll tell me what they're up to, maybe he won't. At least it'll give us something a little more concrete to go on. Is that fair?"

"Yes, Mr. Gordon, that's fair."

"Okay, quit worrying, Dillon. Leave this to me now, y'hear?"

But Dillon couldn't quit worrying. All through the afternoon he worked on his files, but his mind was elsewhere recalling Myriam's fear-stricken voice, her stories about the camp in the Adirondacks and the crazy colonel in his crazy castle, it was the stuff movies were made of. He waited for Gordon to call him back, but the call never came. At five-thirty he cleared his desk and drove home to the apartment through the evening traffic. He hated the apartment when Myriam wasn't in it. It was like a prison, caging him in. He'd always loved the place before, with Myriam's frilly bits and pieces strewn all over the bedroom, her stockings and blouses dumped unceremoniously on dresser, table or floor, her car keys, which she lost endlessly, cradled in the ash-tray or dangling from the wardrobe handle. She had no sense of order, but whirled into everything with the fury of a battering ram, hurling clothes and accoutrements in all directions. Dillon, despite his passion for floppy sweaters and casuals was a meticulous man by nature, a trait he was not especially fond of, for anything in his metabolism so diametrically opposed to Myriam disturbed him, and now that he had the apartment spruce and tidy he discovered that he hated it. It was like living in a mausoleum, he thought – cold, impersonal, devoid of life.

He cooked himself a TV dinner from the icebox, then settled down in front of the television set to watch the re-run of the afternoon ballgame, but somehow his mind wouldn't concentrate. All he could think of was Myriam's phone call. Why hadn't Gordon contacted him? Was he, Dillon, about to be reprimanded for speaking out of turn? Well, hell, he didn't give a damn. If they were really up to what Myriam claimed they were up to, then somebody had to start shouting his mouth off. Sometimes the Company behaved as if it were a law unto itself, and that bothered Dillon. Nobody should be above the Constitution, not even the President. And above all, nobody should be organising revolutions in friendly civilised countries, that was a sneaky way to behave. Why hadn't Gordon called? Even if he, Dillon, were in the doghouse he deserved an explanation. Surely anyone deserved that. He had a good mind to phone Gordon at home. Gordon was one of those men who kept a strict dividing line between office hours and leisure hours. He hated being disturbed in the evening, but dammit he should have called, he owed Dillon that.

Dillon got out his diary and looked up Gordon's number. He picked up the phone and dialled. A strange voice answered.

"Could I speak to Mr. Gordon, please?" Dillon said.

"I'm afraid Mr. Gordon isn't here."

"Do you know when he'll be back?"

"Who's this?"

"I'm – ah – my name is Dillon Harris. I work with Mr. Gordon. He promised to call me this afternoon. Is his wife there?"

The voice at the end of the line hesitated momentarily.

"Mrs. Gordon is lying down right now," it said. "This is Ed Richardson, I live next door. I guess you haven't heard the news, Mr. Harris?"

Something cold touched Dillon's skin. "News?" he murmured.

"Mr. Gordon had a terrible accident this afternoon. He fell down the elevator shaft at work. I'm afraid he was killed instantly."

"Jesus," breathed Dillon. He stood with the receiver in his hand, staring at the wall, his face stunned.

"Mr. Harris, are you still there? I'm sorry if it's been a shock to you, Mr. Harris."

Dillon put down the phone. He remained for a long moment

staring into space while shivers ran up and down the length of his body. Dillon was no fool. There were accidents and accidents, and what had happened to kind gentle thoughtful Mr. Gordon was nothing less than cold deliberate murder, of that he felt certain. Elevator shaft bullshit. How could you fall down an elevator shaft for Christ's sake? Dillon pulled himself together with an effort. If they'd grilled Gordon, they must know where he'd got the story from. Goddamnit, they could be on their way to the apartment this very minute. He had to get out fast.

Dillon grabbed a suitcase and threw in a few odds and ends, enough to keep him going for several days if necessary. He switched off the lights and TV set, and was about to take the elevator down to the underground parking lot when the thought occurred to him that they might be watching his BMW. Even if they weren't, they probably had its number. If he took the car, he could be easily traced. No dice, he thought. He needed to disappear, get out of sight until he had time to think this out. He changed direction and went down the janitor's staircase into the alley at the rear. He took a bus to the downtown Greyhound depot and bought a ticket to New York City. He had nearly an hour to wait before the coach was due to leave, so he found a phone booth, dialled the number of the *Washington Post* and asked for the Features Department. There was a click, and a voice came on the line. "Features here," it grunted.

"I'd like to speak to Sid Davidson," said Dillon. His hand holding the receiver was still shaking.

"Mr. Davidson is off-duty at the moment," the voice said. "Is this a friendly or a business call?"

"Well, it's kind of a mixture of both."

"Mr. Davidson left a number where he can be reached if the matter is urgent."

"Well," said Dillon, "I'd – ah – appreciate it if you could give me that number, ma'am, because what I have to talk to him about is very important indeed."

The girl reeled off a number and Dillon scribbled it on the back of a cigarette packet. He still had no clear course of action in mind beyond the certainty that so long as he kept his information to himself he was in deadly danger. He dialled again. A girl's voice, soft and seductive said, "Hello?"

"Is Sid Davidson there?"

"Who wants to know?"

"Dillon Harris."

"Hold on, Dillon Harris, I'll see if I can find him."

Dillon drummed his fingers on the booth window. He felt slightly nauseated, the tension inside him creating a hollow where his stomach should be. He peered through the glass at the other passengers thronging the waiting room, a party of nuns with neat little suitcases, a man and his wife having an argument by the coffee machine, two negroes in air force uniform, elegant and aloof, neither speaking to the other. After a moment, Sid Davidson's voice came on the line

"Hey, Dillon, how ya doin', old buddy?"

"Listen, Sid, I've got to talk to you."

"Well, it better be good, cousin. I have had a very hard day and am just about to smooth out a few wrinkles, know what I mean?"

"Sid, I've got a story, a hot one."

Sid sighed. "Jesus, Dillon, I hope it's better than last time. You put me in a very embarrassing position, you know that?"

"Sid, this is the biggest thing since Watergate. It'll make your byline a household name."

Sid chuckled. "Same old Dillon. Every time you phone, it's to transform my career. And I'm the kind of dumb son of a bitch who always swallows the bait. Okay partner, shoot."

Speaking tersely, Dillon went through everything that had happened. He told Sid about Camp Fremont, about Myriam's talk with Joseph Spengler, her trip to Britain and her meeting with Savage. He mentioned his discussion with Gordon and Gordon's subsequent death. He left nothing out. Every detail he could remember he included. When he had finished he listened to Sid breathing deeply down the line.

"Dillon," Sid exclaimed, "what kind of stuff are you feeding me here?"

"It's the truth, dammit."

"Truth? It's dynamite, Dillon. Are you serious?"

"Your're damned right," Dillon snapped. "Listen, Sid, a man is dead tonight because he didn't take me seriously enough."

"That was an accident, for Christ's sake."

"In an elevator shaft?" Dillon yelled. "Who falls down elevator shafts in this day and age? That's straight from Chicago, Sid."

The line was silent for a moment. Dillon could almost see him thinking, his round podgy face creased in concentration. After a moment, Sid said, "Look, kid, you can't expect me to print this without checking it out. They'll burn my balls off. I got to do some digging around first, okay?"

"Dig all you want," Dillon said. "Only watch yourself, Sid. Those boys aren't playing games."

"Where can I reach you? Still the same number?"

"No," said Dillon. "No, I'm getting out of town."

"You're kidding."

"Kidding, hell. I'm scared, Sid."

"Dillon, what the hell are you talking about? Things don't happen that way any more."

"Don't tell me how things happen," Dillon growled. "I know how things happen. I'll call you tomorrow at the office. Nine sharp. How's that?"

"Don't let me down, Dillon."

"Go easy, Sid," Dillon said, and hung up.

He slept through most of the journey to New York and arrived on 42nd Street at four o'clock in the morning. The sidewalks were drenched with rain and practically deserted. A pair of hookers huddled in a doorway hoping for a trick from the disembarking passengers. They made off when a police prowl car came cruising by.

Dillon spent the next few hours in the all-night coffee shop filling in time. When daylight came and he judged it respectable enough, he strolled down the block to the Travelodge Motel and booked himself a room.

Inside, he drew the curtains, hung the 'do not disturb' sign on the door and lay dozing on the bed for thirty minutes. At nine o'clock he called the *Washington Post*.

"I'd like to speak to Sid Davidson, please," he said.

"Who's this?" a voice enquired.

"My name's Harris. I promised to phone Sid at nine sharp."

"Well, Mr. Davidson won't be in today, Mr. Harris."

Dillon frowned. "That's crazy," he grunted. "He wouldn't let me down like that."

"Are you a friend of Mr. Davidson?"

"We were at school together."

There was a pause. Then the voice said, "Mr. Harris, I'm sorry to tell you Mr. Davidson was killed early this morning in an automobile accident."

"Killed?" Dillon echoed weakly.

"I'm sorry, sir. We'll be printing the story in our second edition if you'd like further details. Can I put you on to somebody else in the meanwhile?"

Dillon replaced the receiver. The room was spinning, its walls rippling in and out as if he was looking at their reflection in a fairground mirror. He got to his feet reeling dizzily, staggered to the bathroom and began to vomit into the wash-basin.

The first thing Myriam did when she got back to Camp Fremont was to see Farran. She was still in a state of some confusion, and worried too that she had dragged Dillon into this mess, for Dillon was like a child sometimes, he leapt into everything with the delicate finesse of a bulldozer. She should have waited, she realised, she should have figured things out first, given herself a breathing space instead of turning Dillon loose in a situation which, if the truth were known, was beyond him.

Farran, on the other hand, was different. Farran was a brooder, a man who never plunged into anything until he was pretty damned sure what he was up to, and if there was anyone in the world who could help her at this moment, Myriam felt sure it would be Farran.

She found him by the gymnasium, dressed in a track suit

with yellow stripes up the sides. He seized her immediately and pressed his mouth on hers, his tongue forcing its way between her lips. She tugged herself free, gasping hard.

"No, Jack, listen to me, this is important."

"This is important too, dammit," Farran growled, seizing her again.

Myriam thrust her palms against his shoulders, tilting back her head. "Let it wait," she whispered. "I've got to talk to you. Do you know where I've been for the past few days?"

"They said you were sick."

"Did you believe that?"

He frowned. "Well, I went to the medical bay but you weren't there."

"I've been in England," she told him.

"What?"

"They flew me over in a special plane."

"You're crazy."

"Not at all. I was on a mission for the CIA."

He stared at her, puzzled. "Hey, what is this?"

"For a department called the Foreign Operations Co-Ordination Board. Have you ever heard of that, Jack?"

"No," said Farran.

"You should. They're the people who're financing your little vacation here."

He released her. "How d'you know all this?" he demanded.

"I know everything, Jack. Everything there is to know. Listen, have you any idea what the FOCB specialise in? Subversion. Replacing hostile governments with friendly ones."

"Well?"

She took a deep breath. He had to be told. Telling Dillon wasn't enough. She needed support here too.

"They're sending you back to Britain, Jack. To start a revolution."

He seemed unimpressed. "Sure, they are."

"I'm not joking."

"I know you're not."

She stared at him in surprise. His face was calm, almost disinterested.

"You mean you knew all along?"

"Sure."

"When we were up by the river and I was struggling to figure things out, you knew then?"

"Yes."

She peered at him helplessly. "Jack, I'm talking about your own country. They want to overthrow the British government."

"Damned right. It has to be destroyed, it's corrupt."

He spoke tonelessly, like a schoolboy reciting something he'd learned parrot-fashion. This wasn't a person she was talking to, it was a programmed robot.

"Jack, you've been brainwashed so much you don't know who you are any more. Every week in Building 3 they tell you what to think. Do you understand? They're using you, Jack, you're just an instrument to them. They've taken you over like they'd overhaul a beat-up automobile. Don't let them manipulate you, Jack. You can fight that. Fight back."

He shook his head. "They're doing what's right, Myriam. Everything they say is right. Britain's going to the dogs and only we can save it. It's our sacred duty."

Myriam gave up in the end. Nothing could shake Farran's stubborn faith in the nobility of the thing he had been chosen to do. Though his natural functions carried on as normal, everything he thought or did was influenced by his dependence on the men who controlled him.

All through the afternoon she fretted, scarcely listening to Julia, the instructor. Whether she liked it or not, she was on her own. Her reservations about telling Dillon had gone now. Dillon was the only hope she had, and she prayed that for once in his life he would handle this just right. Nevertheless, the fact remained that here at Camp Fremont she was helpless and vulnerable.

When evening came, the woman called Julia called her from the dormitory. Myriam felt a stab of unease as they crossed the square, walking quickly, the fading sunlight dazzling their eyes. This was irregular, and any break in routine, any little thing at all, frightened her more than she cared to admit. Oh

Dillon, she thought, what have you done? If he'd run true to form, gone jumping in feet first, then they must know by now she'd been talking out of turn. Julia's face looked stern and determined.

"Where we going?" Myriam asked.

"Building 3."

"For what reason?"

"Just a talk."

It was not the first time Myriam had been in Building 3, but usually she was secreted out through the side door while the other girls went through their indoctrination sessions. This time, Julia led her down a narrow corridor into a large over-heated room with walls of stripped pine. Seating units in soft moleskin formed an L-shape around a central dais. On the platform itself, a trio of conical pendant lamps dangled over a leather-and-chrome medical bench. A doctor and two nurses studied her curiously as she entered, and a fourth man, medium-sized, compactly built, rose from his chair and took off his spectacles, cleaning them with a handkerchief.

"Miss Coldman?" he said.

"Yes."

"Sit down, Miss Coldman. My name's Howard Mackinson. I work for FOCB."

Myriam chose one of the L-shaped seating units. Every nerve in her body was tingling. She was uncomfortably aware of Julia standing close to her left elbow. The man called Mackinson replaced his spectacles and sat opposite. He studied her mildly.

"You have a friend named Dillon Harris, right?" he said.

Myriam felt something lurch inside her. She peered at the man, fascinated by his too-pale skin. It had an unhealthy, almost plastic texture, as though it had been moulded to his skull as an afterthought.

"Is something wrong?" she murmured.

"In what way, Miss Coldman?"

"Has anything happened to Dillon?" Her voice was shrill, unnatural.

The man shook his head. "Not that I'm aware of; he has, however, disappeared."

"Disappeared?"

Myriam's mind worked furiously. Phoning Dillon had been the action of an idiot. He had no control. He barged into situations with both barrels blazing, it was all he understood. Whatever he'd done, they must realise she'd betrayed her trust.

"He left his office two days ago and hasn't returned," Mackinson said. "As you know, Washington can be a violent town, Miss Coldman, and we've been working in close liaison with the police. However, if it makes you feel better, there've been no homicide victims fitting Harris' description."

"Thank God," Myriam breathed.

"The thing is this, have you any idea where Harris might have gone? Does he have any friends in different parts of the country, friends he might be inclined to visit if he were, say, disturbed about something? We've already checked all his known relatives."

Myriam hoped the man wouldn't notice her fidgeting fingers, or the thin sheen of perspiration on her cheeks and throat.

"Dillon doesn't have many friends," she said. "He's not a good mixer."

"In your experience, are there any particular places he's expressed a fondness for? Childhood memories perhaps?"

"Not that I'm aware of."

"In that case, have you any idea why he would take off without leaving a forwarding address and without contacting his colleagues or superiors?"

"He could have had a breakdown. People do."

"You mean a nervous breakdown, Miss Coldman? Is Harris an emotional young man?"

Myriam looked at him coolly. "Mr Mackinson, if you're from FOCB then I assume you already have a comprehensive file on Dillon. I think you can answer that question better than I can."

Mackinson sighed. He leaned back in his chair, crossing his

legs and studying her with a cool professional appraisal. Myriam felt her skin crawl. The smoothness of his face looked like scar tissue, bland and rubbery, not human at all. Only his eyes were real. They peered out of that shiny expanse like tiny beetles.

"Miss Coldman, you know what we're engaged in here?"

"Yes."

"It's an operation of the utmost delicacy. You've been chosen to play a part in that operation. For a girl who's spent her entire career in Personnel, that's quite a privilege. You do think of it as a privilege, Miss Coldman?"

Myriam didn't answer. Something about the man frightened her. His very blandness was a kind of threat, for she knew it was a game they were playing, a tactical encounter with the moves mapped out beforehand.

"When you joined the Company," Mackinson said, "one thing was impressed upon you through every day of your initial training, the need for secrecy. When you betray the Company, Miss Coldman, you betray your country, too."

Myriam felt a surge of indignation. "Hold on, Mr. Mackinson, maybe I'm naive, but I don't see anything in the Bill of Rights which says I have to help in the suppression of a nation with whom we're not at war."

Mackinson glared at her. "Since when did you have the authority to make pronouncements on matters of national policy? Just who do you think you are, Miss Coldman? God?"

"I think I'm the only one around here with any shred of conscience at all," Myriam snapped.

"Conscience?" echoed Mackinson. "What's conscience? We're pro's, Miss Coldman, we can't afford such luxuries."

He looked at the others, as if calling on them to witness her ingratitude. "You're a disappointment to us, Miss Coldman. To Mr. Spengler, to the department. If I had my way, you'd be neutralised immediately. As it happens, you're needed for more urgent work ahead. Until this moment, we've taken your loyalty as a Company employee for granted. That's all changed now. Dr. Forbes?"

Before Myriam realised what was happening, Julia stepped

behind her seat and seized her in a vicious neck lock. Gasping for breath, Myriam struggled hard. "Don't touch me," she hissed.

One of the nurses began rolling up her left sleeve. Myriam tugged her arm free and swung it in a wild arc, missing the nurse's jaw by a hair's breadth. Julia intensified the pressure on her throat as Myriam choked desperately for air. "Hold still, damn you," Julia snarled.

Trapped and helpless, Myriam watched the needle slide into her defenceless vein. She watched the doctor pumping the drug into her system. The room blurred, lost its clarity. She was floating somewhere just below the ceiling looking down on the scene below. They were lifting her onto the medical bench. Fools. Didn't they realise she wasn't there any more. She was up here, hovering above their heads, and they couldn't even see it. She had to laugh at that. She opened her mouth and began to chuckle, letting herself go, accepting peacefully as oblivion took her.

Myriam remained in Building 3 for five days and five nights. When she was finally returned to the dormitory hut, she had to be led by the hand as though she were blind. For hour after hour, she sat on her bunk staring into space, her eyes devoid of emotion. The other girls tried to coax her through the routine tasks of day-to-day living, but their words had no effect. She sat peering at the wall, all traces of normality drained from her, benumbed and indifferent like a mindless unanimated corpse.

SEVEN

Greece, Thursday July 21st.

The Athens office of the Kozani Shipping Company looked across the old part of town, commanding a fine view of the Acropolis and the blue skies beyond. Horace B. Theymour scarcely noticed the scenery, however, or the sunlight slanting off the foliage which tumbled over the balcony outside. His attention was focused on the man sitting in front of him, small, dapper, heavily jewelled, sixty-eight years old, Bonacas Kozani, sole-owner of one of the largest merchant shipping fleets in the world.

"Let me explain why I'm here," Theymour said, crossing his legs with a smile. "I represent the government of the Island of Taigu in the Indian Ocean. You may or may not be aware that Taigu is suffering its worst drought for several centuries, with the people facing the ravages of famine. We need food supplies urgently. Unfortunately, our own shipping fleet is much too tiny to cope with the demands of a starving population. I would therefore like to charter as many of your vessels as is practical until our crisis is over."

Kozani looked grieved. His eyes moistened as if from pain, and for a moment Theymour had the feeling he was going to cry.

"I have read of the drought in Taigu," said Kozani, "and sympathise with those who are suffering there. Unfortunately, sympathy is all I can offer. My ships are being used to ferry food to Britain. The British merchant fleet has been immobilised by industrial action and though the Royal Navy is running an emergency shuttle service, they can only concentrate on the barest essentials. Without my support, Mr. Theymour, Britain would be dangerously near starvation level."

Theymour kept his voice deliberately casual. "Your sense of duty toward the British government must be very strong," he said.

"It is not a question of duty, Mr. Theymour, but of humanity. Governments do not concern me. People do."

"The inhabitants of Taigu are also people, Mr. Kozani, and they are also hungry."

Kozani spread his hands. "I am distressed, believe me, Mr. Theymour. I wish I could help. The British agreement is not an ideal one from our point of view. Because of their dock strike, we are obliged to unload our cargoes off-shore, a time-consuming and costly business."

"But a highly lucrative one nevertheless," Theymour remarked. "I imagine the British are only too willing to pay through the nose to keep their precious food filtering in."

Kozani looked affronted. He sat back in his chair. "My company is a business concern not a charity," he said. "We are not without compassion, Mr. Theymour. We keep Britain supplied with her needs, but I see no crime in asking a reasonable return for our service."

Theymour was instantly apologetic. "Please don't get me wrong, Mr. Kozani. I was not condemning your enterprise. In fact, I'm a firm believer in healthy competition. And since the people of Taigu are more desperate than the people of Britain, they're willing to pay more for what they require. I am authorised by our President to offer you, not in sterling but in American dollars, a fifty cent increase on every hundred pounds of food delivered. The only proviso being that all your ships be diverted immediately."

Kozani stared at him in astonishment. "That I cannot do, Mr. Theymour," he exclaimed. "There are contracts, agreements . . ."

"The British have their navy, Mr. Kozani. That's better than nothing. In Taigu we are utterly defenceless. We need your help and we need it now."

Kozani looked confused. Theymour watched the various emotions flicker across his face, surprise, disbelief, greed, cunning.

"You put me in a difficult position," he complained. "A decision like this I cannot take alone."

Theymour picked up his hat. "Of course," he said. "I understand perfectly. Take your time, Mr. Kozani. I'll look around the town and return this afternoon. Think it over carefully. When you come down to it, there is, as a businessman, only one conclusion you can come to."

Oman, Wednesday July 27th.

The rain that had fallen since daybreak began to die off in the late afternoon, and leaving the shelter of the caves they moved steadily south, following a jagged shark-tooth ridge higher into the mountains. The man called Wahibar rode in front, his razor-scraped skull gleaming with moisture, his huge backside wobbling in the saddle like a sack of loose potatoes. Roger Leynard, tall, loose-limbed, fair-haired, twenty-seven years old followed close behind. In the west, arid mountains showed stark and clear in the daylight. They were part of the vast Hajar Range, ten thousand feet high, with furrows along their flanks where rivers would flow in wintertime. To the east, Leynard could see a dry gravel plain, unbroken except for a cluster of distant date trees. Even at eight thousand feet, the air was stifling and oil oozed in blobs from his saddlebags.

The man called Wahibar rode without speaking, his brutish face locked up tight like a sealed container. Leynard looked at his watch. It was nearly four o'clock. "How far now?" he demanded in fluent Arabic, nudging his horse alongside.

Wahibar stared at him coolly. His eyes were incalculable, the eyes of an animal: rage, hate, love — one look would encompass them all. "You must learn to be patient," he grunted. "First we must see if we are welcome."

Leynard frowned. "I thought you were one of Al Salalah's lieutenants?"

Wahibar grinned evilly, his gold teeth flashing in the sunlight. "I will be welcome," he said evenly. "It is you they may wish to kill."

Leynard glared at him. There was something repelling about the man. His yellow eyes, his fastidiously shaved head

91

carried an air of menace. "Let me remind you of your promise that I would not be harmed," he said.

Wahibar nodded with mock seriousness. The sun shone on his skull, illuminating a ragged scar which ran from the crown to the tip of his left eyebrow. "A man's promise should be kept only with his friends," he grunted. "You would not blame the lion for breaking its promise to the gazelle."

Leynard reached inside the bag dangling from his saddle-horn and brought out a .32 Colt Detective Special with a two-inch barrel. He turned it over in the daylight to let Wahibar get a good look.

"If any promises are broken," he said evenly, "this lion will end up with quite a headache."

Wahibar looked impressed. "You are a strange man," he said. "You tell me you are a journalist, yet you carry arms like a combatant."

"Simple insurance."

"You do not trust me?"

"Should the gazelle trust the lion?"

Wahibar grinned. "With such teeth, the gazelle has little to fear," he said.

Trees brushed low across the trail. Traces of mist hung in the air like drawn-out strands of cottonwool. They skirted a valley where naked shepherd boys tended flocks of spindly goats. Mud-walled houses perched on the steep mountain slopes. Soon the valleys grew wilder until there were only the twisting tracks of dried-up riverbeds and scattered clumps of thorny vegetation. Dust rose in the air, clogging their nostrils.

At six o'clock, Wahibar called a halt. The place he had chosen seemed no different from a dozen others they had passed on the long ride up. The hills swooped into a small defile, flanked on one side by a snatch of acacias. The earth was dry as ground bone.

"Why are we stopping?" Leynard asked.

"We must wait until they come for us."

"But how will they know we are here?"

Wahibar dismounted, his face implacable. "They know," he said simply.

Leynard took out a handkerchief and wiped his glistening cheeks. He felt uneasy. "Does Al Salalah understand that I come to talk and for no other purpose?" he asked.

Wahibar stared at him in amusement. His thick lips twisted into a grin. "Al Salalah himself will decide what you come for," he murmured.

Leynard could see the scar across his shaven skull, and something cold and constricting moved in his chest. He watched Wahibar take the horses down to a nearby stream and hobble their forelegs so they could graze and reach the water if they felt like it. Wahibar washed himself carefully, bathing his hands and feet and the top of his head, then he swept the ground, knelt down with his forehead touching the earth, and began to recite the opening verse of the Koran. His voice sounded strangely soothing on the silent hillside.

Leynard sat in the shade of an acacia and watched the shadows lengthen. The sky was the colour of heated brass. It crouched above their heads like an enormous inverted bowl, hot and dry, offering no escape. A bird fluttered to earth, made a few sporadic hops and disappeared over a rocky rim. The mountains were blue and gold with a heat haze rising between them, leaving only their jagged tips visible.

An hour passed, then: "They are coming," said Wahibar.

Leynard felt his mouth seize up. There were eight of them altogether, scarecrow men in scarecrow clothing mounted on bony horses. He saw haggard eyes, stubbled cheeks, ragged trousers. On their heads they wore cotton *shemaghs*, and across their saddles, resting casually like bits of harmless shiny plastic lay Armalite AR 180 automatic rifles.

One came up, then another. Wahibar went to meet them and for several minutes they talked excitedly. Then Wahibar led the horses up from the water. "Get mounted," he ordered. "Al Salalah waits for us in the valley."

Leynard swung into the saddle and they moved off, following a track which curled close along the wall of a steep ravine. Below, ghaf trees clustered the rocky floor. As they descended, Leynard saw water running from a deep fissure in the fractured cliff. Bushes sprang out of everywhere, their gnarled roots clutching the parched earth like thirsty jaws. He spotted the ruins of a crude stone fort which had at some time long ago guarded the position of the well. Armed sentries sat in the turrets, their faces hidden by black dust masks. Below, camels squatted in the shade, chewing monotonously.

As they moved lower, mud huts sprang up around them like marvellous enchantment. Smoke from cooking fires rose in the air in slender white columns. A shout went up, and in an instant they were surrounded by people – men in ragged turbans and djellebas, women in yashmaks, children in bits of dirty linen, their heads plastered with henna as they trotted barefoot in front of the horses.

The eight guerrillas fanned out to flank Leynard on each side, keeping the crowd well back. The mud huts parted around a clearing forming the shape of a rough heart. At its tip stood a building which was larger than the others, its walls constructed not of mud but of stones, sepia-coloured, the roof fashioned with plaited grass. On its verandah, a man stood waiting. His face was jagged and uneven, swelling outwards to prominent cheekbones, then sinking into deep hollows tracing both sides of a thin crooked mouth, and ending, almost by accident, Leynard thought, on the jutting thrust of the chin. It was an inelegant face, and the inelegance was made more apparent by the eyes which were small and oddly out of focus. He was shorter than Leynard, but even so there was something compelling about him as he stood there, and Leynard's heart thumped in his chest as he reined in his mount.

"*Salaam eilicumbe*, Al Salalah," he murmured.

The man ignored him. "Who is he?" he asked softly, his voice surprisingly gentle.

Wahibar cleared his throat. "His name is Roger Leynard. He is an American journalist."

"Who told you to bring him here?"

Wahibar spoke again, speaking very rapidly this time and in one of the mountain dialects Leynard could not follow. Al Salalah listened without taking his eyes off the American. Leynard had the sensation of being dissected, as if in some

94

mad dream he was lying on a slab while scalpels peeled away his face.

Al Salalah waited until Wahibar had finished, then said, "Come inside."

Leynard dismounted and followed him into the hut. He knew the next few minutes would be crucial to his very existence, and breathed deeply in an effort to bring his pulse rate back to normal.

The hut was hot and stuffy, the air tinged with the scent of stale food. There were a couple of crudely constructed chairs, a table, a rusty exercise machine and a folding campbed. Filled water skins hung from the rafters like bloated slugs.

Al Salalah dropped into a chair, his strange out-of-focus eyes studying the American coldly. "I am trying to think of a reason," he said, "why I should not kill you."

"Your man promised me a safe return," Leynard said.

Al Salalah shrugged. "When one lives like the fox, one must act like the fox. I cannot be responsible for the promises of my men. I do not wish to kill you, but there are some things which must be done in duty. You see those people out there? It is not my life I gamble with if I let you live, it is theirs too. Is it right I should ask them to take such a risk?"

Leynard breathed deeply. "Killing me would be a great stupidity. I come not as a journalist, but as the representative of a friendly government. Your war against the Sultan has ground to a halt because you no longer have the means to sustain it. I come to offer you that means."

"What can you offer me?" Al Salalah demanded with contempt.

"Guns, ammunition, heavy artillery, APWs and, most important of all, boats. Gunboats. With experts to train your troops how to use them."

Al Salalah frowned. He gave the impression of a man folded in on himself, introspective and brooding.

"Boats?" he echoed. "Our war is fought in the mountains, not on the ocean. For what would we require boats?"

"Your war was doomed from the beginning, Al Salalah. For eleven years, your people fought a bitter struggle against the

Sultan's forces, but not even your training in Moscow could equip you for the expertise of the British army. It was the members of the British Special Air Service Regiment seconded to the Sultan who smashed your revolution."

Al Salalah did not answer. Leynard took his time, judging the tempo perfectly. He knew he was talking for his life. "The time has come for a new revolution," he said. "Britain has problems of her own. She can no longer worry about what happens on the other side of the world."

"You cannot be sure of that," Al Salalah growled.

"No," smiled Leynard, "but Al Salalah can."

He took a deep breath. He had reached the crux of his argument, the whole reason for his being here. Everything depended on Al Salalah accepting his next proposition.

"With gunboats," Leynard explained, "a small party of determined men could block the narrow bottleneck of the Strait of Hormuz, down which the giant oil tankers from the Persian Gulf must pass. Without oil, Britain would be like a snake with its venom drawn. Al Salalah could carry his war into the Sultan's camp without fear of interference. From disorder and disobedience, a new pattern would emerge."

Al Salalah's eyes were unblinking. "And in return for all this," he said, "what would you expect to gain?"

Leynard looked at him, his face honest and sincere. "Only the knowledge that justice has been done," he answered.

Al Salalah rose and strolled across the hut. Hot air wafted in through the glassless slit. Leynard could hear the murmur of voices outside, smell the cooking fires. He felt like a man trapped in a cage with a tiger. Al Salalah had that scent about him, the scent of unpredictability. Leynard wondered if, in his more intemperate moments, he might not savage an arm or a leg. He seemed capable of it.

"When I was a child," murmured Al Salalah, "I had a dream one night. It was a dream I have remembered all my life. It was dark and I was running. The country was very bare, very stony and without moisture. The villages I came to were filled with dying people. There was a famine in the land. Corpses littered the wayside, their cheeks ravaged by the stamp of hunger. Mists hung about the mountains. No one would go into the mists for they were afraid of the unknown, but I was young and desperate to escape the stench of death, so I went alone. In a world of darkness I came suddenly upon a great valley carved out of the mountain fastness. It was a valley unbelievable in its richness. From end to end its belly was choked with an unbroken sea of corn. In the moon's glow, the corn was silver. It swayed at my feet, a vast ocean of corn, enough to feed a continent. I remember thinking, this is what I have been born for. I must lead my people to this valley of silver corn."

He paused. His eyes, strangely sad, looked moist and luminous. Shadows hung beneath his cheekbones. He picked up a dish of dates, crawling with wasps. "Sit and eat with me," he said.

Leynard nodded, relief flooding through him. "*El Hamdhu Lillah*," he said. "To Allah be praise."

On Friday, July 29th, the following four-line advertisement appeared in all British newspapers still in production;

EX COMMANDOS, PARATROOPERS, SAS TROOPS
RAF AIRCREW WANTED FOR ADVENTUROUS
HIGHLY PROFITABLE WORK ABROAD. FOOD
AND CLOTHING PROVIDED FREE. WRITE BOX 204.

Predictably, in view of the gloom which hung over Britain, the replies ran into thousands. Each was answered by a circular letter stating a time, date and place where the applicant would be interviewed to assess his suitability. Because of the petrol shortage, a man called John Dipton spent three weeks cruising around the country in a car stocked with US gasoline, receiving would-be mercenaries in rented hotel rooms in ten major cities. Out of the flood of hopefuls, five hundred and seventy-four were eventually selected. On August 19th, they received a further circular letter instructing them to gather at pre-arranged marshalling points near their homes where they were picked up by USAF buses and transported to American air bases.

By this time, Dipton's mysterious recruiting drive had

attracted the attentions of both the press and Special Branch, but the former were unable to pursue their investigations due to lack of mobility and the latter got no further than the air base gates. An official statement from the American authorities said the men were being hired by a US industrialist to form an anti-communist police force in an unspecified African country.

Meanwhile, the new recruits were flown across the Atlantic and shipped to Camp Fremont where they spent the statutory first few days in Building 3. Care was taken to obliterate all indications that the newcomers were in the USA. American flags and notice boards were taken down, even the name of the camp itself was temporarily removed from above the gate. The men were kept scrupulously apart from the other trainees, eating in a separate mess food carefully prepared to suggest French or Spanish influences. Out of the original five hundred and seventy-four, one hundred and eighty-one failed to respond to indoctrination and were flown immediately back to Britain. The rest were segregated into a special training area where they were given military uniforms and divided into squadrons. These were:

Intelligence and Sabotage Teams
Penetration Teams (Fully Operational)
Air Crew
Missile Strike Force Units

Their training during the first four weeks covered all aspects of tactical warfare:

squadron operations
small group penetration
demolition deployment
single operative assignments
psychological warfare techniques
interview and interrogation techniques
non-nuclear weapons usage
missiles and military strategy

The training was conducted under the approving eye of Colonel Richard Savage and the men were given the title of the '300 Brigade', although in CIA records they were listed officially as Unit G. Colonel Savage himself had been airlifted to Camp Fremont some weeks earlier where he met Joseph Spengler who had travelled up specially from Washington and now made no secret of his department's interest in covert-action operations in Britain.

"We lied to you," he admitted. "There is no Texas billionaire named Horace B. Theymour. We needed to find out how far you were prepared to go."

Savage regarded Spengler mildly. He decided from the start that he did not care for Spengler, but then most people disliked Spengler initially, and their dislike generally grew as their association grew. Spengler had decked himself in a brightly checked Mackinaw jacket which had clearly come straight from the clothing store. It looked incongruous on his very lean frame. His elongated skull seemed to emerge from the heavy collar like a missile head fired from an underground silo.

Savage's manner was haughty and superior. "Why, may I ask, have you gone to such trouble? I'm sure the British authorities could have handled things admirably if they considered me a threat."

Spengler laughed out loud. He tucked his hands in his Mackinaw pockets and strolled to the window, peering out at the rain sweeping the Camp Fremont rooftops. "We're not doing this for the British authorities, Colonel," he said. "The deal Miss Coldman put to you still stands. But it's a tricky situation from our point of view. I mean, how would the American people feel if they knew we were dealing with activist elements out to smash democracy in Britain?"

Colonel Savage frowned. "How d'you mean, activist elements?"

"Why, you, sir."

Savage stared at him with surprise, then drew himself up to his full height. "Are you suggesting I'm a traitor?" he demanded.

"Of course not, Colonel. You're misinterpreting everything I say. We know you're doing this because you care about your country, because you're alarmed at the way things are going.

We're alarmed too. If Britain plunges into disorder, or if the wrong kind of government takes power, we'll be out on a limb. Our military installations in Britain are vital to the security of the United States. Okay, we could pull out, lock ourselves up inside our own continent, but that would make us so vulnerable the reds would laugh their socks off. We need some kind of order restored over there, Colonel, and we need it fast."

He paused as the door opened, and a young sergeant in shirt sleeves brought in two mugs of coffee. Spengler waited until the sergeant had retired, then offered one mug to the colonel, took out a small phial of saccharine tablets and dropped two into his own cup.

Savage regarded him carefully. "I have a feeling," the colonel said, "that Miss Coldman omitted to tell you I am not pro-American."

Spengler nodded. "We got the message."

"I want this firmly understood, Spengler. I will not be a US puppet. I will struggle most vigorously to oppose any American influence on the British way of life."

"That doesn't concern us, Colonel. We're talking about survival. Military survival. All we ask is that our current Defence Agreements be honoured, and if necessary strengthened. That's in both our interests, yours as well as ours."

Savage sipped his coffee, peering at the raindrops tracing uneven patterns down the windowpane, his autocratic face lost in thought. Spengler stood studying him in silence. He had already decided the colonel was a fool, but that scarcely mattered as long as Savage appeared convincing to the British people and, properly handled, Spengler felt sure he could be very convincing indeed.

Later, Spengler took the colonel on a conducted tour of the camp. Gusts of wind swept rain into their faces, stinging their cheeks and forcing them to turn up their collars against its assault. The surrounding hills had been wiped out by curtains of rolling mist and the trees around the perimeter fence dripped mournfully, their trunks glistening with moisture, their branches soggy and limp.

They stood in the mud and watched men in khaki denims

running through an assault course which included barbed-wire tunnels, treetop rope-pulleys and water-filled ditches.

"What d'you think of them?" Spengler asked.

Savage sniffed. "Bit rough around the edges," he said. "They'll have to do better than that."

"Give them time, colonel. They haven't settled in yet. I promise you, within a month you won't recognise them."

"A month?"

"Sure, no need to rush. Let's face it, the moment isn't ripe for you to make your appearance yet. I mean, in Britain you're still regarded as a kind of crank."

As Savage glared at him indignantly, Spengler chuckled and held up his hand. "Don't be offended, Colonel. If we're going to work together, we have to be honest with each other You do have the support of some right-wing sections of the community, but both the government and a pretty sizeable lump of the population see you as a misguided eccentric. We have to prepare the way for a shift in public thinking. First, we'll push the people further into confusion, and when they're confused enough we'll push them into anger, and when they're angry enough, we'll give them you as a focal point, some-one who can channel their fury into a definite means and end."

They began to pick their way across the surface of churned-up mud, their boots sinking deep in the soggy slime, the spray lashing their faces. As they leaned heavily into the wind, a swirl of geese rose yelping above their heads, sweeping westward across the treetops. The moisture seemed to curl out of the ground itself, swirling around their feet in columns of twisting mist, draining the density from the air. They paused at the edge of a small compound flanked by warning flag em-placers. Inside the perimeter, a party of men wearing gas masks and NCB protective clothing were grouped around a large tanker equipped with multiple sprays and nozzle attachments. They looked like creatures from another universe, and in the drifting fog and rain Savage was shaken by a sense of unreality.

"What's going on here?" he demanded.

"This is our nuclear, biological and chemical warfare section," Spengler told him. "Those men are learning how to detect contamination and how to operate in a contaminated environment. The truck is a Soviet-built BRDM-rkh reconnaissance vehicle. It's equipped with emplacements for forty warning flags, which can be fired into the ground by propulsion cartridges. The tanker it's pulling contains formaldehyde and ammonia for spraying on to infected areas."

Savage frowned. His face seemed to harden into an unflinchable mould, the skin drawing tight across its frame of projecting bones.

"No one mentioned chemical warfare," he said. "I intend to *save* my country, not destroy it."

Spengler chuckled. "Not you, Colonel. You won't be using chemicals or biological agents, but we have to prepare ourselves for anything the enemy may throw at us. That's basic common sense."

Savage considered for a moment, then nodded shortly. "You're quite right," he agreed. "Things could get a lot dirtier than we've bargained for."

They turned toward the main training area, skirting a small copse of trees and making a detour around a heap of glistening oil-drums. The sound of barked orders hung on the rain-sodden air.

"This plan you've got for slicing the country in two," Spengler said, "that's quite something. Think it'll work?"

Savage looked affronted. "Mr. Spengler, I have been a soldier for nearly forty years . . ."

"Will it work, Colonel?"

"Of course, it'll work. Do you take me for an imbecile?"

"No revolution in the past quarter of a century has succeeded by a direct confrontation with the army," Spengler insisted. "Politically, militarily and economically, the urban areas hold the key, because that's where the greatest section of the people live. You're a gentleman who thinks he's going to fight a gentlemen's war. Drive your front across the neck of Britain and the RAF will blast you out of existence."

Savage's lips fluttered helplessly. Spengler's air of icy logic seemed to unnerve him. "They wouldn't . . . they couldn't," he muttered. "They'd be squandering innocent lives . . ."

"What lives? You said yourself that whole area is isolated. You'd be sitting up like targets at a skeet shoot."

They ducked under a wire fence and strolled between rows of rain-soaked barrack huts. Telephone cables hung mournfully like dripping shrouds. Savage's feet were slurping inside his boots. He felt thoroughly miserable, and Spengler's bluntness discomforted him even more. Spengler himself seemed lost in thought. When he spoke again, his voice was soft and speculative, as if he were talking to himself.

"On the other hand, most urban revolutionary struggles drag on for years and end up getting nowhere. The advantage of your idea is that you would be a definite presence, the people would know where to find you, you'd become a rallying point. What we have to do is take steps to see that the RAF no longer has the resources to blast you too severely, and that you have the means to counter attack if they do. You need aircraft. That's beyond question. The problem is, you also need somewhere to launch them, and that's not easy in the Cheviot Hills. Even if you build an airstrip, the RAF could take it out in their first attack. We're going to supply you with half a squadron of Hawker Harrier jump jets. They're the perfect machines for your kind of war, because they operate from any available stretch of grass. Mind you, they're not easy to fly. Our marines have been crashing them at the rate of one a month. Hawker pilots have to be the very best. There's no radar, no reliable navigation system, get the hover wrong and the damn thing can roll right over on to its back. However, some of your volunteers attended the RAF Advanced Flying School in Anglesey, and I'm hoping we'll find at least one or two with the necessary skills and aptitude. We're also going to supply you with Ground-Air-Missiles, Seismic Detection Sensors, tanks, artillery and helicopters. Most of the equipment will be British- or Soviet-made. The rest will be carefully vetted to see that no marks or trade numbers can identify them as American in origin. In some cases, even the basic designs may have to be altered. Meanwhile, your men will be put

103

through a crash training course carried out by the finest instructors we can muster."

They stopped to watch a group of soldiers busily unloading a massive rotatable rocket launcher from a cross-country trailer.

Savage stared at it wordlessly.

"It's a Soviet Guideline anti-aircraft missile," Spengler told him. "It was one of these little babies which brought down the U-2 plane flown by Gary Powers over the Soviet Union in 1960. They're somewhat out of date by today's standards, but still lethal enough to treat with respect. Two of the booster fins have gyro-controlled rudders for course-setting. The sustainer is fuelled by nitric acid and kerosene, and can be steered by computer to intercept its target."

"Very impressive," Savage admitted.

Spengler peered up at him, grinning wryly. "By the time your men take the field, Colonel," he said, "they may not be the biggest army in the world, but you can bet your ass on one thing – they'll be the best damned equipped sons of bitches ever to fight for life and liberty."

EIGHT

The frightening thing about Spengler's formula for the collapse of the British system lay not so much in its ruthlessness as in its startling simplicity. In the beginning, the project had no clear title. Among the operatives of FOCB it was known by the number of its file cover, K20431, until some more imaginative figure gave it the nickname of 'The Doomsday Dossier' and the name stuck; before long everyone was calling it that, both on and off the record. The aim of the Dossier was no different from the aim of any other revolutionary movement, namely to create in Britain – through the process of agitation, subversion, rioting, economic manipulation and diversionary diplomacy – a state of such confusion that an armed takeover would become feasible.

Spengler had calculated right from the beginning that Britain was in dire straits and only the slightest push would be required to send her over the edge, so he set out with a plan which carried three distinct phases. Phase One was aimed at destroying the final shreds of credibility which held the teetering faith of the British people together. Its purpose was to create in each individual the feeling that his world was disintegrating into chaos and disorder. It was put into operation on Monday June 6th, the anniversary, Spengler noted with sardonic irony, of that triumph of Anglo-American co-operation, the D-Day landings.

He began by putting pressure on the few remaining American industrial concerns still operating in the British Isles to either withdraw or shut down until the economic crisis was resolved. They took little persuading. In fact, even Spengler had to admit he'd been surprised by the willingness of "those commerce carnivores" to co-operate, which seemed to suggest that they'd been looking for an excuse to crap out all along. Companies from other countries were offered alternative sitings in different parts of Europe, with tempting financial backing if they agreed to pull up stakes immediately. Since the flight of foreign capital had progressed with the increase of inflation, it was not difficult to persuade investors that their interests could best be served elsewhere. The effect on the British money markets was instantaneous.

However, economic pressure was only the first of Spengler's weapons. On August 2nd, the first batch of trainees from Camp Fremont was flown to the British Isles. These were civilian operatives who specialised in the disruption of basic services and the penetration of trades union organisations. Their targets were the power stations. Each group was given three weeks to bring the nation's electricity grid system to a standstill. Since almost half of the generating capacity of the British electricity supply came from only twenty strategic power stations based in south Yorkshire and the Trent Valley (among them Eggborough, Drax, Ferrybridge and High Marnham), it was these stations which were selected for special attention. The Camp Fremont trainees got themselves jobs where they could, mixed with the power men in leisure hours where they couldn't and, through a system drilled into them over weeks of painstaking indoctrination, proceeded to create an atmosphere of turmoil and unrest.

In the end, only about eight thousand of the country's thirty thousand manual workers employed by the Central Electricity Generating Board actually went on strike, but they were enough. Though the blackout wasn't total, the government was forced to introduce a rigid system of electricity cuts which began in the third week and demonstrated the awesome vulnerability of the grid system to infiltration and disruption. Care was taken to ensure that no section of the population was without power for more than twenty-four hours at a time, for the authorities considered it essential that some kind of link be maintained between themselves and the people. That link became television. By this time, only the BBC was still in operation, for the Independent Broadcasting Authority had closed down months before, due to lack of advertising revenue.

Meanwhile, the fresh uprising in Oman which had shut off the Strait of Hormuz and prevented all but a handful of oil tankers getting through from the Persian Gulf brought British industry to its final shutdown. The government invoked emergency powers aimed at conserving the last drops of precious fuel. It became illegal for a private citizen to possess either petrol or oil. The penalty was ten years' imprisonment. Television and radio stations interspersed their programmes with instructions on alternative energy sources. Scientists gave lectures on how to use wind to create electricity, how to power houses with water wheels, how to produce methane gas out of pig manure and how to get the most out of a wood-burning stove.

Spengler's second line of attack, the shutting off of Britain's vital commodities, was the most telling and, sad to say, the most simple move of all since many of the staples of life were already being supplied directly from the USA. The American air-lift operation was brought to an immediate halt, together with the millions of dollars being paid out in US aid. Foreign ships carrying food supplies to Britain were diverted to other ports on the promise of high monetary rewards. Action of this kind would have been devastating at the best of times; Britain, being such an overcrowded little island, was never more than seven or eight weeks away from famine. But with food stocks already stretched to their limit, the British people knew, for the first time in centuries, what it was like to face starvation. Rationing became even more stringent. The provisions available in the shops were scarcely enough to keep body and soul together, and everyone realised that when supplies ran out there would be nothing left. Many of the elderly died from malnutrition.

However, this slow hiccupping route to disaster was not by any means allowed to proceed unchallenged, for by this time a new mood had begun to emerge among the people. If Spengler had anticipated a total disintegration of public energy and spirit, then it soon became clear that he had badly miscalculated. The air of disillusionment and melancholy which had hung over the early stages of Britain's collapse now gave way to a deep sullen anger. It was as if the population, instead of breaking under its hardships, had actually begun to blossom, welcoming the challenge, and seeking out the cause of its discontent with an enthusiasm and determination that was utterly electrifying. People who had been previously sunk in apathy and despair were filled with a bold new sense of purpose. All over the country, aspiring new leaders sprang up, galvanising listeners with memories of Empire days.

For those who still had money to buy books, the works of Kipling, Talbot Mundy and Sapper replaced the popular fiction of the period, and musicians churned out songs extolling the virtues of Britain's past glories and bulldog spirit. Within a month, this wave of national fervour had reached fanatical proportions. Printed copies of Nelson's Trafalgar speech fluttered from billboards all over London. Slogans like 'England Expects' and 'Mother of the Free' lost their banality in a wave of new-found patriotism. Sometimes this devotion to crown and country exploded into violence when right-wing elements encountered anarchists and savage brawls broke out. The truth was, the British people were spoiling for a fight. They'd had enough of calm acceptance. As their living standards collapsed, they were filled with a need for action and looked around desperately for an adversary. Had they found one, had they managed to isolate the cause of their misfortune, the chances are they would have shaken Europe until its teeth rattled. As it was, no one seemed able to work out with any degree of certainty in which direction the enemy lay, or if indeed there was an enemy at all beyond the politicians whom they blamed anyhow. But in the regions, pockets of para-military units appeared with alarming frequency, drilling with wooden rifles, dressing in makeshift uniforms and expressing a fierce devotion to the Union Jack. The authorities, dismayed by such militarism, moved in swiftly to break these units up, and only in the cities, where left-wing extremist groups were being formed almost day by day, was there any clear sign of opposition to law and order.

A group of housewives in Lancaster organised a movement called 'Daughters of the Empire' which set out to promote the principles of British resilience and ingenuity. In one week, its numbers rocketed from fifty-two to one thousand and forty-nine.

None of this did much good in a practical sense, of course, though it did rekindle a sense of hope for a while, a feeling that all could not be lost if national unity prevailed, but much of this motivating force was dispersed as the weakness which hunger generates began to take hold.

Radio and television programmes switched their emphasis from energy sources to the problems of survival. Experts gave details on how to make salads out of chopped dandelion leaves, how to set rabbit snares, bird traps, where to look for wild berries, roots and hedgerow plants. However, sixty million people can't be satisfactorily fed on wild foliage, and in the country areas farmers had to set up shotgun patrols to guard their crops from hordes of hungry scavengers.

The government, worried about the threat of disease engendered by lack of proper nutrition, sent doctors and health workers to visit all sections of the community. They carried out tests, keeping a wary eye on the appearance of any new virus or malady.

Agencies such as Oxfam struggled to bring in food and medicine for the poor, and one newspaper reported triumphantly that five and a half million children were getting three meals daily out of foreign charities. Nevertheless, the sight of youngsters with sunken cheeks and other attributes of deprivation became a common sight. The people's faith in their own administration, already sorely taxed, finally broke down altogether as the hunger in their bellies slowly and inexorably intensified.

On Saturday, August 20th, Farran was shipped back to the British Isles on board an S22 heavy transport plane which dropped him, together with the thirty-four fellow ex-Camp Fremont trainees (who formed the Fourth Infiltration Unit of the '300 Brigade') at Bakewell US Air Base in West Sussex, from where he was driven overnight in a car sporting US Embassy number plates (to ensure immunity from the petrol restriction law) and deposited in the early hours of Sunday morning in a small boarding house off Ladbroke Grove in London.

It was over three months since Farran had been in England, and the changes he saw there both shocked and amazed him. Living conditions had been bad enough at the time of his leaving, but now there was a general air of impoverishment and seediness which seemed to seep through the London streets like a malignant odour, defying even the summer sunshine. Never had Farran seen London look gloomier, and the sight of boarded-up shopfronts, abandoned cars and hungry people roaming restlessly in the hope of finding a supermarket not yet sold out, wrought in him the chilling conviction that even in the midst of plenty, no nation was far from the abyss.

Nevertheless, despite this despondency, Farran was pleased and relieved to be back home, for the conditioning procedures in Building 3 during the final weeks of training had taken on a new and distinctly unpleasant feature. Though no explanation had been given, the reasons lay in the fact that the Camp Fremont techniques, like all induction methods based on theories of hypnotic suggestion, needed to be repeated day after day to remain effective. The doctors knew that once the trainees were turned loose, their carefully nurtured response patterns would fade and disappear unless some means could be found to reactivate them. To this end, Farran and his companions were placed individually in sensory-deprivation chambers for twenty-four to thirty-six hours at a time. These chambers had no windows and no furniture. A solitary bucket served as a lavatory, and two vacuum flasks provided nourishment, one containing water, the other a vanilla-flavoured high-protein mixture which had been carefully drugged to induce a state of high suggestibility. The temperature was kept at a constant sixty-six degrees.

Once the subject had sunk into a stupor, tapes of popular danceband music were piped into his cell. Each prisoner was provided with a different tune to which he and he alone was conditioned to respond. Thereafter, that tune became the trigger device which, when heard, automatically plunged him into a deep hypnotic trance. At the end of each music session, new and potent images were fed into his subconscious mind by a strong, deliberately monotoned voice. As each man departed to carry out his allotted tasks, he was given a small recording machine and a selection of cassette-tapes with which he could, without realising it, avert any chance of his subconscious mind re-establishing its own identity.

Though Farran worked alone, he was part of a seventy-man team scattered around the cities of London, Birmingham, Manchester, Liverpool, Newcastle, Edinburgh and Glasgow, with the job of locating and co-ordinating the activist extremist groups springing up in the urban areas as a consequence of poverty and privation.

Farran lived quietly, making his daily excursions into the streets where he sought out pockets of resistance among the crowds of workless humanity in Ladbroke Grove and Notting Hill. Once a week he was visited by a man called Romney, an American who spoke with an immaculate cockney accent and who arrived on a bicycle carrying a rucksack loaded with tinned meat and vegetables, dried bread and canned US Army iron rations. Half of the provisions were for Farran, the other half for the anarchists he contacted.

Romney also delivered fresh cassette tapes which Farran obediently played each morning on his portable recorder. Each tape began with the tune to which he had been conditioned to respond, and ended with the same monotonous voice breathing out his instructions.

There was, by this time, no doubt in Farran's mind that what he was doing was both honourable and right. The doctors had planted the seeds of revolt deep into his subconscious, the tapes reaffirmed these teachings daily, and if any further stimulus was needed, the sight of suffering people convinced Farran that salvation could only be reached through disorder and rebellion. He saw himself as a shining crusader fighting the chains of poverty and exploitation.

In the first fortnight, he contacted and negotiated with four major anarchist groups, all of whom treated him with cautious suspicion but accepted nevertheless his offer of food, and agreed to carry out the stipulated distribution of activist literature. This was made up largely of pamphlets, printed out of the country and delivered to Farran each week together with his tapes and provisions. They followed a basic formula.

Citizens of Britain,

Criminal mismanagement has brought this country to its knees. The split between government and people has left its mark on every level of our society. Unemployment is rife, our children are starving, our country impoverished. Production is non-existent, economic development at a standstill. Armed forces are needed to overthrow the catastrophic excesses of the ruling group. The nucleus of these forces already exists. Guerrilla units have arisen to revindicate the honour of Britain and bring the people to redemption.

AIMS OF THE NATIONAL LIBERATION FORCES OF GREAT BRITAIN (THE 300 BRIGADE)

1. To establish a government capable of leading our country through the grave crisis now impending.
2. To unite and organise all elements interested in the restoration of law and order, and the high ideals of British democracy.
3. To enforce respect for national sovereignty and independence.
4. To defend the national heritage, its integrity and wealth.
5. To protect the interests of the people, their livelihood, welfare and institutions.

> Colonel Richard Savage,
> National Commander of the 300 Brigade,
> the military arm of the Revolution.

Not surprisingly, some of the anarchists, the more militant ones, recalled Colonel Savage from earlier publicity as a fascist-bastard-who-ought-to-be-stood-up-against-a-wall-and-shot but, as Farran pointed out, the basic aim of all believers was the overthrow of the system, and a true revolu-

112

tionary never hesitated to use any instrument, no matter how repugnant, in the pursuit of his objective. Since Colonel Savage had the power to unite the people, he should be utilised until such time as he could be replaced with a more desirable leader. Moreover, on such occasions Romney managed to include a couple of extra cans of stewing beef in the weekly provision supply, and that generally swung the argument. Soon, pamphlets proclaiming freedom, justice and most important of all, the name of Colonel Savage fluttered from practically every lamp-post and telegraph pole in Greater London.

But by this time Farran's activities had begun to be noticed by the FC5 Squad, that section of the police force set up at the height of the crisis and given special emergency powers to deal with civil disobedience. Farran had been warned to expect police scrutiny, but as the weeks passed by without incident, his natural caution subsided so that when the arrest came he was taken by surprise.

They picked him up at half-past four in the afternoon outside a cinema on Westbourne Grove. There were two of them, big men in dark grey raincoats who made him stand with his palms against the wall while they searched through his clothes. Then they took him to Harrow Road police station and left him to stew for a while in a tiny cell. After about an hour, a thickset medium-sized man in a blue suit led Farran down a narrow corridor into what was clearly an interview room. It was small and badly lit. There was no furniture apart from one hard-backed chair which stood in the centre of the floor, and a light bulb dangling from the ceiling. The walls were plastered, the floor was stone and had at some time long ago been painted red. There was a fireplace with the remnants of ash in the grate. There was a window which faced south toward the river. A man was standing by the window. The man was big and heavy-shouldered, but graceful. When he moved, there was a smooth preciseness in his actions. His hair was clipped short, military style, and his face looked lean and hard as burnished steel.

"Who is this man, sergeant?" he asked.

"I don't know, sir," said the man in the blue suit. "I don't know who he is."

"Ask him who he is, sergeant."

"Tell the commander who you are."

Farran stared from one to the other. He had been warned to expect interrogation, had been carefully schooled in all methods of interview techniques, but this cold autocratic opening bewildered him. He said warily, "Jack Farran."

"Where do you live?" This from the commander.

"Ladbroke Grove."

"Where is Ladbroke Grove?"

"402 Oxford Gardens. Room 1A."

"Married?"

"No."

"Do you have a job?"

"No."

"What about friends?"

Farran hesitated. "What kind of friends?" he asked.

"Do you have any friends?" the commander repeated as if he hadn't spoken.

"Yes, I have friends," Farran grunted.

"Where do they live?"

Farran hesitated again. This wasn't the Britain he used to know. The police practically made their own rules these days, for the government believed that in the face of poverty and despair, order must be maintained above all else. He'd heard rumours of the FC5 Squad, ugly rumours. But the worst of it was, they'd caught him with his pants down, as helpless as a trembling virgin.

"How the hell do I know where they live," he snapped. "They live all over the place, it's a big city."

"Where do they live?"

Clearly the commander intended to go on repeating himself until he got an answer. On impulse, Farran said, "Chelsea."

"Are your friends in Chelsea like your friends in Notting Hill?" the commander demanded.

"I have no friends in Notting Hill," Farran answered.

"We know you have friends in Notting Hill," the commander said evenly. "We've seen you with your friends in Notting Hill. Until today, we did not know about your friends in Chelsea. Are they scum too? Do they spread the poison of gloom and discontent?"

"I don't know what you mean."

"He doesn't know what I mean, sergeant."

"He's not very quick on the uptake, sir."

"Do you see them often, these friends in Chelsea?" the commander murmured.

"Couple of times a week."

"How long do you stay?"

"That depends."

"On what?"

"On what we're doing."

"Printing leaflets?"

"What leaflets?"

"Anti-government leaflets."

"I know nothing of any leaflets."

"He doesn't seem to know what I'm talking about, sergeant."

"Perhaps he doesn't know about the posters either, sir."

"Ask him about the posters, sergeant."

"Tell the commander about the posters."

"What posters?"

"He says he doesn't know about the posters, sir."

"Do you think we've got the wrong man, sergeant?"

"I think that's hardly likely, sir."

The commander stared at Farran, his face hard and unyielding. "You did say you live off Ladbroke Grove, didn't you?"

Farran didn't answer.

"You did say you live off Ladbroke Grove, didn't you?" No reply.

"Ask him where he lives, sergeant."

"Tell the commander where you live."

Farran said, "Ladbroke Grove." He said it like a child reciting.

"Say 'sir' when you speak to the commander."

"Ladbroke Grove, sir."

"Ask him if he has any friends, sergeant."

"Tell the commander if you have any friends."

"Yes."

"He says yes, he has friends, sir."

"Where do they live?"

"Chelsea."

"Ask him if he's proud of his country, sergeant."

"Tell the commander if you're proud of your country."

"Yes," said Farran.

"Sir," the sergeant snapped.

"Yes, sir."

"Ask him if he considers a man who is proud of his country should mix with anarchists, parasites and agitators who want to see Britain driven to the wall?"

Farran did not answer.

"I believe I've upset him, sergeant," the commander said.

"He does seem a little down in the mouth, sir."

"Ask him if he's upset."

"The commander would like to know if you're upset."

"No."

"He says no, he's not upset, sir."

They kept it up for more than three hours. The commander walked backwards and forwards across the room. He stood at the window, stood behind the chair, strolled to the door. He made a point of never standing in one place for longer than a minute at a time. He walked stiffly, back straight, head erect. He held a ruler in one hand which he slapped repeatedly against his thigh.

Farran could scarcely believe it was happening. The scene belonged to a nightmare from some fascist police state, not freedom-loving England. He sat hunched in the chair, staring at the floor as the atmosphere in the room grew thicker. He felt drained and defenceless. Only an odd stubborn streak kept him going.

"Why has your ration book scarcely been used?" the commander demanded.

"I . . . the shops are practically empty."

"But your ration book shows only seven coupons missing.

116

Seven coupons in six weeks. By any normal standards, you ought to be dead. Unless of course, someone's feeding you."

"Well . . . yes."

"Your friends in Chelsea?"

"Yes."

"On what?"

"Whatever's going."

"Bread?"

"Yes."

"Boiled ham?"

"On occasion."

"Is it good?"

"It's okay."

"Where does it come from? The warehouses ran out of ham ages ago."

"Well . . . maybe it was beef."

"I thought you said it was ham."

"Beef."

"I think sergeant, correct me if I am wrong, but I think he said it was ham."

"I'm sure of it, commander."

"I believe he's lying to us, sergeant."

"I believe he is, commander."

"Your name *is* Jack Farran, isn't it?"

"Yes."

"And you do live off Ladbroke Grove?"

Farran didn't answer.

"He won't answer me, sergeant."

"Perhaps he's thirsty, sir."

"Do you think so?"

"He has a thirsty look."

"Ask him if he'd like a drink of water."

"Do you want a glass of water?"

"No."

"He says no, he doesn't want a glass of water."

"Is he sure?"

"Are you sure you don't want a glass of water?"

"No, I don't want a glass of water."

"He says no, he doesn't want a glass of water, sir."

"You do live off Ladbroke Grove, Farran?"

Farran remained silent.

"Hit him sergeant," the commander said evenly.

The sergeant stepped forward and hit Farran between the eyes with his clenched fist. There was a sound like wood splitting and Farran's head flicked back like a whiplash. Blood spurted from his nose, splashing over his chin and down the front of his shirt.

"You do live off Ladbroke Grove?"

"Yes."

"Yes, what?" snapped the sergeant.

"Yes, sir."

The commander put his hands in his pockets. He had a look of infinite patience. "Who's employing you, Farran?" he asked pleasantly.

Farran remained silent. He felt stunned and sick.

"Your friends in Chelsea, are they employing you?"

"There are no friends in Chelsea. I made that up."

"He made it up, sergeant."

"Perhaps he made it up about the ham too, sir."

"Where is the literature coming from, Farran?"

"What literature?"

"Where is Colonel Savage?"

"Who?"

"Your friend."

"What friend?"

"Perhaps he made it up about the colonel, sergeant."

"He seems quite adept at making things up, sir."

"I think he's lying to us."

"I think he is, sir."

"Hit him, sergeant."

The sergeant hit Farran twice in the face. He used his fist hammer-fashion, jerking Farran's head viciously from side to side, and the heavy ring on his finger split the jaw open, sending blood streaming down his jacket.

The commander said: "Not pleasant, is it, Farran?"

"No, sir."

"You won't lie to us again?"

"No, sir."

"Where is Colonel Savage?"

"I know no Colonel Savage."

"Who's printing the underground literature?"

"I don't know."

"You mix with the people who distribute it. You go to their little meetings. You preach revolution and disobedience, spread disorder and unrest."

"It's a free country," Farran growled.

"Free country? Do you really think so? Stand up, Farran. Let me show you how free this country is."

With a speed and ferocity that was chilling, the commander stepped forward and drove his knee into Farran's crotch. Farran choked. His body sagged, he crouched over, clutching himself. The commander gripped his hair with one hand and jerked his head downwards. At the same time he brought up his left knee and smashed it full into Farran's face. There was a distinct crack as the nose bone broke. Farran sank to his knees and began to vomit on the floor.

"Freedom is a luxury for those who obey the law," the commander said. "For the vermin who gnaw at our society there can be no freedom. They have to be rooted out and destroyed so that the rest of decent humanity can go on living again. Under the Emergency Powers Act, I can lock you away for twenty-eight days without bringing charges. Think yourself lucky our prisons no longer have the provisions to cope with scum like you. Personally, I'd be happy to lock you in a cell and let you starve to death. Let us catch you in our sights again and I'll demonstrate just how unpleasant I can really be. Get him out of here sergeant, and fumigate the room. I can't stand the stench of treachery."

When he got back to his bedroom Farran, stunned and battered, packed his nostrils with cotton wool and moulded his nose into some semblance of its former shape with his fingertips. Next morning he visited a doctor at St. Mary's Hospital, a friend of his landlady's, who complimented him on a fine re-mould job as he expertly re-set the bone and structured it with plaster. The doctor was an Indian who regarded everything with Indian equaminity.

"That is the trouble with you British," he said, "you are too bloody complacent. No one ever believed it could happen here. Secret trials, police brutality, torture and interrogation, such anomalies belong to countries who do not understand the meaning of democratic rule. Alas, when the downward slide begins, it is very swift. You have learned the lesson so many western intellectuals are forced to face. No nation is immune."

Farran felt no resentment at what had happened in the police station. He regarded it as justice of a sort, for he deserved to be punished for having ignored the warnings of his instructors that Britain had changed, that the police had new far-reaching powers, and that sooner or later he would be subjected to their attentions.

Though he felt stiff and sore from his beating, he actually enjoyed outwitting the various 'tails' the plain-clothes men assigned to him; it gave an added spice to what was becoming a dreary existence, and it made him feel, to some small extent, more like a true revolutionary. He had to admit he did not care for the dissidents he contacted, but then his likes or dislikes had no real place in the great scheme of things and he continued to do his job thoroughly, receiving instructions and fresh cassette tapes from his weekly visitor and supply officer, Herbert Romney. Then, one afternoon in late September, quite unexpectedly, Romney did not turn up. In his place instead (and Farran could scarcely believe this, and actually whooped with delight when he opened the door) came Myriam, who had been flown in from Camp Fremont to take over the co-ordination of the various 'sleepers' scattered around West London.

Myriam was as delighted to see Farran as he was to see her, for it was many weeks since they'd parted, and Myriam had missed him more deeply than she would ever have believed possible. They spent the rest of the afternoon celebrating their reunion in bed, and thereafter she returned nightly, although she kept her flat in Lancaster Gate as a base.

Myriam had long since recovered from her reaction to the

brainwashing sessions in Building 3. Now she was as dedicated as Farran to the armed struggle in Britain. Each morning she played her music tapes on a portable cassette machine, renewing the behaviour patterns ingrained in her subconscious. The only difference, and it was a very slight one, lay in her inner conviction that she was oddly out of alignment. It was something she couldn't describe, something she couldn't quite put her finger on, a feeling of gaps opening up in her psyche like the dark holes in space which scientists endlessly puzzled over, a deep-rooted belief that bits of her didn't quite come together as a jig-saw puzzle will not come together if several of its pieces are missing.

She had strange dreams from time to time, and in them another man emerged, elusively familiar. He was big and volatile, a shambling bear of a man whom she knew was her lover, yet Myriam felt convinced that the only lover she'd ever had was Farran. Soon the dreams began recurring, and in each one the same unidentified man haunted her memory like a ghost from the inner recesses of her brain. She never mentioned this to Farran, or to anyone else for that matter, for the ideological conflict in which they were immersed was too important for personal considerations, and she carried on with her job, acting as a link between the various guerrilla teams, distributing supplies, cassette tapes and instructions with the unquestioning devotion of a computer.

One day she arrived at Farran's flat brimming with excitement at the news that the students of London's universities, carefully penetrated and subverted over a period of many weeks, had decided to take to the streets the following Monday. The universities, like many other institutions, had clung to at least an illusion of normality, conducting their courses as though the world outside, and the pressures tearing at it, scarcely existed. But it was in the student unions that some of the deepest unrest had been felt, and since this would be the first open act of rebellion, both Myriam and Farran saw it as a significant step in their personal struggle. That night, they made love with a strange humility, as if what they were doing had become a religious rather than a physical experience, a culmination of all they had worked toward, but as the first tremors of climax shook Myriam's body, Farran seemed suddenly to disappear and in his place, like a spectre come from the past to torment her, lay the man from her dreams, strange, disturbing, hauntingly familiar.

NINE

Monday dawned with that bright over-real clarity that only comes with the early autumn. The sun, even at eight o'clock, carried a muffled warmth that gave Londoners a sense of the world renewing itself. The streets and buildings looked too vivid to be believed, like those sharply-etched paintings which display so much detail no human eye could possibly take it all in.

Over the streets of London there was a holiday atmosphere as if the problems of poverty and deprivation had been put aside for the moment while the people enjoyed the spectacle of students baiting the forces of authority, finding in it an entertaining diversion from the rigours of staying alive.

Farran and Myriam left their flat in Ladbroke Grove and walked to Piccadilly Circus where the main gathering was scheduled to take place at ten a.m. The itinerary, as Myriam understood it, was to march from there along Piccadilly to Hyde Park Corner and then down to the gates of Buckingham Palace, though what purpose such a march would achieve was difficult to define since the Royal Family had not been in residence for many weeks and could scarcely be blamed for the current crisis even if they had. But, as Farran pointed out, the actual destination was unimportant so long as the students and the people united and demonstrated their solidarity.

All the way to Piccadilly Circus, people were on the move, drifting along the pavements with a sense of excitement and anticipation. The mood was a gay one. The crowds laughed and shouted. It was rebellion, but rebellion with a difference. Spirits were high, not angry. Farran realised this was the first time since his return to London he had not been overwhelmed by the gloom and despondency of the city's streets.

"You'd almost think they realised," Myriam whispered with excitement. "You'd almost think they knew the Revolution was coming."

"Maybe they do," said Farran. "Maybe they're just so bloody fed up with struggling and starving that they're willing to accept anything now, anything that'll get them out of their apathy."

"Look, the TV people."

A group of dismal-faced young men in shabby trousers and pullovers picked their way through the lines of abandoned vehicles in the middle of the road, hauling cameras, batteries, gun-mikes and recording equipment. In contrast to the gaiety of the crowd, they looked like a funeral procession, and watching them, Farran understood why. The petrol restriction law had hit the news teams too. All events had to be covered on foot, and Farran knew dragging heavy television equipment halfway around London was no picnic. They would work for their money that day.

"Don't you feel proud?" Myriam whispered, squeezing his arm.

"Proud?"

"It's what we've struggled so hard for. Our first big success."

"Not mine," said Farran. "This is the student division."

"It's all the same in the long run. What one group does, the next group inherits."

"Oh, sure," said Farran.

As they approached Piccadilly Circus, Farran spotted units of the newly-formed riot police, backed up by their 'black marias'. The police and the armed forces were the only people who still had petrol. Even so, they used it sparingly, and Farran was surprised to see so many vehicles in evidence. The army was there too, keeping in the background as much as possible, their carbines slung casually across their shoulders as they watched the crowds with implacable faces or whispered messages on two-way radio sets.

Farran studied the riot police thoughtfully. This would, he knew, be their first testing ground since their formation nearly four months before. Close up, they looked surprisingly young as they stood in platoons of thirty or more, untouched by the frivolity of the crowd, their faces grim and expectant behind their gasmasks, white helmets, riot shields and heavy hardwood batons.

Units of Red Cross men waited on the opposite side of the street, their black uniforms distinguishable by white armbands and shoulder webbing. Like the police, they seemed on edge, as though they feared the glorious autumn day was about to erupt into violence and bloodshed.

As he emerged with the crowd into the Circus itself, Farran saw the reason for the tension. The whole central island, including the area around the Eros statue was a sea of bobbing, milling heads. Banners proclaimed: 'DOWN WITH INJUSTICE AND STARVATION'. 'GIVE US A GOVERNMENT WHICH IS AWARE OF OUR NATION'S WEALTH', 'FORGET THE CRIMES AND MISTAKES OF THE PAST, EATING IS NOT A PRIVILEGE, IT IS A BASIC HUMAN RIGHT', 'VICTORY TO THE PEOPLE'.

The students had built barricades across the entire width of the street, dragging wrecked and abandoned vehicles over the thoroughfare, digging up paving stones, ripping out the metal-mesh pedestrian barriers and re-erecting them around their crudely constructed fortress so that they were protected on four sides. Clearly, the idea of the march had been abandoned, and now they swayed and jostled behind their makeshift palisades, hurling abuse at both army and police with an air of happy self-righteous delight. Absurdly, some of the onlookers were busy taking photographs. Even in the depths of hardship, Farran thought, the ordinary acts of living took precedence over the major ones. As they watched, a bottle hurled from the centre of the island sailed through the air and shattered on the concrete four feet from a police inspector. He leapt back startled, while both students and crowd hooted with derision. An ugly rumble rose from the riot squad and Farran, standing well away from the white-helmeted platoons could feel their aggression reach him across the jostling people. Further down the street, he could see a squadron of mounted policemen getting ready to charge if things got out of hand. If was clear to Farran, as it must have been to anyone with an ounce of perception, that the noisy demonstrations would soon erupt into something far more serious, and with the mood of the riot squads as it was at present, all the pent-up frustration of the past few months could well break loose in a wild burst of ferocity and confusion.

"We'd better get back a bit," he said.

"Back?" Myriam echoed. "Jack, we ought to be out there. This is our fight as much as theirs."

"Don't be stupid. We can't afford to get mixed up with this. What happens if we get injured, or the scuffers pick us up? We'll leave gaps, that's what, and who's going to fill them? We've come too far to blow it all on one little demonstration."

Myriam seemed mollified. "You're right, Jack," she whispered. "Let's move."

They elbowed through the watching throng until Farran was satisfied they were far enough away to beat a hasty retreat if they had to, then they stood with the other spectators enjoying the sunshine, enjoying the sight of militant students thumbing their noses at authority, enjoying the knowledge that the seeds of their revolution were at last beginning to take fruit.

At twelve noon, the gaiety came to a bloody end. It began with students dropping molotov cocktails from the roofs of buildings around the Circus perimeter. They exploded in clouds of flame and smoke, creating momentary confusion among the riot police. Troops quickly isolated the culprits, arresting them as they fled to the streets below, but by this time the main body of demonstrators, encouraged by the bomb blasts, began bombarding the police with a barrage of stones, bottles, bricks, bits of wood and anything else they could get their hands on. The air was heavy with missiles and, as they watched, Farran saw several policemen hit the ground and lie motionless until their comrades dragged them to safety. He scanned the rooftops again. Soldiers were moving along the concrete parapets. There was no sign of the fire bombers.

"Where did they get the petrol for those molotov cocktails?" Farran hissed.

"From me," Myriam said blandly. Farran looked at her.

By this time, the police in the square had begun to retaliate. Gas grenades exploded in puffs of white smoke. Farran caught the acrid scent of tear gas carried on the wind.

"It's started," he whispered. "There'll be a charge any second."

The words were hardly out of his mouth when, with a ragged cry, the first wave of riot police hurled itself at the barricades. Farran saw the crowd surge backwards, heard screams, cries of anger and alarm. Through the confused jumble he saw the white helmets dancing, the batons falling, the bodies lying. The tear gas fumes grew stronger, making his eyes swim. He took out a handkerchief and mopped his cheeks. The students milled around in confusion, their ranks broken and disorganised as the riot squads thrust them backwards out of their makeshift fortress and into the open. Above the bobbing heads, mounted policemen swung their batons wildly, their faces twisted, their arms going like windmills as they chopped and hacked, pounded and slashed, swaying in their saddles with the fury of attack.

A young boy weaved out of the swirling throng, his arms held forward defensively as he struggled to find direction. He moved like a blind man, sliding one foot in front of the other. From the tip of his crown to his chin he was a mass of bloody flesh. As Farran watched, a group of riot police set about him like demons. The boy slid to his knees and within seconds the heavy batons had pounded him to the ground.

Farran heard a scream and saw a young girl, her face paralysed with fright, struggling to get away. A policeman leapt forward and swung his baton in a wide arc. There was a clunk like a hammer striking wood and the girl sprawled in the dust. She tried to get to her feet. The policeman stood above her, his face twisted with rage, and began to raise the baton again. A student wielding a pickaxe handle belted him hard between the eyes and he hit the concrete, rolling over backwards, his helmet disappearing beneath the scurrying feet. The girl staggered back into the crowd.

As Farran watched, scarcely daring to breathe, a new wave of missiles was launched from behind the barricades, falling among the policemen like lethal rain. With a roar of triumph, the students increased the ferocity of their attack until bit by bit the riot squads were driven back and the demonstrators had re-occupied the central island.

In the next hour, the police made six charges in all. Each time they were repelled under a bombardment of bottles, stones and bricks, and soon the entire Circus began to resemble a battlefield, with missiles everywhere, broken glass, discarded batons and Red Cross men moving in and out to ferry off the injured.

By mid-afternoon, the high spirits and hot tempers had begun to cool, and things might have ended there, or at least petered out until some semblance of order could be restored, but just before three o'clock, while the riot squads were busy re-organising themselves, there came a sudden sharp crack from behind the Eros statue. The sound reached clearly to Farran's ears, reverberating across the square. A young lieutenant perched on one of the army vehicles flipped over backwards and hit the concrete with stunning force. He struggled to get up, his face dazed and hurt. His mouth was open, but no sound emerged. Blood was spreading in a dark stain across the front of his combat jacket. He pressed both hands against the spot as though trying to hold it in place. The blood oozed out between his fingers and he fell back motionless, his eyes staring at the sky.

Farran felt a sickening fear crawl up his spine.

"Jesus," he choked, "they're *shooting* out there."

For a moment, the whole Circus was hushed, as though the suddenness of the shot had stunned them all equally, police and rioters alike. The shouting ceased, the missiles stopped, the swirling crowd came to a standstill. All eyes centred on the solitary blood-soaked corpse sprawled in the gutter. Then, like a series of jumping jacks going off at once, a whole fusillade of shots rang out, all of them coming clearly and unmistakably from the centre of the students' ranks. A policeman spun across the pavement, his arms and legs thrashing the ground. A soldier dropped where he stood, his face ground into a mush-like pulp.

With shrieks of panic, the students broke ranks and began to run for the Circus peripheral. The shooting went on, the snipers picking out targets among the army vehicles and firing between the ranks of fleeing demonstrators. Then the army rifles opened up their sound deep and hollow like cows coughing in a field at night. People screamed as the students began falling, their bodies littering the ground like carelessly strewn confetti. In their frenzy to escape, others stumbled over them, rolling and twisting in a forest of whirling limbs. Farran saw a young girl crawling for cover, her left arm dangling from a couple of muscle fibres.

He seized Myriam's wrist. "Who set this up?" he shouted.

She stared at him, her eyes bright with alarm. "What are you talking about?"

"Your bloody field force, is this their idea?"

She shook her head, refusing to believe it. "No, Jack, no. They wouldn't . . ."

"Like hell," growled Farran. "Nobody gets into a shooting match with the army unless they're bloody crazy. Somebody wants a massacre out there."

The first wave of students reached them, and suddenly the action they had been watching was all around them, they were spectators no longer. Farran felt himself being carried helplessly backwards as the crowd broke in terrified confusion. He saw a woman go down under the stampede and seized Myriam tightly, holding on to her sleeve like grim death. He smelled again the scent of tear gas fumes, heard the sharp crack-crack-crack of rifle fire and saw the bodies falling, the hurt, the dazed, the dying and the dead.

"Let's get out of here," he shouted.

He began to run, still holding Myriam's arm. Ahead, the road was blocked by a squadron of mounted policemen. They looked grim and determined as they waited, with batons raised, for the panic-stricken escapers to come within striking range.

"We can't make it, Jack," Myriam gasped. "We can't make it."

Farran dragged her into a doorway, his mouth convulsed, his brain scarcely registering the people hurtling by. There was no escape that way. Not unless they wanted their skulls broken. It was crazy, all of it crazy. This didn't happen in England.

The door they had stopped against had a wide glass panel through which Farran could see the bolt on the other side. Without hesitation he drove his fist straight through the glass and slipped the catch free.

"This way," he gasped.

His hand was bleeding, but he didn't give a damn. He hadn't even felt the pain. All he could think of was the need to escape, to find some way out of this stampeding nightmare. They were in a large dusty room where huge cartons stood perched one on top of the other. The floor was stone. Cobwebs cluttered the ceiling. From outside came the muffled sound of shouts, screams, gunshots.

"What is this place?" Myriam whispered.

"Looks like the storeroom of a shop," Farran said. "Maybe it'll bring us out on a back road."

He moved quickly between the packing cases, dragging Myriam, glad to be away from the horror of the world outside.

They found a corridor and clattered down it, looking for an exit.

"Oh Jack," Myriam sobbed, "it was horrible."

"Yeah," said Farran.

"Those poor poor people."

"Forget them. Think about us. We're not out of this mess yet."

It hadn't taken much, he thought. A bit of careful timing, a few judicious gunshots and the whole bloody powderkeg had exploded. So much for English tolerance and moderation. When it came to the push, chaos and panic were universal.

They found a short flight of stairs, and then another corridor opening into a smaller room, just as dusty as the first, but filled this time with rolls of heavy carpet. There was a door opposite. Farran was making toward it when he heard the scrape of boots outside, the muffled staccato sound of barked orders. He pulled Myriam back.

"Somebody out there," he hissed.

"Riot squad?"

"Troops, I think. Sounds like."

Myriam's face darkened. "Bloody murderers."

Farran stared at her angrily. "They were firing in self-defence," he said. "No soldier in the world's going to watch his friends shot down and not squeeze off a round or two."

"They're murderers, all of them" Myriam maintained, her face pale and tense.

"And what about your friends on the student infiltration unit," Farran asked with exasperation. "They started all this. Aren't they murderers?"

Myriam didn't answer. She looked as though she was ready to burst into tears. Farran hoped not. That was all he needed at this moment, a hysterical female.

He shuffled to the door and pressed his ear against it, listening for sounds from outside. He could hear distant shouting and scuffling, but in the immediate vicinity things seemed reasonably still. There was no window and no keyhole. Nothing else for it, they would have to take a chance. He eased back the bolt and creaked the door open an inch or two. They seemed to be in some kind of mews or narrow street. He could see dustbins against the opposite wall. He turned to look at Myriam. Her face was still pale, but to his immense relief she looked calmer, more composed.

"Okay," he whispered, "let's go."

They ran into the sunlight and in that instant Farran knew he had made a mistake. There were people in the alley, soldiers, not in front but behind. He could see the opening nearly forty yards ahead and realised at once they would never make it. A voice rang on the air, harsh, commanding. "Stand still, you two. Stop at once or we fire."

Farran slithered to a halt. Myriam stood beside him, gasping hopelessly. Her eyes looked wide and frightened. Farran peered back. A party of troops was loading casualties on to an ambulance. A young officer in lieutenant's uniform came striding briskly toward them.

"Where d'you think you're going?" he snapped.

Farran breathed deeply, struggling to gain control of himself. "We're trying to get out of here," he said, "away from the shooting."

The lieutenant peered at him closely, then at Myriam. "What's your name?"

"Farran."

"This your wife?"

"Fiancée."

"What is this, Nigel?" asked another voice, and Farran turned to see a major with a swagger stick strolling casually toward them. He was slim, thirty to thirty-five years old, moustached, suntanned.

"Good afternoon, sir," the lieutenant said, saluting. "We caught these characters behaving suspiciously. They were hiding in one of the buildings back there. When they spotted us, they tried to make a run for it."

"Bloody right," Farran snapped. "What do you expect with half Piccadilly Circus littered with dying people?"

The major studied him curiously. "Who are you?" he demanded.

"My name's Farran. We're not part of the demonstration. We're spectators, like most of the other poor sods out there."

The major shook his head in irritation. "Damned fools. None of them with a ha'porth of sense. Nor you either. Don't you realise our job is difficult enough without having hordes of idiot onlookers under our feet? What did you come for?"

"I don't know," Farran shrugged. "A bit of excitement, I suppose. We didn't expect it to get out of hand."

"Well, I hope you're satisfied. You've just witnessed the collapse of British restraint. From now on, things can never be the same again. Where did you think you were running to anyway?"

"We were just. . . . I suppose we just wanted to escape," Farran murmured.

132

"You'd have ended up right in the thick of it," the major said. "Where do you live?"

"Ladbroke Grove."

The major looked at the lieutenant. "Simon, is that ambulance heading for Harrow Road?"

"I believe so, sir."

"Any room?"

"Oh, I'm sure they can squeeze in a couple more."

The major turned back to Farran. "We'll give you a lift at least as far as Queensway. But next time, use your bloody heads and keep away from trouble. It's difficult enough sorting out the real agitators without having to put up with a bunch of gormless observers as well."

The ride back in the ambulance turned out in one respect to be worse than the riot itself, for it was filled with wounded people, both soldiers and civilians, and the entire journey was punctuated by the groans of their suffering.

Farran and Myriam sat with two young medics who were trying to administer a plasma transfusion to a young private with a dressing on his chest the size of a football. His face was ghastly, his skin covered with a faint yellowish sheen that made it appear strangely luminous. As they were passing the Edgware Road, one of the medics said, "You can forget that. He's gone."

The other, a small plumpish man with tousled gingery hair, glared at Farran and Myriam with a look of pure hate.

"Did you see enough today?" he exclaimed. "Did they put on a good show for you?"

Myriam gave a choking sob. The medic shook his head in disgust. "You make me sick," he growled.

Back in their room, Farran flopped into a chair, his entire metabolism in conflict. The feelings of compunction and self-reproach which even the meticulous attention of Building 3 had failed to fully extinguish inside him, now rose to assert their rightful place, and finding that place occupied by other more foreign emotions immediately engaged them, plunging Farran into a bewildered stupor. He felt bitter, confused and disgusted.

133

Myriam went into the kitchen and made some coffee. When she came out, he saw she had been crying.

"Jack?" she whispered.

"What?"

"All those people dead. That shouldn't have happened, Jack."

"It was planned," Farran said angrily. "The whole bloody thing was planned. That was no spontaneous shooting. It was a cold deliberate provocation and it worked just the way your friends wanted it to work."

She sat on the floor at his feet. "You can't be sure, Jack."

"I'm sure."

Tears sprang from her eyes and began to roll down her cheeks. Something was happening to her, something she didn't understand.

"Jack, I'm so confused. Feel my arm. I'm like that all over. Numb. Tell me what we're doing is right. It is right, isn't it Jack?"

Farran sighed, staring at the ceiling. A great hollowness seemed to open up inside him, like an ancient wound beginning to hurt again.

"I don't know," he said. "I just don't know any more."

In early October, a number of strange consignments began arriving at American air bases all over the country. They came in sealed containers, like large coffee cans, and on their sides were names like 'Crabmeat Casserole', 'Never-Fail Rice', and in some instances, 'Industrial Wool'. The cans were transported in discreet loads to the ten major cities of Britain. They contained a relatively new substance called CX3. CX3 was a type of explosive which combined both magnesium and white phosphorus, so that as well as being light, malleable, and carrying strong 'blast probability', it also included a high incendiary potential. In secret factories tucked away in rented rooms in the middle of Britain's most thickly populated urban areas, teams of carefully trained operatives worked night and day converting their supplies of CX3 into deadly home-made bombs. Most of the bombs were small enough to be carried in an ordinary shopping bag or suitcase. All were capable of producing widespread devastation. In FOCB records, their object was listed as being "to kill, neutralise and demoralise".

Some of the bombs were packed with hundreds of small irregular-shaped pellets called flechettes, to produce a fragmentation effect. Some contained a jellified oily mixture called sarium which, on detonation, produced a fire that was difficult to control, rather like the results of an airborne napalm attack.

Within a month, each of Britain's larger cities contained, scattered through its suburbs and council estates, enough CX3 bombs to turn it into a battlefield. Spengler's war was ready to begin.

TEN

The scent of brine hung like a pall above the rows of drum-like vats at the Chattahoochee Pickling Company in northern Florida. There were times Dillon felt sure that smell would remain with him for the rest of his life. It seemed to lodge in every nook and cranny of his person, polluting his nostrils, permeating his hair – even, he felt sure, emanating from his pores when he perspired, which was often, for his job entailed unloading millions of cucumbers, onions and cauliflowers which arrived by truck from the fertile farmlands on the Chattahoochee River and had to be dumped into the tubs for salt-curing, a process which lasted over a period of three months. Dillon worked shirtless under the late autumn sunshine, his big rawboned body tanned and glistening. He had learned to move in a kind of rhythm, unloading a truck at a time, hauling the heavy packing cases across the courtyard and stacking them on the forklift conveyor to be ferried to the vats. It was boring work, repetitive, unstimulating, physically exhausting, but it had allowed him to fade out of existence and for the first time in three months he felt blissfully secure. There was no reason why anyone from the CIA should look for him in rural Florida, and certainly not at the Chattahoochee Pickling Company. All things considered, Dillon felt he had done a pretty good job of disappearing, although he recognised that until he could find a way out of his predicament, the odour of pickled cucumbers was going to have to be lived with.

Gasping sweatily, Dillon dumped his last packing case on to the forklift just as the lunchtime whistle blew. With a sigh of relief, he mopped his gleaming face and wandered up to the shack to pick up his coffee and sandwiches. Some of the other men were already in there, eating, playing cards or generally fooling about. They were glad to be in the shade, glad of any respite, no matter how brief, from the endless unloading and dumping. It was, Dillon thought, a hell of a way to make a living, with no future in it that he could see, except the privilege of staying alive. For that alone, he could put up with anything, even the smell and, if he was honest with himself, only one thing spoiled his new-found sanctuary, and that was the thought of Myriam. Was she still alive, and if so, where?

Dillon's first move after his flight from New York had been to hire a car and drive to the Adirondacks looking for Camp Fremont. But after eight days of cruising around those lonely hillbilly roads, he'd been forced to admit defeat. If Camp Fremont truly existed, the authorities had managed to obliterate every hint of its whereabouts. For days on end, he'd pulled into isolated gas stations, asking questions, checking maps, but coming up always against the same blank wall of ignorance and rejection. Camp Fremont? Never heard of it. He might as well have asked for the Kingdom of Camelot.

At last it became clear to Dillon that it was high time he got the hell out of there, and started concentrating on saving his own skin. He disposed of the hire car and moved south on foot, picking up lifts as he went along and doing occasional jobs when he needed the money. His brain was in a turmoil. It wasn't easy to turn his back on Myriam when for all he knew she needed him desperately. Come to that, maybe she was dead already. Maybe they had done to her what they'd done to his boss Brad Gordon, and his friend from the *Washington Post*, Sid Davidson. But Dillon wouldn't allow himself to think about that. Myriam was alive. She had to be alive. Sooner or later, when he'd figured this thing out, he would come up with a way of helping her, but right now he had to concentrate on survival, otherwise they'd fix him just like they'd fixed Brad and Sid.

He crossed the border at Niagara and worked on the tobacco harvest on the shores of Lake Erie, labouring in the fields under a blistering sun. When the harvest was over, he moved steadily south, bumming rides all the way, developing a natural cunning which helped steer him clear of the law. Near Owensboro, Kentucky, he worked in a sawmill, hauling lengths of timber off a conveyor belt and stacking them in piles for transportation. At Talladega, Alabama, he shifted furniture and painted housefronts. At Laurel, Mississippi, he hauled shingles for a roofing firm. Meanwhile, his physical appearance gradually changed. He let his hair grow long and neglected to shave. Soon he was sporting a heavy beard, and with the tangled mop on his skull, began to resemble a not-too-amiable gorilla which had by some freakish accident been decked out in human clothing. Naturally, this helped little in picking up rides, but by now Dillon was beginning to accumulate a little spending money and as his confidence grew he switched from hitch-hiking to travelling on Greyhound coaches.

At Chattahoochee he adopted the name of Thomas Martin, and with the job at the pickling plant felt his transformation was finally complete. Not that it made him feel much better. Safer maybe, but there was still the unalterable fact that Myriam might be alive and needing him, and that somewhere men were working, without the knowledge or approval of the American people, toward the destruction of their closest ally. He couldn't skulk in his den for ever. Sooner or later, he had to figure out a course of action and pursue it. All his life, he had reacted to every problem in the same way, by charging head-long in and hoping for the best. Unfortunately, his bull-like eagerness had already resulted in the deaths of two men for whom he felt both affection and respect, and he did not intend getting into that ballgame again. There had to be some other way, direct but sensible, something he could do that would fix the whole rotten business and get both Myriam and him off the hook. He was thinking of this as he entered the lunch room. There was a smell of coffee, cigarette smoke and human sweat. Girlie calendars peered down from the walls. The men were crowded around the table, eating sandwiches and playing poker. Their hard hats hung from pegs by the door.

"Those dummies," one of them was saying, "the way they go on sometimes, it's like nobody else in the world existed."

"Yeah," another murmured, "you'd think it was God Almighty, instead of the President."

Something stirred in Dillon's brain. "What's that?" he asked.

"Those schmucks in New Orleans, they think they're the clean-up hitters in the whole bastard line-up."

"No," said Dillon, "about the President."

The man looked at him. "Don't you read the papers? He's visiting New Orleans tomorrow. They're carrying on like it's the greatest thing since Independence. But there's only one reason he's making that trip. He knows damn well if there's an election in July he'll lose Louisiana. He wants to run his vote total as high as he can get it."

Dillon felt a tingle of excitement. Of course, the President. The one man in the country he knew he could trust. If he, Dillon Harris, could somehow or other get to him, the President could straighten out the whole awful bag of shit. It was a crazy idea. After all, he would be guarded day and night, but Dillon had to try. For Myriam. For Brad and Sid. For the country goddamnit. It was his Godgiven duty. Crazy or not, there was no other way, and this opportunity had been dropped in his lap like a gift from heaven.

Dillon quickly made up his mind. He left his sandwiches where they were, and went at once to see his boss Miles Anson, a small bony scarecrow of a man who had started out regarding Dillon with hostile suspicion (because of his hairy looks), but who now trusted him with the bond a father might feel for a son. He smiled as Dillon stepped into his office.

"Hello, Tom," he said, using the name Dillon went by, "something on your mind?"

Dillon shifted his feet uncomfortably. "I'm sorry to do this, Mr. Anson, with the bean harvest coming in and all, but I'm going to have to quit."

Miles Anson frowned. "Quit, Tom? You crazy?"

"I have to go to New Orleans," Dillon said. "It's very important, Mr. Anson. I mean, I wouldn't walk out on you this way unless it was a matter of life and death."

"You make it sound very dramatic, Tom."

"Mr. Anson, it's so goddamned dramatic it frightens me every time I think about it."

"Some relative sick? Friend maybe?"

Dillon shook his head. "I wish it was that simple, Mr. Anson, I really do. Please don't ask me any questions and then I won't have to lie any, which is what I'll do if you start pumping me."

Miles Anson sighed and got to his feet. He was wearing crumpled dungarees, for his job was divided between the office and the pickling plants outside. He took out a handkerchief and blew his nose. "I like you, Tom," he said, "I was going to put you in charge of the assembly line in a week or two. Listen, supposing we play it this way. You go to New Orleans and do whatever it is you have to, and I'll hold the job open for seven days. How's that? If you're not back by then, I'll start looking around for a replacement."

"I don't like to cause so much trouble," Dillon said.

"No trouble, Tom. Like I said, you're a good worker, reliable and conscientious, and I'll be sorry to see you go. Get back before next Tuesday and the job's still yours. Now I can't be much fairer than that, can I?"

"No, sir, Mr. Anson, I guess not."

That evening, Dillon took the bus to New Orleans. He travelled overnight, hoping to sleep in one of the reclining seats, but an unexpected thunderstorm kept him awake well into the early hours. Lightning flashed and rain pounded the highway in a relentless tattoo. The passengers peered through the windows, uttering breathless 'oooohs' and 'aaaahs' at each rippling bombardment. Dillon sat thinking miserably of Myriam. It always hit him worse at night. Sometimes he would lie for hours, not sleeping, wondering if he had abandoned her. If they'd hurt Myriam, he thought, there wasn't really much point in living any more. The only thing that kept him sane, kept him intact as a person was the belief – one he clung to with desperate urgency – that some day they would be re-united. Meanwhile, as the news from Britain grew steadily more depressing, Dillon had given up reading newspapers. The knowledge that he, and only he knew what was really going on sometimes became too much to bear, and he had to put it out of his mind as a man might ignore the pain of a tumour he can do nothing about.

Now, in the stormladen night, the enormity of what he had embarked on disturbed him. How the hell was he, Dillon Harris, going to get to see the President? The whole population of the Mississippi Delta would be in New Orleans tomorrow, and every single human being would have one thought in mind, to get as close to the President as he possibly could. He had no clear plan of campaign. Come to that, he didn't even know where the President intended to be. It was a sorry start to a highly unlikely escapade, and his gloominess increased with each rain-sodden mile.

The woman sitting next to him smiled pleasantly. "You going to New Orleans?" she asked.

"Yes, ma'am."

"Home town?"

"No, first time there."

"I come every fall," she said. "My daughter's studying at Tulane. She spends her vacations working on the campus so this is practically the only time I get to see her. You know the President'll be there tomorrow?"

"Yes, ma'am, I know."

"He's doing the prize-giving at the university. I've got his itinerary right here."

She showed him a week-old copy of the New Orleans *Times-Picayune*. On its inside page was a list of the places the President intended to visit. Dillon felt his pulses quicken.

"Mind if I look at that, ma'am?" he asked.

"Of course not."

He spread the paper out, going down the official functions, mentally considering and rejecting each in turn. It was going to be tricky. The President would be watched every second, from the time he stepped off his plane to the time he stepped back on again. Getting close to him would be tough enough, but actually engaging his attention, making him listen while he, Dillon, told him what was happening at FOCB seemed beyond the bounds of even Dillon's fertile optimism.

141

All right, he told himself, you started this merry-go-round, now see it through. *Make* the President listen. He's the only chance you've got.

Peering down the list for a second time, Dillon saw the President planned to lunch at Luc's, a Creole restaurant which specialised in crawfish bisque, oysters and soft shell crab, and which stood on Dauphine Street in the old French Quarter. A restaurant would be better than out on the street, Dillon reasoned. Less people, less harassment. And if the President was eating, maybe he'd have time to listen too. The question was, how could he penetrate the security system without endangering his own hide? It would need careful reconnoitring.

The coach arrived in New Orleans at six-thirty in the morning, and Dillon strolled down Canal Street with apprehension lying inside him like a leaden weight. Even at that early hour there was a sense of excitement and anticipation. People milled about on the sidewalks, clutching homemade banners and paper flags. Strips of bunting hung across the full width of the street. Placards proclaimed: "Welcome to the Home of Jazz, Mr. President". Buses rumbled by, making for destinations with names like 'Desire' and 'Elysian Fields'. Helicopters hovered above the rooftops, their rotors filling the air with an incessant buzzing. Dillon's spirits fell again. The impossibility of his situation was becoming plainer every second. The combined resources of the police, the FBI and the CIA were being aimed at keeping interlopers out of the President's way, and he alone, Dillon Harris, one man, was crazy enough to think he could penetrate the system. He needed a headshrinker.

Dillon found a 24-hour hamburger palace and ordered a plate of eggs and grits, with hot coffee. The place was full of men in dungarees on their way to work. They read the morning papers and talked about the President's visit. Dillon wished he was going to work too. He envied them their non-involvement. Maybe he was playing this all wrong, risking his neck on an impossible gamble. Screw it, he thought, quit acting like a jerk. You've got to go through with it. There's no other way.

With breakfast over, he went and strolled into the narrow streets of the New Orleans French Quarter. The quaint old buildings with their ironwork balconies gathered around him like an intricate maze. He passed hordes of curio shops, their windows still shuttered in the early morning. Sunlight shimmered on the sidewalks.

Along Bourbon Street, the stripjoint doors were wide open, and Dillon could see the dinginess of the bars inside, empty now in the daylight, the tables piled on top of each other as the floors were swept and the glasses washed. He turned into Dauphine, and strolled along casually, hugging the shade of the overhead balustrades. Even at eight o'clock, the sun seemed ready to blind him with a blaze of white light.

When he got to Luc's, there were men hovering about all over the place, mean-looking men in light summer suits and conservative ties. He guessed they were SS, secret servicemen seconded from both the FBI and CIA to maintain security throughout the President's visit. Though there were still several hours to go, they had the restaurant sealed up tighter than a pickle jar. Dillon took out his cigarettes, stuck one in his mouth and lit it up. Not even a mouse could sneak through there, he thought. What wild notion had made him believe he could take on the finest security machine the country had to offer? If he wasn't careful, he stood a damned good chance of getting himself shot.

There was another thought worrying Dillon. It was just possible that one of the SS men might recognise him. After all, some of them worked for the Company. It wasn't beyond the bounds of possibility that they'd once belonged to FOCB, and if that was the case they must know he was a wanted man, a man who needed to be silenced. For a moment, Dillon felt his hands tremble. He paused in the doorway of a tiny curio shop and peered back down the street, wondering if he should retrace his steps and go back to Chattahoochee. It wasn't such a bad life when you thought about it, and any life at all was better than oblivion. Then Dillon thought about Myriam, and he knew he had to go on. He'd wasted too many weeks already, skulking like a rat in his hole. The time for running was over.

Taking a deep breath, Dillon strode purposefully up the sidewalk until he drew level with the restaurant door. At that precise moment, a man with a skin the texture of buttermilk, smooth and shiny, stepped into his path and asked for a light. Dillon stared at him in confusion. The man was Paul Zahl with whom he had worked four years ago in Langley, Virginia. He offered his cigarette and Zahl took it, lighting his own as his quick eyes danced all over Dillon, hard and suspicious. He was wearing a cowhide safari jacket, and close, Dillon noticed he was sweating slightly.

"Paul?" Dillon whispered.

The man frowned, surprised to hear his name mentioned. "Yes, what can I do for you, friend?"

"Paul, for Chrissake, don't you recognise me?"

Zahl's expression changed to blank astonishment. "Dillon?" he murmured, "is it Dillon?"

"Of course, it's Dillon. Who the hell do you think it is, Abraham Lincoln?"

"Dillon, what are you doing under all that fuzz? You look like a neanderthal man, for Chrissake."

Dillon's mind was in a whirl. Paul Zahl of all people. This was an unexpected stroke of luck. He trusted Zahl almost as much as he trusted Myriam. They had been good friends together in Langley, and he knew beyond any shadow of doubt that Zahl had never worked for FOCB, although of course, as Dillon was only too aware, the news of his disappearance might have been passed to other departments. He seized Zahl's arm.

"Paul," he gasped, "thank Christ I've found you."

But Zahl wasn't even listening. He was staring at Dillon transfixed, while a mixture of emotions flitted across his face, wonder, disbelief, puzzlement. "Dillon, an awful lot of people are very anxious to talk to you. I mean, where have you *been* for the past three months?"

"Paul, forget that. We're in the seventh innings and the

144

light's going okay? I've got a favour to ask and I haven't much time."

"Well, won't you at least tell me where you've been hiding yourself?"

"Not now, Paul. Maybe later, but not now. How many of these guys out there are SS?"

"All of them, except the character in the tux. He's the manager. The President's lunching here today."

"I know that," said Dillon. "Paul listen, I've got to see the President."

Zahl's face didn't alter. "Sure," he said, "I'll give him a call and tell him you're coming. Maybe he'll cancel his afternoon appointments so you two can shoot the bull about old times together."

"Paul, don't give me that smart-ass crap. I'm in a jam. I've got some information, something terribly, terribly important that I can tell only to the President direct."

Zahl's face was unmoved. There was a ragged tear on his forehead just above the nose, an old scar Dillon remembered from earlier days. "You'll have to do better than that, old buddy," he said, "this restaurant's like Fort Knox today. If I let you in there, they'd cut my balls off."

"Please, Paul," Dillon cried, "I know it's risky, but you've got to chance it."

"Why should I?"

"I can't tell you," Dillon said helplessly, "I can't tell you a damned thing except that this is so big it'll blow your mind. Trust me, dammit. You want to know where I've been for the past three months? Okay, I've been on the lam. On the run, get it? There are people who want me dead because of what I know. That's how big it is, and that's why I can't say any more."

"Dillon, you've flipped your lid," Zahl murmured.

"Let the President decide that," Dillon insisted. "Just get me in there, Paul, that's all I ask."

Zahl raised his eyebrows. The scar on his forehead was a different colour, pinker, brighter; it always turned like that when he was disturbed or upset. He studied Dillon carefully, his eyes moving from head to toe. "How far d'you think you'd get?" he grunted. "You look like a man who's been marooned on a desert island for twenty-five years. Even if I did sneak you in, they'd grab you before you'd walked ten feet."

"I'll have a shave and a haircut," Dillon promised, "and I'll buy a suit. Two hours from now, you won't even recognise me. Come on, Paul, we're friends, aren't we? We've always been friends. What have you got to lose?"

"My head, that's what."

"Listen, when the President hears what I have to say, he'll give you the Medal of Honour. You'll be a national hero, Paul."

Zahl tucked his hands in his pockets and sighed. "Okay," he shrugged, "maybe I'm crazier than you are, but get here at noon and if I can squeeze you in through the service door I'll do it. But just remember one thing when they drag you down to that padded cell. It wasn't me, old buddy."

"Thanks, Paul," Dillon said. "You're a good kid."

"Yeah," Zahl echoed drily.

"Just one thing more. Don't tell anyone you saw me here. No one, understand? This is between us, you and me."

"Who'm I going to tell, for Chrissake?"

"Good man, Paul. I'll be here at noon."

Dillon's brain was buzzing with excitement. The whole situation had suddenly reversed itself. By the most extraordinary coincidence, he had run into the one man in the world he could trust to help him. If things worked out, both he and Myriam could be clear by nightfall.

He made his way to a department store where he bought a sports jacket, trousers, white shirt and dark blue striped tie. He stopped at a barber's shop and had his tangled hair trimmed into a crewcut. Then he checked into the YMCA, showered, shaved, and changed into his new clothing. He felt all his nerve-ends tingling. The prospect of meeting the most powerful man in the world was a disquieting one. After all, what did you *say* to a President, for Chrissake? "Like the soup, Mr. President? Would you care to hear about the revolution in Britain?"

146

He'd better get smart. He'd have about ten seconds to grab the President's attention, maybe less. By then they'd be on to him, the SS men. His only hope was to say something in the first sentence that would make the President stop them dragging him away. Everything depended on his luck. He had never thought of himself as needing luck before, but he needed it now, he needed all he could get.

At ten minutes to twelve he left his key at reception and strolled across Canal Street back to the French Quarter. With the official visit now imminent, the controlled excitement of the early morning had changed to pandemonium. The streets were filled with a vast throng of restless spectators, all waiting expectantly. Uniformed policemen struggled to hold the crowds in check. Along the rooftops, orange spots marked the presence of special marksmen who studied the sea of heads with cool professional eyes. A film crew stood on the streetcorner, preparing to go into action. The sound recordist pulled down his headphones.

"They've just left the levee," he said.

The director checked his watch. "That's about four minutes away. We could get the sync piece in the can, if you're ready."

"Okay."

Dillon elbowed his way through the crowd until he had reached a point directly opposite the restaurant entrance. His whole body was aching with the strain. Sweat broke out between his shoulder-blades, soaking his new white shirt. A group of schoolchildren waved placards in his face declaring: "We Love You, Mr. President".

Then somebody yelled, "They're coming," and a wave of ragged cheering echoed across the rooftops.

The fleet of limousines cruised slowly up the street, flanked by motor cycles and piloted front and rear by police cars with lights flashing and sirens screaming. Dillon felt his pulses quicken. He was pleased at that, pleased that after all he had gone through he could still get that slight aura of hysteria which showed he was human.

The motorcade drew up in front, and the waiting crowd surged impatiently against the police barriers. All four doors of the President's limousine burst open simultaneously, and secret servicemen tumbled into the street, tense and watchful. Then Dillon felt his heart thump as the familiar figure of the President emerged, dapper and graceful, hair tousled by the wind, face creased but boyish as he beamed smiles at the excited crowd. The wave of cheering reached a crescendo. For almost a full minute, the President stood there, both arms outstretched as if to embrace the deafening applause, then, to the apparent consternation of his security men, strolled straight across to the delighted onlookers and began to move along them, laughing, chatting, shaking hands. The New Orleans District Attorney followed a little more discreetly, displaying an indulgent smile at his President's excesses, and behind him came a thin elderly man who looked, Dillon thought, as if he could not see any point in such a circus and did not know what they were all doing here anyhow.

A group of schoolboys jostled for the famous presidential handshake. Arms reached out to touch him as he passed by. The President went on grinning and moving gracefully along the barriers, oblivious it seemed to the urgent whispers of his secret servicemen. The film crew followed his line of advance, trying to move in as close as possible without getting under the great man's feet. The sound recordist dodged in and out between the security guards, using a gun mike to pick up impromptu conversations between the President and the crowd. The police were now having considerable trouble in keeping the spectators in check.

Outside the restaurant, the other members of the party had gathered together in a tight little group, amused by their President's ebulliency. The press secretary, a stately man in a wool-flannel suit waved the camera crew back. It was his job to keep things on schedule, and he was clearly worried they would run behind time.

An all-black jazz band from one of the nearby jazz dens began to play a zipped-up version of 'Hail to the Chief', but no one seemed to notice. They were too busy cheering the President who, still waving, was being shepherded into the restaurant by the beaming District Attorney.

Dillon let another ten minutes go by until some of the hullaballoo had died down, then he elbowed his way over the street to the service entrance. Zahl was standing by the door, his face pale and worried. "Where the hell have you been?"

"Sorry, Paul, I was watching the show out there."

Zahl tugged him into the doorway. "Get your ass in here fast," he growled. "I'm taking a risk out here, you know that?"

"I know it, Paul, and I appreciate it."

"Okay, slap your hands against the wall and spread out, feet apart," Zahl ordered.

Dillon stared at him in surprise. "What the hell for?" he demanded.

"Because I'm telling you to, that's what the hell for. Maybe you're packing heat. You think I'm going to let you near the President with a loaded gun in your pocket?"

"Oh, for Christ's sake, Paul . . ."

"No," said Zahl, "this is for my sake. I don't intend living the rest of my life with the knowledge that I let in the President's assassin."

Dillon stood with his hands on the wall as Zahl carefully and professionally frisked him. "How long have you known me?" Dillon asked, "Eight years? When did I ever point a gun at anybody?"

"We do this my way or not at all," Zahl answered. "Straighten up and turn around."

Dillon did so. Zahl pinned something to his jacket lapel.

"What's that?" Dillon asked.

"Special pass. It'll get you through the kitchens. After that, you're on your own."

Dillon smiled at him, and his voice softened to a gentler tone. "I want to thank you, Paul."

"Don't thank me," Zahl growled, "just get it over with and get the hell out. Every second you're in there, my goddamned stomach is ready to blow sky-high. Now, move."

Dillon turned and made his way up the corridor, feeling something inside him expanding as if he was about to rupture himself out of sheer tension. His whole future depended on the next thirty seconds.

The corridor ended and Dillon found himself in the kitchen. It was filled with people, all in various stages of panic and confusion. Dillon recognised the manager who was busy bellowing at one of his chefs. An SS man in a mohair jacket glanced at Dillon as he entered. The pass pinned to his lapel seemed to satisfy him.

Dillon's skin was creeping as he looked around. He wanted to laugh crazily, to hurl cups and plates about the room in one moment of glorious abandonment.

A tray with three bowls of soup on it lay on the table. Without pausing in his stride, Dillon picked it up and walked on into the dining room.

An SS man stationed by the door looked up, and Dillon felt his palms turn icy. He recognised the man. His name was Soames, he had once worked for FOCB. Dillon felt his senses reeling. There was no doubt in his mind the man would recognise him in turn. Shaved and crewcut, he had lost his earlier immunity.

Dillon felt fear sweep his body. You blind stupid asshole, he told himself, you should never have come. The idea was crazy from the beginning.

He started to cross the floor, walking straight-backed, head erect, the tray clutched across his chest like some form of bizarre banner, keeping his gaze fixed on the little group of people clustered around the dining table at the far end, as if by some remarkable sorcery he could make himself invisible.

He saw the President, dapper and smiling, leaning forward to illustrate some point or other. The people at the table laughed, their laughter echoing across the empty restaurant, hollow and discordant. Beyond the table, two further SS men tucked themselves discreetly against the far wall. The President's personal bodyguard.

Dillon felt as if he had withdrawn inside his own skull. He strode on, desperate to get there, his legs moving by instinct almost, for no feeling seemed to exist beyond his thighs. It was like walking through liquid butter. Christ, he had to reach the President before that bastard stopped him.

"Just a moment, please," said a voice from behind his head.

Dillon quickened his pace, pretending he'd misunderstood. Jesus, the restaurant seemed as long as a football field. He'd die of panic by the time he got there. The tray, clutched in his hands was beginning to tremble, the soup bowls clattering noisily. He resisted the urge to break into a run. Twenty yards to go. Why doesn't the President look up, for Chrissake? If only he would look up, then maybe he Dillon could take a risk on shouting across the final stretch. But he had to have the President's attention first.

"Excuse me," the voice called from behind, louder now, more insistent.

Dillon ignored it. Fifteen yards. The President was deep in the process of telling some joke or other, beaming across the dining table while the other guests leaned forward to catch what he was saying. A spasm in Dillon's chest almost brought him to a halt. Jesus, that's all I need right now, he thought, a goddamned heart attack. He forced himself to concentrate on not walking too quickly, but trying at the same time to lessen the gap between the President and himself before that lunatic behind took it into his mind to start cutting rough.

Sweat streaked his belly and chest. His mouth felt dry as cinder. Even if he made it, he had no guarantee he'd be able to speak straight, and everything depended on his first few words.

"The man with the soup tray," shouted the voice from behind, loud, commanding, instantly dramatic, "stand right where you are."

Jesus Christ, it was like the movies. Dillon swallowed. Everyone in the room was watching him now, the President, the luncheon guests, the two SS men who were moving cautiously forward from the far wall. What did that idiot have to shout like that for? Now, they saw him as a potential threat. There was already a trace of unease in the President's eyes. He, Dillon, had to make contact and make it fast. Throwing caution to the wind, he began to run. The soup bowls clattered. He shouted as loudly as he could, "Mr. President . . "

But his words were lost in the general confusion, for goddamnit those stupid dummies at the dinner table were actually diving on to the floor, for Chrissake, and the two SS men were running forward, pushing the President to the ground, and oh-my-God those were guns they were hauling from under their jackets.

"Look out," came the voice from behind, "that man's armed."

Armed? thought Dillon, insane with panic. Armed with three stupid bowls of soup, while those two lunatics crouching behind the dining table were getting ready to blast his head off. Without thinking twice, Dillon threw the tray directly into the faces of the two SS men and made a dash for the door. His feet slithered on the polished marble. The big man, the one from FOCB was blocking his route, crouching, both arms outstretched, the pistol in his fist aimed unerringly at Dillon's stomach. That crazy idiot bastard's going to kill me.

Dillon swivelled in mid-stride and changed direction toward the window. He saw the spurt of flame as the gun went off, felt the heat of the bullet zip past his shoulder. Oh, Jesus.

That window was miles away. It hovered in his vision, a great oblong of blessed light and freedom. If only he could make it, dive headlong through that implacable glass. On the sidewalk he'd still have a chance. In here, he was dead meat.

Dillon saw the window dancing crazily. He saw the wrought-iron balconies on the buildings across the street. He saw the pale blue of the sky above the rooftops. Then something erupted inside his skull, a blinding paroxysm of light that demolished his vision, jarred his nerve-ends, and somehow, though he could not remember falling, he was on the ground with a terrible weight grinding into his spine. There was no pain, thank God, only a curious numbness which came creeping up through his forearms and thighs. Dillon could feel dampness against his eyelids, and opening them saw the blood. There was blood everywhere, his own blood. He was dying. Crazy. He wanted to laugh at the irony of it. He'd blown the whole thing, ruined his one big chance. Jesus, couldn't he ever do anything right? Only he knew the truth of the monstrous conspiracy that was being conducted out there, and he was fading into oblivion. Who would save Myriam now, he wondered?

He saw the legs of the SS man standing above him. He saw the slick of his own blood. Then he relaxed, laid back his head, closed his eyes and never saw anything ever again.

ELEVEN

On Wednesday, November 30th, Joseph Spengler flew from Washington to Camp Fremont to speak to Colonel Savage. Spengler was in fine spirits. So far, his highly complex plan had proceeded bang on schedule, everything dovetailing neatly into place with what seemed to Spengler almost awesome accuracy. Spengler prided himself on his methodical mind, but this was the largest and most sophisticated project he had ever undertaken, and even he had to admit he was surprised by the smoothness with which it had progressed.

He chatted freely with the pilot all the way from Washington, and then with the driver who ferried him from the airstrip deep into the snowclad Adirondacks. Spengler noticed quite a change in Camp Fremont when he arrived at the gates. The central section of camp, the part which had been used to house Farran and his friends now stood deserted. Only the western area where Colonel Savage and his mercenaries trained with their ground-to-air missiles still buzzed with life. This portion had been scrupulously cordoned off from the rest, and considerable trouble continued to be taken to ensure that no clear evidence existed to give the recruits any indication they were in the United States. The deception was not a hundred per cent successful, Spengler realised, for the half-dozen ex-RAF pilots training down at the airstrip could hardly fail to notice the USAF planes flying in and out daily, but half-a-dozen men out of nearly four hundred were little enough to worry about, he reasoned, and steps could be taken to ensure their discretion when the time came.

Camp Fremont had changed in more than the deployment of its personnel however, for the lush greenery which surrounded it in summer had given way to thick powdery snow.

The windows of the army huts displayed patterns of mottled ice, and the roadways were rutted where tyres had carved channels through the frozen mud.

Spengler waited for Colonel Savage in the Camp Commander's office. He was feeling pleased with himself. Though the greatest test was still to come, Spengler was a great believer in the old sporting cliché that a good start led to an even better finish, and his optimism had grown steadily with each report his agents sent in.

He was humming softly when the door opened and Colonel Savage entered. Savage looked lean and fit, his cheeks flushed from the mountain air. He was dressed in drill trousers and a camouflaged combat jacket. On his head was a small beret. Tall and erect, he looked every inch the soldier.

Seeing Spengler, his eyes became haughty, but Spengler cared little whether people liked him or not. Qualities like friendliness and amiability did not exist in Spengler's world.

"Would you like a drink, Colonel?" he asked.

"I should love a drink," Savage said.

Spengler walked to the bookcase and took a large bottle of Scotch from behind it. He filled two glasses and handed one to Savage. "How d'you think your men are shaping up?" he enquired. "I realise four months is a rather restricted training period, but time has never been on our side, you know that."

"They're doing all right," Savage said cautiously. "I've no complaints."

"Good. It may interest you to know their instructors feel they're now ready to take the field. Would you feel confident enough to test your newly-formed army in action?"

"I might," said Savage, choosing his words with care. "To be honest, I'd be happier if they had another couple of months to find their feet. Some of those missile units are new and unfamiliar."

Spengler strolled to the window and breathed on the frosted glass, clearing a tiny circle with the side of his hand. He peered at the snow outside. "I wish that were possible, Colonel," he said, "but we're moving out the heavy equipment tonight. I want your men standing by ready for transfer tomorrow or the day after."

Savage said nothing for a while. He cradled his glass in both palms and studied Spengler thoughtfully. "Short notice, isn't it? Couldn't you have given us more warning?"

"Sorry, Colonel, it wasn't planned this way. More a question of knowing when the time was ripe. It's ripe now, Colonel. Like a plum ready for picking. Four months ago, your revolution would have blown up in your face. The British government would have crushed you inside twenty-four hours, and the people wouldn't have known a damn thing about it until it was all over. But we've been carefully preparing the way, tightening the screws here and there, putting an economic lock on Britain until the people are so giddy they'd be prepared to accept anyone who offered discipline and stability, even Adolf Hitler."

"You're mad," said Savage.

Spengler sighed. He said, as though explaining to a child: "All revolutions are the same, Colonel. They have the same ground rules. First, you create anarchy, then you offer order. Until now, we've been employing economic pressures. From tomorrow, we introduce terror. We're going to bring every British city to its knees, Colonel, and while that's happening, while the government is trying to deal with the war in its streets, we'll be moving your men and equipment into position for their war on the land. We've given the people a taste of confusion. Now we're going to let them taste fear. By the time you make your move, they'll be so dizzy you'll seem like a light from heaven."

Savage's face had gone very pale. "How do you intend to conduct this . . . terror?" he asked softly.

Spengler smiled. "Know how many men you need to bring a city to a standstill, Colonel? Two, that's all. Two men distributing carrier bags filled with explosive at carefully chosen strategic points. Tomorrow night, we'll be sending three hundred into the streets of London alone. Imagine that. Some of them are Camp Fremont trainees, the rest are activist elements recruited inside Britain. We're launching a bombing

156

campaign throughout the country that's unprecedented in history. By dawn on Friday, every major city will be in flames. It'll make the wartime blitz look like the Fourth of July."

"You damned lunatic," the Colonel hissed, staring at Spengler with loathing and disgust. "The people in the cities aren't soldiers, they're civilians. They don't deserve to die."

Spengler frowned. "Hold on, Colonel. Our targets have been specifically chosen to avoid unnecessary suffering. Our aim is to destroy property, intensify a sense of chaos and turmoil, create an *illusion* of widespread death. With enough bomb-blasts and fires, the people will be paralysed with panic. They'll feel that their civilisation is crumbling, and that's when you make your appearance."

"This is a dirtier game than I'd bargained for, Spengler."

"I warned you, Colonel, I warned you right from the beginning it wouldn't be a gentlemen's war. People *will* be killed, we can't avoid that. We're struggling hard to keep the numbers down, but without some loss of human life nobody's going to take you seriously."

"If you'd left this to me . . ."

"If we'd left it to you, it'd have been a fiasco. The dirty tricks are our department, Colonel, just concentrate on fighting your revolution. You start by establishing control of the Cheviots. Think you can do that?"

Savage nodded coldly. "I've gone over the strategy a thousand times," he said. "I could do it blindfolded."

"Good. Once the key villages are occupied and the roads sealed off, you must sit back and wait for the government to make its move. Be sure of one thing Colonel, they'll hit you with everything they've got. In Britain today, nobody has time to sit around negotiating. They'll use the RAF to blast you out. You've got only a half-dozen pilots with Hawker Harrier jump jets but you do have artillery and ground-to-air missiles, and the RAF is desperately short of fuel. If you can survive the first assault, chances are they'll have to withdraw. After that, they'll send in the army, probably a Quick Reaction Group of about two hundred men, with a back-up of a further four hundred and fifty. They can get nearly a thousand troops into the field inside twenty-four hours, which means you'll be heavily outnumbered, but since you control the roads and valleys you can use the hills as a buffer zone, and with the sophisticated weaponry we're supplying, force them to retreat. Once that happens, Colonel, you'll be free to commence your push to the west. The hydro-electric plants are already in a state of chaos. Your troops can occupy the pumping stations which supply water to the big towns and put them out of action. With neither water nor electricity, the large communities will become untenable, allowing your columns to enter and take command."

Colonel Savage stood in silence. Spengler leaned forward and refilled his glass. "What's wrong, Colonel?" he asked. "You look green around the gills. This is a time for rejoicing. Everything you've dreamed of is about to happen. Aren't you happy?"

Savage looked at his Scotch. His eyes were filled with a strange sadness. "I don't expect you to understand this, Spengler," he said softly, "but for the first time in my life, I feel ashamed."

At half-past four on the afternoon of Thursday, December 1st, Jack Farran rolled over in bed and looked at his watch. "It's time," he said softly.

Beside him, her head propped by the pillow, Myriam nodded. She was staring at the ceiling, displaying no sign of emotion. Farran allowed himself a sigh. It was the moment they both had been dreading.

"I'll go first," he said.

He went into the bathroom and used the shower. He dressed himself in corded slacks, a thick seaman's pullover and a padded anorak. Then, while Myriam bathed, he boiled the kettle in the kitchen and filled two mugs with instant coffee. She wandered through in bathrobe and slippers, drying her hair with the towel. Farran pushed one of the mugs into her hand and she sipped slowly, saying nothing. What was there to say, Farran wondered? They'd gone through it all a thousand times before, in conversations which left them taut

158

as bowstrings, for any deviation from their conditioned patterns had the strangest effect, as if they were being split in two. Farran walked to the window and drew back the curtain.

"Black as pitch," he said. "How short the light gets in December. One minute it's afternoon, the next it's night."

"Dark's good for what we have to do," said Myriam.

Farran shrugged. He felt as if some elusive part of his personality was struggling to reassert itself. Myriam was the same. Ever since the Piccadilly Riots, they'd viewed their roles with increasing disquiet. And yet, the strange thing was, neither had ever considered rebelling, as if the future was pre-ordained and could not possibly be avoided, no matter how it might repel them.

"Maybe they'll call it off," Myriam said hopefully. "A sort of last-minute reprieve."

"Why?" asked Farran. "Because you want them to? Don't be so bloody stupid."

"It happens," she said. "A change of heart, a new strategy."

"A bloody miracle," retorted Farran. "Listen, nothing's going to stop it, so put that from your mind. Might as well accept the bastard."

Myriam poured herself more coffee. She moved slowly, as if defeat had wrought in her a hopeless lassitude. Farran rubbed the back of his neck. "I feel rotten," he confessed. "Weak all over. Scared."

"I'm frightened too," said Myriam. "What if things go wrong?"

"No," said Farran. "We've planned too hard. Nothing can misfire, that's the godawful truth."

Myriam finished her coffee and got dressed, then they moved into different rooms and, following instructions, played their cassette tapes as a final stimulatory boost. Ready at last, they said goodbye at the front door. It was a cold night with a touch of frost on the ground. Farran kissed her gently on the lips and squeezed her hand. "Take care," he whispered.

"You too," she said, "I'll see you in the morning."

"That's right. In the morning."

Farran turned and walked briskly along the pavement without looking back. He felt as if any slackening of pace would destroy his already wavering resolve. At least Myriam would be out of the thick of it, he thought, unless something crazy happened. Quit worrying about Myriam, start worrying about yourself. Not just about survival. Survival is something you can handle. Start worrying about guilt. It lingers on long after the deed itself is over, and you'd better learn to live with it, friend, because it's going to be a close and constant companion.

The headquarters of the Popular Movement for the Liberation of Britain, the PMLB, occupied two rooms above a grubby antique shop in the Portobello Road. Faded posters advocating mass insurrection, the organising of strikes and demonstrations, and the establishment of a United Confederation of Oppressed Peoples fluttered from the front door. The corridor was unlit, uncarpeted and smelled of urine. Upstairs, the place was filled with people in donkey jackets, sweaters and tattered anoraks who squatted on the floor or perched on packing cases waiting for the call to go into action.

Stacked against the far wall were vast numbers of plastic carrier bags. They were arranged in orderly rows, and in front of each row was a figure chalked on the floorboard.

"That's the detonation time," explained the PMLB leader, Jerry Rambaud, short, thickset, ginger-haired. "Each bomb has its timing mechanism pre-set, so all you need to do is activate the clock when the bag's set down. It's simple enough. Just slip you hand inside the opening and flick this little lever here."

Farran nodded approvingly. "Good," he murmured. "The fewer complications, the less chance of a slip-up."

Rambaud looked at him. "Who goes first?"

"Please yourself. Draw lots if you like. We move off in teams of four, every twenty minutes. The first units start with targets in the immediate vicinity, gradually extending their sphere of operation as the night goes on. We work by rota, each team getting back to base as quickly as possible for the next assault. Only those with two miles or more to cover qualify for transport. The rest will have to take their chances in the confusion."

"Can't we start now?" Rambaud asked.

Farran looked at his watch. "We have to co-ordinate our movements with the other units throughout London. If anyone jumps the gun, the whole system is thrown out of alignment. We've still fourteen minutes to go."

Rambaud shrugged. "Well, let me wish you luck," he said.

"You too," Farran murmured.

"And power to the revolution."

Farran looked at him mildly, his breath leaving clouds of steam on the frozen air. "Stuff the revolution," he said as he settled down to wait.

The first bombs went off at nine p.m. Myriam heard them as she drove along the Bayswater Road. They sounded like distant firecrackers, their sharp staccato coughs blurring one into the other like a sustained roll of explosions rather than a series of individual blasts. It's started, she thought. Farran had been right. There'd been no reprieve. Lunacy, that's what it was, a lunacy too overpowering to fight, for neither she nor Farran seemed capable of pulling out, which was the craziest thing. Why didn't she just drive right now, right this very minute straight to the nearest police station and tell them the whole story from the beginning? What story, she asked herself? What have you got to tell, what do you even *know*? That a revolution is being conducted by somebody you can't quite remember, aimed at something that was never made quite clear? They'd laugh you out of their office and you know it.

Myriam's indoctrination in Building 3 had been extensive and thorough, but not thorough enough to prevent her harbouring emotions which came into conflict with the tasks she'd been conditioned to perform. This created a kind of see-saw situation in her brain. She felt that by using a little willpower she could hit back at whatever it was controlling her, if only she could grasp what that thing might be. However, parts of her memory had been extinguished, so that now she saw gaps in her past as the migraine sufferer might see gaps in his vision. But at least she realised there was something wrong, which was in itself, she felt, a victory.

Myriam's role on the night of December 1st, was to act as a courier, ferrying bomb-carrying terrorists from one target to another in a car sporting CC plates, CC standing for Consular Corps and therefore having diplomatic immunity from the Petrol Restriction Act.

It wasn't easy picking a route through the lines of abandoned cars or piles of uncleared rubbish which had gathered steadily in the gutters since the dustmen's strike, but still, Myriam reasoned, she would rather be doing this than what Farran was doing, tucking plastic bags filled with explosive around deserted supermarkets and public buildings. Driving was different. With driving, you had less involvement. It was only a transport job after all. There was no finger on the timing mechanism, you were removed from all that. And without the involvement, there would be far less guilt. At least she hoped so. She couldn't take that now. She had enough to contend with, worrying about Farran.

The picking-up and putting-down of the bomb carriers was a scrupulously timed and carefully regulated operation that had been drilled into Myriam's brain over a period of nearly two months. She had to arrive at each rendezvous exactly on the dot, not a minute too soon, not a minute too late. There, she picked up her teams, generally four-strong, and ferried them to their next assault point, a destination locked in her brain like a cross on a streetmap that could never be forgotten. All she had to do was keep her timings right, and for the first two hours she found it easy, picking her way from point to point with the accuracy of a homing pigeon. She heard the bombs popping as she went, but always in the distance, discreet rumblings, outrages far removed from herself. That was Farran's lot, those lunatics from PMLB who were intent on blowing up the whole damned universe if they got half a chance. She hoped Farran was holding them in check. She hoped they were sticking to their brief, distributing the bombs in deserted shopping centres where no one would get hurt.

It was just before eleven when Myriam drove into her first stricken area. She spotted the glow from half a mile away, a great pool of crimson hanging above the streets like the heated bottom of a copper pot. She noticed fumes billowing, growing stronger by the second, smelled their pungent scent in her nostrils. She saw sparks, flames, columns of smoke slithering into the sky, then suddenly the streets were crammed with people, panic-stricken, desperate to escape. They came from all directions, their faces demented, their movements irregular, half-crazed with terror. Two nuns, their robes singed and blackened by smoke, struggled to help a woman whose coat-sleeves smouldered as she screamed hysterically.

A man with a scarf wrapped around his mouth scuttled across the road clutching a small child. The child's face was thrust against her father's chest, and Myriam could see the tiny spine rising and falling as she gasped for air. Ease up, Myriam told herself, they're scared because they don't know what's happening. You do, so stay loose.

An old woman screamed as she drove past, and then continued screaming, standing with one hand clasped tightly to a lamppost, her withered face glowing in the orange light. She looked sub-human, demoniacal, a figure conjured up from fantasy. Myriam turned her head away. People were trying to wave her down, desperate to escape the inferno. She kept one hand on the horn, aiming directly at them until they were forced to leap for safety. She'd done away with compassion, she'd done away with everything except the need to keep on the move, for the frenzy around her intensified her response patterns, forcing her on when every fibre in her body wanted to stop.

For the next two hours she went through a kind of nightmare, picking up her charges, setting them down on target, driving on to the next rendezvous with dazed determination. She felt the whole world had gone mad and only she retained a modicum of sanity.

Farran waited on the street corner. As far as he could tell, the road seemed empty, the little shops and cafés shuttered for the night. There wasn't a soul around, except for a solitary tramp who was squatting on the pavement trying to sing like Caruso. His voice sound cracked and discordant on the night air.

"You'd better get out of here, dad," Farran said. "It's going to be hotter than hell in the next few minutes. Go on, get moving fast."

The tramp stared at him without comprehension. His lips were smeared with spittle. He sang on, oblivious to Farran or to any kind of interruption whatsoever.

Farran checked the street again, then whistled shrilly. The other members of his team appeared, moving side by side up the pavement, each man carrying two plastic bags, one in each hand. They looked, Farran thought, like a music hall comedy team, and he stared at them with exasperation.

"Couldn't you have spread out a bit?" he said. "You're like the bloody Keystone Cops with that little lot. If the scuffers were about, they'd nab you in an instant."

One of the team members peered curiously at the tramp. "Who's he?" he demanded.

"Some old bugger. We'd better drag him out of here before he gets his head blown off."

"Jesus," the man moaned, "as if we didn't have enough to think about."

"Fan out," Farran ordered. "Everybody keep well apart. And don't forget to set your charges."

He walked into the empty shopping centre, his footsteps making a hollow clatter on the mock-marble floor. The store windows were nearly all empty. Tattered newspapers, torn cartons and cigarette packets littered the ground. It was dark and quiet, and in spite of himself Farran shuddered. There was a strange oppressiveness under the empty arches. Without people, it was like being trapped in a vast and echoing mausoleum.

The precinct grew steadily darker as he moved inside, until he had to put one hand against the wall and feel his way along. Balls, he thought. This is far enough. If I go any further, I might not find my way out. He put down the first of his packages and gently slid the lever from left to right, one down, one to go.

He felt happier retracing his steps. The precinct had seemed like a prison, holding him in. He placed his second package in

164

a butcher's doorway, activated the timing mechanism and hurried back to the pavement. The others were already waiting, their faces pale and nervous.

"What the hell kept you?" said one.

"Just doing my job," Farran snapped.

He looked at the tramp. "We'd better drag this old codger out of harm's way."

The tramp however did not wish to go, and in the end they had to carry him, struggling furiously, from one street to the next. When they were satisfied he was safe from the blast, they deposited him on the pavement and began to walk briskly in the direction of Shepherd's Bush. Farran took out his cigarettes. He put one in his mouth and lit it. The ground seemed suddenly to shudder beneath their feet as behind them the world erupted in a tremendous explosion. The tinkle of glass reached their ears as windows were shattered by the white-hot rush of air. The explosion was quickly followed by another, then another and another, the reverberations echoing across the rooftops like rolls of distant thunder. Without turning back, Farran glanced at his watch.

"Bang on target," he said simply.

Myriam switched off her headlamps for the night was bright as day. She drove through areas where entire streets were ablaze, flames licking out of the rooftops, leaping between the buildings, growing, expanding with terrifying force. Smoke drifted across her windscreen. She peered out in awe as fire picked its way up shopfronts and department stores, billowing out of window frames, setting chimneys and towers in stark relief as it crawled higher and higher toward the sky.

She passed a group of firemen frantically unrolling hoses. Columns of spray traced the air, curling into the heart of the blaze in clouds of hissing steam.

Nothing was real any more, nothing she could put a name to. The ravaged streets seemed to suck her into a vortex of madness and pandemonium. Sweat oozed from her pores. Her chest felt tight. She couldn't stand the suffocation, the fumes, the scent of blazing timber. Let me get out of this, she thought.

For God's sake, let me get out. But there was no escape and she knew it, not until her job was done. A long night was what they'd promised. A dirty bloody terrifying night, and they'd been dead right. Nothing in her life could equal it and she hoped nothing ever would again. She was driving by instinct now. People pressed against the car front hoping to force her to a halt, but she nosed relentlessly through. Their hands jerked at the door handles, tried to smash the windows. A man's face squeezed hard against the glass, mouth and nose distorted, eyes bulging with terror. She turned her head away, driving on, keeping her brain in neutral. Cold and aloof. Untouched. The only way to survive.

She spotted the roof of the White City Stadium and drew in to the kerb, peering frantically through the smoke for the men she had been sent to collect. There was no sign of a friendly face, only clusters of terrified humanity scrambling along the pavements in aimless despair. Parked at the roadside, Myriam's car looked no different to the hordes of abandoned vehicles, and the crowd ignored her. She checked her watch. Where on earth had they got to? This operation was geared to split-second timing. If anyone failed to rendezvous right on the dot, the entire plan was thrown out of schedule.

A family of Arabs scampered by, the men in robes and pointed sandals, the women in djellebas, their faces hidden by heavy cowled hoods. A dog, half-crazed with fear, scuttled crab-like across the street. Myriam waited, fuming with impatience. Should she press on, move to the next rendez-vous point, or remain here?

Suddenly she heard a commotion at the end of the street and, peering through the smoke, spotted two men running towards her. One was injured, with blood streaming down his cheeks. He ran with his left arm hooked around his companion's shoulder, dragging his leg helplessly like a cripple. Behind them, screaming with hate, ran a mob of twenty or thirty people. Myriam knew at once that these were the men she was waiting for. Without hesitation, she started the engine, reached over and unlocked the rear door. Cruising along the kerb, Myriam could see the relief in the men's faces as, gasping for breath, they tumbled into the rear seat, filling the confined space with the scent of sweat and fear. Myriam did not wait for the door to shut for the mob were upon her in an instant, leaping on to the bonnet, hammering the windscreen with their fists, pressing their crazed angry faces against the glassy surface. Slamming her foot on the accelerator, she leapt through their ranks, forcing them to leap for safety as she shot across the road and skidded wildly around the nearest corner.

"What happened?" she demanded, gripping the steering wheel fiercely.

"They spotted us," one of the men gasped. "We were just on the point of setting the charges when some old idiot saw what we were doing. They nearly tore us limb from limb."

"Your friend's hurt," Myriam murmured.

"They hit him with a brick," the man said. "Fortunately, he was only stunned. If he'd fallen, they'd have kicked him into pulp. They're out for blood, that mob. I've never seen such madness."

Myriam shuddered. Never, she thought? Was their own madness any more meaningful because it lacked the mindless fury of the mob? Forget that, she told herself, just concentrate on what you're doing, otherwise you'll never get through this night.

But somehow, bit by bit she did get through it, reaching her check points with impeccable accuracy, switching off her brain with cold-blooded determination. There was nothing to think about, nothing but the job in hand. Soon it would be over. Then she could relax, find Farran, weep her heart out. Not long now, she thought, not long now.

Notting Hill Underground Station. Rows of empty ticket machines, a shuttered newspaper kiosk and a handful of people huddled in the subway, hiding from the panic and confusion outside. Farran slipped his plastic bag behind the telephone cubicles and flicked the lever into position.

"Bomb," he bellowed. "Everybody out, there's a bomb down here."

With terrified screams, the people darted for cover. Farran smiled grimly to himself and walked back to the street. In two more minutes it would all be over. This was his last call. He felt a wave of almost overwhelming relief. Jesus, what a night. Slipping his hands in his overcoat pockets, he crossed the road toward Smith's bookshop. The air was heavy with smoke, the pavements bustling with running people, frantic to escape the blast. Never had Farran seen such chaos and disorder. The sky above London was the colour of heated bronze. A distant crackle of flames rang in his ears like static on a radio transmission.

As he reached the bookshop, a man stepped out of the doorway halting in his path. Farran frowned and hesitated. There was something familiar about the man's outline, but his face was obscured in drifting smoke. Farran started to speak, then something solid struck him in the upper body and before he realised what was happening, he was on the ground, the sky tilting crazily far above his head. He screwed up his eyes, dazed and breathless as he struggled to grasp this unexpected phenomenon. My God, he thought in disbelief, the bastard's shot me.

Two o'clock in the morning was the time of Myriam's final pick-up. The meeting place was engraved in her brain. Goldhawk Road, opposite the tube station. Here at least there was a merciful respite from the constant pandemonium, for the bombs had just been set and the streets were as yet still untouched. A solitary figure waited by the kerbside. She frowned. Only one, she thought?

Turning quickly, she slithered to a halt and reached over to unlock the rear door. She peered curiously at the man who clambered in. "Where are the others?" she asked.

He shrugged. He was tall and slender, his face smeared with grime and sweat. Tiny craters marked his cheeks, the legacy of some ancient skin disease. He made a nodding motion with his head, and peering out Myriam felt a stab of shock as she spotted three bodies tucked against the shopfronts. They were laid out neatly, almost reverently, partially hidden from her view by piles of uncleared refuse. Oh God, she thought.

"What happened?" Her voice was barely a squeak.

The man didn't answer. Instead, he withdrew one hand from his raincoat pocket and showed her a gun. It was a 9 mm Beretta Brigadier. She stared at him in horror. "You?"

He nodded.

"Why?"

"Orders," he said, and her wrists turned icy.

"You were *told* to do that?"

He nodded again. His face was a curious yellow colour, as though he was about to be sick.

Myriam turned to her driving. The man was clearly in a daze, the result of some kind of mental reaction. But what on earth was going on? Her mind churned madly. A man ordered to kill his own companions, it was the craziest part of this whole crazy escapade.

"Where you at Camp Fremont?" she asked on impulse, watching him in the driving mirror. He nodded. Sweat traced uneven lines through the dirt on his cheeks, and his eyes gleamed brightly. He looked vaguely unhinged.

Building 3, Myriam thought. It had to be Building 3. They'd conditioned him, given him his orders under sedation. His act of murder had to be part of some strategy set in motion months before. And yet it still didn't make sense. What possible purpose could be served in wiping out three of their own people?

It was quiet when they reached the dropping-off point on the corner of Kildare Terrace, but thick columns of smoke were drifting about, carried by the wind. Someone was waiting as she drew to a halt, a woman. Half-obscured, she stood motionless, watching Myriam through the windscreen, small, slightly-built, middle-aged. Myriam felt a stab of unease.

Like a robot, the man clambered from the car, moving awkwardly as if he was no longer in full control of his limbs. He straightened, smoke wafting into his face. There was a look in his eyes Myriam couldn't quite decipher. The sickness was still there, the dazed expression was still there, but now there was something else, an air of such hopelessness that Myriam felt her insides freeze. The woman raised one hand and Myriam realised with a chill of alarm that she was clutching a revolver.

"No," Myriam shouted.

Too late. She heard the shot almost simultaneously. The man's face seemed to crumple inwards, the nose and part of the upper mouth vanishing before her eyes. He pitched backwards, hitting the ground like a felled log. Myriam's legs seemed to turn into slime. Fear, shock, disbelief, horror, the emotions tumbled through her in dizzy procession.

The woman on the pavement swung her gun in a wide arc. Oh my God, thought Myriam, she's going to kill me too. She hurled herself sideways as the shot went off almost in her face. She heard with windscreen explode with a bang. Missed, she thought, leaning across the passenger seat, but only for a moment. One step was all the woman needed. There was no place left Myriam could hide. A careful aim, a quick squeeze on the trigger and she was done for. Move, you dummy, her brain screamed. Pull yourself together and get the hell out of here.

Half-crazed with terror and still crouching low, Myriam rammed the gear into its slot and thrust one heel on the accelerator. The car leapt forward like a bullet, and with her stomach plunging she eased her head just high enough to see through the shattered windscreen, both hands clutching the steering wheel for dear life. She could see the woman in the driving mirror, perched in the centre of the road, aiming carefully. There was a spurt of flame and the rear window burst in a shower of glass. Myriam felt hysteria beginning to engulf her. She skidded wildly sideways, taking the corner far too fast but mercifully squeezing through with inches to spare, one mudguard scraping a garden wall. Made it, she thought. Sweet God in heaven, I've made it. The woman was out of sight, but still Myriam drove like somebody crazed, rocking and swaying as she weaved in and out between the abandoned cars. She felt she was losing control. Not yet, she thought, later maybe, but not now. She had to think, figure out what those bastards were up to. For reasons best known to themselves, they were systematically destroying their own operatives.

170

Oh God, she thought, Farran. His face leapt into her vision. What if he too was marked down for assassination? There wasn't time to ponder why. She had to reach him before they did, the murderous bastards.

Myriam drove straight to PMLB headquarters. The rooms were deserted, the plastic carrier bags with their deadly contents had all disappeared. A girl in a tattered anorak sat perched on one of the packing cases, staring glumly into space. Myriam shook her by the shoulder.

"Where's Farran?" she demanded.

The girl looked at her, focusing her eyes with an effort. Drugs, Myriam wondered? Or was she so knocked out by the chaos outside, she scarcely knew where she was any more?

"Jack Farran," Myriam insisted, "has he been here? Do you know where he's gone?"

The girl shook her head. Tears glistened on her cheeks. Myriam left her and ran back to the car. Think, she told herself, for Christ's sake try and remember where Jack said his targets would be. She felt sure the last was at Notting Hill Gate. He should have returned by now, unless they'd got him. Her stomach seemed to freeze. If they'd hurt Farran she'd make them pay, she'd find a way of doing it, find out who they were, get them one by one if she had to. They'd remember the day they'd murdered Jack Farran for the rest of their miserable lives.

She found Notting Hill Gate in a state of uproar. People were running in every direction, crazy with terror. Their shouts and footsteps rose above the crackling of blazing timber. She cruised slowly, her eyes scanning the demented faces. Hopeless, she thought, it was hopeless. How could she pick one familiar figure out of that milling mob? She turned the car around and tried again. Nothing. Oh Jack, what have they done to you?

Smoke whirled through her shattered windscreen. It seemed to curl out of the ground itself, draining the density from the air so that everything looked flat and featureless. People lurched out of the fumes with terrifying suddenness.

She saw a man running, staggering, holding on to the shopfronts for support. Blood soaked through his clothing at the shoulder. As she watched, he pushed himself up and began to run again. Her heart jumped. Farran. In the hazy confusion she almost hadn't recognised him. Thank God.

Myriam skidded to a halt and threw open the door. "Jack," she bellowed.

Farran spotted her, crossed the pavement and slid panting into the passenger seat. Without wasting a second, Myriam swung into the road, steering madly through the scattered crowd. Farran's eyes were wracked with pain. His face looked ghastly. He sucked hard at the air.

"Are you badly hurt?" she hissed.

He tried to speak but nothing happened. He swallowed, tried again. "It was Toby Wexler," he croaked. "He . . . shot me, for Christ's sake."

"We'll look at it later," Myriam said. "Right now, hold on to your seat."

He stared at her weakly, his cheeks gleaming. "Where are we going?" he murmured.

"Anywhere," she grunted. "They're killing off their operatives by relay. We've got to get out of here, out of London, out of the whole stinking area."

By far the most complex and precarious part of Joseph Spengler's plan for the armed struggle in Britain was the operation which took place on the night of December 1st when, in order to maintain compartmentation (the CIA phrase for keeping everyone involved as much in the dark as possible), all operatives with an overall knowledge of aims and objectives were systematically eliminated. It was an operation of such precision and magnitude that even Spengler's methodical brain reeled at its conception. For success, it depended on so many factors coming together at just the right moment that only an idiot, or a crazy optimist would dare gamble on the whole thing going like clockwork. Joseph Spengler was just such an optimist.

Those of the Camp Fremont recruits who had responded most favourably to indoctrination procedures had been selected for special treatment during the last six weeks of their training. In the heady atmosphere of Building 3, new and startling suggestions were inserted deep into their subconscious. After the bombings on the night of the 1st, each of these carefully prepared specimens carried out, without malice or forethought, the task that had been allotted to him, namely to dispose of those members of his immediate circle who, in the opinion of FOCB headquarters, knew too much for their own good. The nucleus of knowledgable operatives having been severely reduced, the executioners were themselves then executed by a team of selected hit men and women who knew nothing at all about the job they'd been called upon to do beyond the names, descriptions and locations of their victims. All things considered, the affair was a remarkable success. By the morning of the 2nd, apart from Myriam and Farran and a bare handful of bewildered fugitives still being tracked down, scarcely anyone remained alive who had any idea of what was happening beyond his own individual role. Spengler's compartmentation concept was almost complete.

Meanwhile, as the cities burned, the mood of the people took a new and unexpected turn. The alarm and despondency which Spengler had prophesied existed all right, but not to any widespread or disabling degree. Instead, large sections of the community rallied together, forming themselves into makeshift fire brigades to deal with the flames still raging in their streets, and cordoning off areas of devastation so that the real firemen, the professionals, could concentrate on making the shells of burnt-out buildings safe again. Though food was scarce, groups of ladies organised mobile catering columns, and miraculously managed to produce huge tubs of soup and tea, which they then distributed by pushcart among the homeless and the suffering. Men from all levels of life banded together and set about the task of cleaning up the chaos created by the bombers, working in harmony, each individual dedicating himself to the same ideal – the re-establishing of stability and order.

The panic of December 1st was lost in a universal sense of purpose, and the air of unity which had begun to blossom during the early stages of Spengler's programme now re-asserted itself with a degree of fervour that was almost mani-acal. What the people had lacked in their previous patriotic outburst had been an adversary. They had looked in vain for a cause to follow, a war to fight and now, like a signal from heaven itself, the truth became clear – an enemy did exist, somewhere in their midst were the men at the root of their misfortunes.

As the fires were gradually brought under control, the authorities found themselves faced with an even more alarm-ing phenomenon – groups of vigilantes who patrolled the streets looking for dissidents, outcasts, anyone at all who might have been responsible for the blitz on their cities. In at least one incident, a party of innocent West Indians was attacked and badly beaten in the Fulham Road. The police did what they could but kept a low profile, leaving the main-tenance of law and order to the troops who finally, in despera-tion, imposed a curfew prohibiting the assembling of groups of more than five people at a time, and forbidding anyone to venture on to the streets after 9 p.m.

While this was going on, unknown to the people and unde-tected by the authorities, convoys of aircraft, tanks, artillery and missile units were being transported from various US air bases in the north of England to the Scottish border. Colonel Richard Savage and his men were landed in relays at Fleet-cliffe Air Base and transferred by trucks to the Cheviot Hills. It was a cold rainy night and, as they moved further north, the rain turned to snow so that by the time they reached the first rolling summits the entire land, as far as they could see, was covered with a blanket of white.

With judgement and dexterity, Colonel Savage deployed his men. His takeover of the terrain was swift, professional and undramatic. There was no resistance. In fact, the reaction of both residents and police was one of surprise, followed by amusement, followed by delight as they realised Savage's men were excellently provisioned and intended to share those pro-visions for as long as their occupation lasted.

Savage spent most of December 3rd moving his heavy

equipment into position. Spengler had warned him that everything depended on being able to withstand the first assault, and Savage divided his men into squadrons, ordering them to dig in and prepare for battle. He used the little town of Wooler as his base, converting the police station there into a field HQ and directing operations by radio. He established 81 mm mortar teams on the highest summits, the men protected by camouflage netting and white clothing which made them invisible against the snow. He sealed off the approach roads with Swingfire long-range anti-tank guns complete with ZB 298s which allowed his troops to pick up targets at night or in fog and smoke. He occupied the College Valley and ordered his half-dozen fighter planes to be serviced ready for take-off. Over the roughest terrain he scattered Striker and Ferret armoured reconnaissance vehicles, and as a safety precaution prepared a helicopter shuttle service for evacuating wounded. Most important of all, he established his Soviet-built Guideline, Grail and Gecko surface-to-air missile systems, at three strategic points on the corners of a massive triangle which governed the aerial approaches to the territory under his control. Most of his equipment was British- or Russian-made. The more sophisticated pieces from the United States had been carefully disguised to obscure their origin in case they fell into enemy hands.

On the afternoon of December 3rd he travelled the area by landrover, watching the perparations with approval, chatting to his men, enjoying the experience of being back in harness, filled with confidence and anticipation for the future.

When he was satisfied everything was ready, he drove back to Wooler and telephoned each of the national newspapers in turn. Then he telephoned the BBC. Finally, he telephoned Westminster direct and gave his message to a stunned and disbelieving press secretary. When he was convinced everything had been done which could be done, he gave orders that he was not to be disturbed except in the event of a direct attack, went to bed and fell into a dreamless sleep.

TWELVE

It was strange waking up in the car with the icy wind freezing Myriam's body through the shattered windscreen. It was broad daylight. Farran, wrapped in her arms, seemed to be burning up. She could feel his heat radiating into her limbs. His head was resting on the leather seat cover, his skin drawn taut across the hollows beneath his cheekbones. She touched his forehead. His pores were moist to the touch, hot and sweaty. Fever. That damned shoulder wound. She'd dressed it as best she could, but the first-aid box in the back of the car wasn't equipped for a .32 slug. She'd managed to stop the bleeding, but Farran needed expert help before his system poisoned.

Myriam straightened and peered around. The deserted highway looked strangely macabre. Such a broad ribbon of concrete and not a vehicle in sight. Flat fields coated with frost reached away on both sides. The sky was like papier maché, grey and soggy. A flock of geese wheeled above her head, flying in formation, their hoarse cries adding a note of melancholy to the chill morning air.

How long had they been on the road? Two days, three? Her mind was a blur, a hotch-potch of wild images. London. The bombings. That woman poised to shoot her. She'd gone over the night a thousand times without reaching any conclusion. What made Farran and herself so dangerous? What did they know that had to be silenced? It was crazy, all of it crazy, but she didn't give a damn any more. All she cared about now was survival.

She eased herself gently out of Farran's arms, clambering from the car without waking him. Shivering in the cold, she felt the pangs of hunger deep in her insides. It was well over twenty-four hours since they'd eaten. They needed food desperately, but first she had to get Farran to a doctor, otherwise she'd have a corpse on her hands.

She walked to the back of the car, unlocked the boot and hauled out a can of petrol. She topped up the fuel tank then climbed into the driver's seat and started the engine. Farran was still unconscious as she pulled into the highway. For several miles she drove through a chequerboard of greens, browns and greys, and not once did she see a sign of human habitation beyond an occasional derelict car or the windowless shell of some building deserted by its inhabitants. There were no cattle or sheep in the meadows. They had all been slaughtered weeks before, and now the land had a cold dead look, as if nothing lived or moved there except herself.

She had no clear idea where she was heading. They'd driven northward, coasting slowly because of the broken windscreen. Farran in his delirium kept insisting on returning to his own home town, Newcastle-upon-Tyne, but she felt it was better to stay in the country, away from towns, away from people.

In spite of herself, her mind kept going back to the chaos of December 1st. The flames, the smoke, the panic-crazed crowds seemed etched into her memory in such a fashion that she almost wondered if it had really happened, or if she had simply dreamt it, or read it somewhere in a book. That was possible, wasn't it? Some things you read were so vivid they became part of your own experience. But she knew in her heart it was no imagining. Farran's shoulder was proof of that.

An uncanny greyness hung above the land. The hedgerows looked withered, their twigs and branches glistening with hoarfrost. Streams trickled in the pasture folds. She saw a tangled carpet of brambles, and beyond them a ploughed field which seemed to stretch for ever, its furrows tightening like the threads of a never-ending loom until they were lost from sight. A narrow track traced the field edge, and at the end of it stood a farmhouse, a dour building of grey stone and even greyer slate, with steeply sloping roofs, and a cobbled forecourt in front of its main door. Smoke curled from a chimney, fading as the wind caught it. People.

177

Myriam turned off the highway and drove slowly along the cratered farmtrack, her eyes watering in the wind.

She knocked at the door, but no one answered. She walked around to the back and tried there, but no sound or movement came from inside the house. The windows were covered with heavy gauze curtains which showed only her own reflection. And yet the smoke was indisputable. A fire meant people. The place was occupied.

Myriam returned to the car and jammed her hand on the horn. The high-pitched shriek blasted her eardrums, drifting across the furrowed fields. The front door opened just a fraction, and a man's voice, sharp and hostile demanded, "What do you want?"

Myriam took her hand from the horn. "Will you help me, please? I have a sick man here."

"Go away."

"Please. He needs a doctor."

"This isn't a hospital."

"I wouldn't trouble you if it wasn't an emergency. Let me use your telephone."

"No doctor around here," the voice snapped sullenly, and the door began to close. Myriam jammed her foot in the crack.

"I'm afraid he might die," she pleaded.

There was a pause, then the voice said, "What's wrong with 'im?"

"He's been shot."

"Shot?" the tone was incredulous.

Myriam sighed. "We've driven up from London," she explained. "We were caught in the riots there."

"The ones on television?"

"That's right. My fiancé was hit by a sniper."

Slowly, the door swung open. The man standing on the step was short, chubby and almost totally bald. Only a few flimsy tufts of hair sprouted above his ears. His face was coarse, unshaved and dirty. His eyes were small and set very far apart.

"You drove up, you say?" he murmured.

"Yes."

"With petrol?"

"We carry our own. In the back of the car."

"How much?"

Myriam hesitated. She didn't like the look of the man, but Farran needed help and this loutish brute seemed the only help around. "Enough," she added non-committally.

"We need petrol here," the man grunted. "We've not seen a drop of the stuff for nearly six weeks."

"I'll give you half a gallon," Myriam offered. "That's fair. Help me and I'll help you."

The man nodded in agreement, opening the door wide. "Okay, come in," he said. "We'd better get your friend out of the cold. We'll see what we can do."

Together they dragged Farran, half-conscious and vaguely protesting out of the car and into the farmhouse sitting room. They laid him full length on a sofa in front of the fire. Myriam was gasping for breath by the time she straightened. The room seemed overcrowded, the walls cluttered with trinkets fashioned out of some fake brassy material. There was a hi-fi radiogram, a television set, a number of assorted armchairs and potted plants scattered all over the place. A woman in a shabby apron shuffled in from the kitchen drying her hands. "What's this?" she demanded, her voice high and sharp.

"Gentleman's hurt," the man murmured. "He's been shot."

"Shot?" the woman exclaimed.

"Hit by a sniper. They've driven all the way from London."

Her eyes narrowed, flitting over Myriam. "How could they?" she demanded.

"With petrol, Hilda. They've got a carload of the stuff."

"Possessing petrol's against the law. Ten years in the nick if you're caught."

"I'm an American citizen," Myriam explained. "My car carries Consular plates. We're immune from the Petrol Restriction Act."

"See," the man murmured, "it's all above board."

The woman sniffed crossly. "Trust the Yanks. Might know they'd find a way around this mess."

"You ought to be grateful," Myriam answered coldly. "If it wasn't for the Yanks, you'd have starved to death months ago. They've been keeping you alive."

"Fat lot of good it's done," the woman snorted. "We're on our uppers now, all of us. In the cities, they say people are dying from hunger."

"That's not true," Myriam said. "It's bad, but not that bad. Not yet. You shouldn't listen to rumours."

The man interrupted. He seemed alarmed at the way the conversation was going. The prospect of petrol had made him forget his earlier hostility. Now he was anxious to please.

"You can use the phone," he offered. "There's a directory at the bottom of the stairs. I warn you though, you'll be lucky to find a doctor. People are afraid to leave their homes."

Myriam hesitated. "Have you any food?" she asked.

The farmer and his wife looked at each other. "Food?" he echoed, as if he hadn't understood the question.

"We'll pay for it."

He shook his head. "It's not a question of money."

"With petrol."

His eyes glittered greedily. "How much?"

"What have you got?"

He glanced at his wife again. Her face was expressionless. "We have a little cheese," he said, "some tinned carrots."

"Bread?"

"No."

"Crackers, biscuits, anything like that?"

"Nothing."

Myriam sighed. Cheese and carrots, hardly a mouth-watering mixture. Still, Farran needed to be fed if he was going to survive.

"I'll give you another half-gallon," she offered. "I daren't risk more. We don't know yet how far we'll have to go."

The farmer considered for a moment, wondering whether to push the price up. In the end, he nodded. He opened a drawer, took out a box of cigarettes and offered her one. She shook her head. He placed one in his mouth and lit it. His beady eyes studied her curiously. She felt herself shuddering.

There was something about the man which physically repelled her.

"How was it in London?" he asked.

"Terrifying."

He scratched his beard stubble, letting the smoke drift from his nostrils in a lazy stream. "They hit all the cities just like that," he told her. "You were lucky to get out. The army's got roadblocks everywhere, keeping people in."

She looked at him. "Does that include Newcastle?"

"Everywhere. They've introduced martial law."

Myriam tried to keep her face impassive. "Who's responsible for it all," she asked casually, "the bombings and such?"

The farmer shrugged. "Nobody knows yet. There's a rumour around we've been invaded. That's why we're staying put."

"Invaded by who?"

"Russia, most likely. So people are saying. Mind you, if you asked my opinion, I'd say it's the Chinks. They've been preparing this for years, haven't they? I mean, what about all these Chinese restaurants, what are they doing here? Spies, that's what. Advance agents. They've been paving the way."

"Is that why people are so afraid?"

The farmer nodded soberly. "That's why," he said.

While his wife went about laying out the cheese, heating the carrots in a saucepan and boiling water for a pot of tea (which mercifully she still had in plentiful supply) Myriam spent half an hour going through the telephone book and calling every GP in the reasonable vicinity. Some didn't bother to answer. Some slammed down the receiver. Others pretended the doctor had gone away, and she was speaking to his brother, or his uncle, or his gardener, or some other unlikely character. It was not, Myriam thought, a reassuring experience. As the farmer had predicted, people in the country were frightened, too frightened to leave the safety of their own homes.

She paused just long enough to gobble the meal the farmer's wife set out on the kitchen table, and force-feed Farran. He looked dreadful. His skin was glistening, his eyes bright, slightly deranged, flitting around the room in a crazy terrified

181

way as if he expected the walls to come tumbling in at any second.

They'd barely finished when Myriam heard the rumbling of trucks on the road outside. The sound was so utterly unexpected, so startling after the silence that none of them moved for several seconds. The rumbling went on, heavy, persistent, sending vibrations along the kitchen floor. Myriam thrust back her chair and ran to the window. She could scarcely believe her eyes. The road was crammed with military vehicles, Chieftain tanks, trucks, personnel carriers, Stalwart transporters, motor-cycle despatch riders, armoured reconnaissance units, staff cars. They stretched bumper to bumper as far as Myriam could see. It looked as though the entire British army was on the move.

"Good God," the farmer's wife breathed.

But Myriam wasn't listening. A column of such dimensions had to include an ambulance or two, and ambulances meant medics. Without pausing to explain. Myriam ran outside, started up the car and bumped and lurched furiously down the narrow farmtrack. She didn't pause to ask herself the purpose of such a massive migration. Her only thought was Farran and the possibility of help ahead.

She reached the road. The column was driving three deep, travelling slower than twenty miles an hour. Calmly and defiantly, she nudged her car forward, edging bit by bit directly into its path. With a fusillade of horns, the slow-moving vehicles slithered to a halt. Myriam remained where she was, blocking the inside lane. A minute passed. She could see the drivers in the nearmost truck, their faces blank and puzzled. A sergeant with a beefy face came running along the cinder verge.

"What d'you think you're up to?" he yelled. "Get that bloody car out of there."

Myriam stared at him coolly, refusing to budge. The sergeant fretted and fumed. He was clearly out of his depth when dealing with a determined and resolute female.

"All right, sergeant, leave this to me." The words were soft and carefully modulated, but they carried about them the ring of command. The man who uttered them was tall, sandy-haired, moustached, thirty to thirty-five years old. He wore a major's uniform. The sergeant saluted and beat a thankful retreat.

The officer leaned against the car, smiling gently. "Young lady," he murmured in a lazy drawl, "I suppose you realise you are causing us a great deal of annoyance."

Myriam said quickly, "Major, I need help. I have a wounded man back there at the farmhouse. He's been shot in the shoulder and needs medical attention urgently. I can't seem to find a doctor anywhere."

The major frowned. "Shot, you say?"

"We were in London two night ago. Some lunatic cut loose with a revolver and my fiancé got hit. I'm afraid the wound is beginning to fester."

The officer brushed his moustache with his fingertips. He straightened and walked around the car, peering at the shattered windscreen and broken rear window. He looked at the numberplate.

"You're from the American Consulate?" he asked.

Myriam nodded.

"Have you some means of identification?"

"I've got my passport, if that's any good," she said.

She fumbled for her purse on the rear seat. Her heart was pounding as the major studied the photograph. She looked a mess, she knew, and the damned picture had never been a good likeness to begin with. If he disbelieved her now, she'd be right back where she'd started. Farran too.

The major scratched his cheek, thinking hard. He was, she realised, quite a handsome man, with a pleasant, evenly-planed face that seemed strangely unlived-in. Not naïve exactly. Just nice. He was smiling when he handed the passport back.

"Thank you, Miss Coldman," he said. "If you wouldn't mind reversing on to the verge, we'll see what we can do. You'll be happy to know we do have medical teams on the column, and handling bullet wounds is one of their specialties. Let's take a look at this fiancé of yours."

The medical crew turned out to be more than considerate. They insisted on carrying Farran from the farm by stretcher, even though he was capable of walking the distance unaided. Inside the ambulance, the doctor, a fresh-faced young man scarcely out of medical college, examined the wound carefully.

"What d'you think?" the major asked.

"Not bad," the doctor grunted. "Slug seems to have been deflected by the shoulder bone. Bit of infection there, but it ought to clear up with treatment. Straightforward probe job actually."

"Can you do it on the move?"

"We could at a pinch, but it'd be safer if we stayed still."

"How long?"

"Ten minutes or so for the extraction. Another ten for dressing."

The major straightened. "Well, I think we can spare twenty minutes," he said. He smiled at Myriam. There were freckles across the bridge of his nose. "We'd better give the doctor some breathing space, it's a wee bit cramped in here. Would you care to join me in the staff car? He'll give us a shout when he's done."

Inside the staff car, the major opened his coat and took out a silver whisky flask. "Scotch?" he asked.

Myriam smiled wearily, and nodded. She felt her body beginning to flag. Worrying about Farran had taken its toll, and now it was pleasant to sit here, knowing he was in good hands, and let herself relax. She liked the major. He looked an honest man. She liked his features, open and direct. She felt comfortable in his presence.

He filled the little silver cap to its brim and thrust it into her hand. He himself drank straight from the flask.

"You believe in being prepared, Major," Myriam said.

The major chuckled. "Never go anywhere without it," he told her. "My number one rule in life is look after the creature comforts, they're what makes living tolerable."

They were parked on the verge of the road, Myriam's own

car twenty yards in front, the ambulance behind. The column of military vehicles trundled steadily by.

"What's going on?" Myriam asked. "The trucks, the men. I've never seen a troop movement like it."

The major grinned. "Some bloody lunatic's started a revolution," he said.

She felt something jump in her chest. "Revolution?"

"Yes. Up near the Scottish border. Retired army colonel."

Myriam reached down and gripped the edge of her seat. Something was happening to her, something strange and unexpected. She felt the past coming back, a memory, a fragment caught at random from the unlit complexities of her mind. She stared at the major, her face pale. "Colonel Savage?"

The major chuckled. "That's right. The old bugger's finally gone over the top. Did you hear it on television?"

"No," she whispered, "it just came to me. Like telepathy."

He reached over and refilled her flasktop. "He's got a whole damned army behind him," he told her, "Aircraft, artillery, the works. God knows where his backing's coming from."

"So what happens now?"

"War. Simple as that. Our job's to wipe him out. No deals, no negotiating. Just the chopping block. They're calling it Operation Overkill."

Myriam shuddered. "Sounds bloody."

The major nodded. "Sign of the times, isn't it? I mean, human life tends to lose its value when a country's backed up against a wall. Same in wartime. People do things they'd shrink from in more convivial moments. Governments too."

Myriam sipped her Scotch. The liquid burned her throat going down, and sent a wave of blessed heat through her stomach. In her mind she could see Savage clearly, a tall man, very dapper, haughty and aristocratic. She knew they'd met, though for the moment the reasons and circumstances escaped her. Still, that would come, she felt certain.

As they were sitting, a grey limousine slithered to a halt just ahead of her parked car. The doors opened and three men got out. One was a brigadier, the other two wore civilian clothes.

185

The first was short and stocky, the other tall and heavy-shouldered with the cadaverous features of someone who had lived his life on a diet entirely composed of meat. The men strode to the staff car and the major clambered out to meet them, saluting smartly. "Can I help you, sir?"

"These gentlemen are from Special Branch," the brigadier said. "Do you happen to know who that car belongs to, the one with the CC plates?"

Myriam felt a sensation like electricity run through her stomach and thighs. As she put down the flaskcap, she noticed her hand was shaking.

"One of the US Consulate people," the major replied. "This young lady here. Her fiancé's having a little extraction in the ambulance behind. He stopped a bullet in London the other night."

The two men in civilian clothes stared at Myriam coldly.

"Would you mind telling us your name, miss?" The tall one asked.

"Her name is Coldman," the major announced. "Myriam Coldman."

She saw a tell-tale flicker in the man's eyes. The name had meant something.

"And your fiancé?"

"Farran," she muttered, "Jack Farran."

The three men looked at each other as though she had said something deeply profound. The brigadier took the major's arm and drew him aside. "May we have a word with you in private?"

Myriam watched them talking by the roadside. The tall civilian was leaning forward as if he could intimidate the major by his sheer intensity of purpose. The major brushed nervously at his moustache. Myriam felt fear stir inside her. The car seemed stifling, she couldn't bear to be enclosed. She clambered into the wintry air. Those men weren't from Special Branch, they were after her hide. Special Branch didn't even know she existed. They were assassins, here to finish her off. Farran too. There were fields beyond the road, reaching as far as she could see. Not much cover. Still, if she made a dash for it there was always a chance of escape. Better than being shot down like a dog. Except that she couldn't. Not without Jack. If she went at all, they went together.

After a few moments, the ambulance door opened and the doctor came out, leading Farran by his good arm. Farran looked a little less pale, but his eyes were still dazed, still disorientated. He moved zombie-like, allowing the doctor to manipulate him across the tarmac. The doctor smiled.

"Well, the wound's clean and dressed, and I've given him a shot to get the fever down. There's still a touch of infection there, so feed him these antibiotics three times daily." He pressed a small phial into Myriam's hand. "I'd get him to a doctor tomorrow or the day after," he added, "to have the dressing changed. For the moment though, there's nothing to worry about."

Myriam breathed a sigh of relief. "Doctor, I don't know how to thank you."

He chuckled softly. "Don't bother," he said. "The army never does."

She looked at Farran closely. She could see by his expression that escape was out of the question. Farran was beyond the reach of normal thought. He was still lost in the peculiar wanderings of his own mind.

The major came back, followed by the brigadier. They'd been joined by the sergeant with the beefy face. That made five to two, hardly an even match.

The major's earlier friendliness had disappeared. He said briskly, "I'm sorry, Miss Coldman, but these gentlemen have a warrant for your arrest."

Myriam regarded him haughtily. "On what charge?"

"Detention under the Prevention of Terrorism Act," the cadaverous-looking civilian said, strolling over to join them. Myriam peered at him. He was going to kill her, she felt sure of it. His eyes told her that. Blank and impartial, they had the look of an animal slaughterer. He was part of the conspiracy bent on their destruction, her's and Farran's. She turned to the major, pleading.

"These men aren't from Special Branch," she said.

"They're imposters, professional killers. They want to murder us."

The major stared at her in blank disbelief. "Miss Coldman, you've taken leave of your senses."

"Please believe me. If you let them take us, we're done for."

The major looked perturbed. "Miss Coldman, I have no choice. They have a warrant . . ."

"A forgery. Their ID cards are forgeries too. They've been hired to eliminate my fiancé and me."

"What for?" the major exclaimed.

"I don't know," she cried. "For God's sake, I don't know. But it's the truth, you've got to believe that."

Got to, she thought? It was crazy. A tale told by an idiot. How could she expect the major to accept such a story, and yet . . . there was something in his eyes which made her feel she was winning. He looked unhappy.

The tall civilian seized her by the elbow, his fingers digging into her flesh. "Come on," he snapped, "get into the car."

She tried to pull back. The major seemed uncertain. Her impassioned entreaty had confused him.

"Are you going to let this happen, Major?" she demanded.

He shook his head, protesting. "Believe me, Miss Coldman, these men carry impeccable credentials. I'm a soldier, I can't take sides."

Godamnit, she had to get through to the man, somehow convince him that only he stood between her and certain death, but how could she do it without sounding crazy? She *was* crazy, she thought, crazy and hysterical, and that was just the way she looked. Still, she had to give it one last try.

"You'd better take sides this time, Major," she cried. "You'd better think about it pretty damned hard. If you let these sons of bitches murder us, you'll have to live with the memory for the rest of your life."

Suddenly, before she realised what was happening, the tall man had grabbed her by the waist, lifted her bodily into the air and thrust her into the rear seat of the limousine. Farran was bundled in beside her, and the small civilian followed, his face cool and aloof.

188

She caught a quick glimpse of the startled major, his eyes now filled with concern, then the tall man slid behind the driving wheel, started the engine and pulled across the line of army vehicles, picking an exit road which led straight across the open countryside.

Myriam breathed out, defeat flooding through her. Damn the major. Why couldn't he have listened? Now she was on her own. Farran's mind was still in a state of shock, which she supposed was a blessing in a way. At least he would go to his death without knowing, she envied him that.

For several miles they drove in silence, winding through endless fields and pastures. "Where are you taking us?" Myriam demanded once. No one answered. The tall man glanced at her in the driving mirror, that was all.

Farms glided by, hydro-electric pylons, rivers. Eventually, the road topped a small hill where heavy woodland cluttered the grassy verge. The tall man brought the car to a halt, peering at the thicket. Thick undergrowth choked the tree trunks.

"This'll do," he said shortly.

He opened the glove compartment and drew out a .32 Colt Police Special. Myriam felt her wrists turn cold. The man opened the gun, checked it was loaded, snapped it shut again. His movements were terse, unemotional. It was hard to believe he was going to kill her. He seemed so casual, so incredibly matter-of-fact.

They got out of the car.

"Stay close," the tall one told his companion. "It's pretty dense in there. We don't want them making a break for it."

He was right about the thicket, it was dense. They moved in single file, the tall man first, picking a route through nettles, scrub and decaying timber. The ground sloped upwards, criss-crossed with fallen trees. Myriam felt her resolution dissolve. She wondered how it would feel, the bullet. Would it be quick? One swift spasm and then oblivion. Would there be pain or just a momentary numbness? The undergrowth grew thicker the further they penetrated. It would take months before their bodies were discovered. If ever. Maybe no one would come here ever again. It would be as if she and Farran had never existed.

She stared at the shoulders of the tall civilian. He looked so normal, so unspeakably ordinary. And yet, he was going to murder her, and he would do it with as much emotion as a chef chopping up vegetables for the pot.

She could run for it, she supposed, make one swift dash into the undergrowth, but that meant leaving Farran, and besides, how far would she get? Three paces at the most, probably less. It was hard to think of running when her limbs were melting out of sheer terror.

They came to a halt in a small clearing. The tangle of brambles looked solid on all sides. The tall killer peered about approvingly. "This is far enough," he said.

Myriam felt the other one draw away, leaving herself and Farran in the centre, exposed and vulnerable. The killer stared at them, his eyes strangely sad. Oh God, Myriam thought, I can't stand much more of this.

"Get on with it," she snapped, "what are you waiting for?"

The man sighed. "Miss Coldman," he said, "this isn't something we enjoy. I don't know why it has to be done, and I don't ask any questions. I obey orders, that's all."

He raised the .32. Myriam felt her throat constrict. Sweet Jesus, she breathed. Her eyes focused on the barrel's opening. It seemed huge, like a sawn-off sewage pipe. Out of that aperture, death would come. Sharp and fiery. One blast for her, one for Farran, then nothing. The end of living, the world extinguished. It was strange she felt no emotion other than fear. Her legs were numb from that, the numbness crawling up her arteries as terror engulfed her, but there was no vision of her past life, no sadness even. Only this hopeless, pathetic fear. Don't let it hurt, she thought. Let it be quick, one swift dissolving flash.

Aayyeeii: there was a sudden tearing sound as the small man, still backing away, pitched through the brush and landed backside-foremost in a muddy pool. He stared up at them in pained surprise. It would have been comical, Myriam thought, if the situation hadn't been so serious.

With a heart-fluttering roar, three mallard burst from the thicket and hurled themselves squealing into the air. The killer with the gun looked momentarily startled. He peered from his companion to the squawking bundles in the sky, bewildered by the unexpected din. Myriam felt her pulses quickening. She glanced at the ground. Half-hidden in the grass lay the rotting branch of some long-dead tree, its bark almost obscured by lichen and moss, its twigs sharp and brittle, ready to snap. Without hesitation she scooped it up and drove it hard into the big man's face. Its jagged end caught him below the left eye, and with an exclamation of surprise and pain he staggered backward, collapsing over a clump of gorse. His pistol sailed through the air, curving in an almost graceful arc before dropping into the bushes. Myriam seized Farran's arm and plunged into the undergrowth, half-leading, half-dragging him behind her. She had no idea where she was going. All she could think of was the desperate need to get away. Branches gouged her cheeks, snagged in her hair, scraped her shoulders, arms and chest. She heard the tall man swearing angrily as he scrambled around in the scrub looking for his gun. Then a shot rang out, the blast deafening in the confined space. Tears streamed down her cheeks as she stumbled on, crossing a narrow stream where icy water washed against her ankles. Her vision blurred with the moisture in her eyes. She caught a glimpse of the sky through the trees, then the ground undulated, its cracks and ditches coated with dense scrub. A second shot rang out, sharp and insistent. Gasping heavily she paused, dragging Farran to a halt. He was swaying on his legs, staring aimlessly into space. She felt a surge of unreasoning anger. It wasn't fair, it just wasn't fair for him to go on like this, letting her drag him along like a helpless puppy. He had to take his share of the strain, he had to. She shook him hard.

"Jack," she hissed, "Jack, snap out of it, hear me? They're going to kill us, Jack. Understand? Either we get away now, or we're done for. Jack, please pull yourself together."

She heard a crashing in the undergrowth and her heart pounded madly in her chest. They were coming. In a blaze of frustration she hit Farran across the mouth.

"Wake up, you gutless bastard," she shouted. "Do I have to look after you like a baby?"

He started, peering at her with surprise and consternation, as if some defective mechanism in his brain had been jerked into working order again. "What?" he gasped.

"Listen."

The crashing was getting closer. The pursuers couldn't move fast through the underbrush and that was a blessing, but then neither could she and Farran, and even worse, they were leaving a trail of broken twigs and debris for their pursuers to follow.

"How many?" Farran demanded.

God, had he really been that benumbed?

"Two," she said.

"Armed?"

"Yes."

"Come on."

He seized her wrist and ploughed into the undergrowth, leaping and stumbling through brambles, brush and crisp brown bracken. The ground sloped upwards in a steep clay bank, and suddenly the thicket ended. One second they were surrounded by trees, the next they were staring across flat fields to a hazy mist merging into the skyline. The sea. It swirled eastwards in shades of coaly-grey. Far out, a steamer chugged sedately south. The coastal cliff was rimmed with clumps of spiky grass. There was nowhere to run to, no escape except by water.

"We're trapped," she gasped.

"Like hell we are," snapped Farran. "Come on."

They clambered over the fence and ran hysterically, the sea and the cliff bobbing in front of them like a distorted vision. The ploughed soil, crisp with frost, dragged at their ankles, slowing them down, making them gasp for breath as they pounded toward the field's perimeter.

Crack crack crack, the shots came in a continuous roll. Their pursuers had broken out of the thicket. Myriam felt sick with fear. She saw a spurt of earth leap into the air on her left and forced herself to accelerate, charging neck and neck with Farran, watching the rise and fall of the fence ahead as bullets whispered close to their skulls. Christ, she thought, I can't go on much longer. Her eyes were blinded by tears and sweat. More shots. How could they possibly miss at this range?

She and Farran were running at a crouch now, Farran bent almost double, the heat from his body communicating itself through his hold on her wrist. Was that fever, or fright? Myriam didn't know and didn't much care any more. Farran's physical condition had lost its importance in the face of such imminent danger. I'm going to vomit, she thought. If I don't stop soon, I won't be able to help myself.

They reached the fence and scrambled over it, faces tense and blood-drained. Bullets smacked into the tarred wood, sending splinters jumping in the crisp air. A few feet of soggy clay lay between the fence and the edge of the precipice. Sixty feet below, they could see the beach, dotted with boulders and clumps of rotting seaweed. The cliff buckled outwards, its sandy rock criss-crossed with tracks of soggy earth. There was no time to hesitate. The clumping of feet on frozen soil drummed in their ears.

"Now," Farran shouted, and they scrambled downwards together, picking a route between the jagged outcrops, digging in their heels for purchase as their feet slipped and slithered down the steep muddy bank. Myriam felt her stomach shudder. There was no stopping their downward motion. She felt helpless, like a child caught on a runaway roller-coaster, terrified of the speed but unable to get off. She could see boulders below, and little furrows in the sand, and pools of water reflecting the pale grey sky. Her vision tilted, she was gasping for breath, and somewhere close at hand she felt faintness waiting to engulf her. Already her knees were buckling.

Farran was picking his way with amazing accuracy. There was no time to assimilate snags or hazards. Everything happened at once. Watch that outcrop. Buttress there. Keep to the left of the slippery slab.

Myriam couldn't understand why they hadn't fallen. It was crazy to descend at this speed, but the decision was out of their hands. Having started, the momentum of their own bodies carried them relentlessly on.

The cliff was all angles, the gradient steepening fast as they slid wildly down to the lower slopes. Myriam felt her whole body shaken out of symmetry. Each step jarred her unmercifully. She felt her left foot go, sliding downwards. She lost her grip on Farran. Oh God, I'm falling, she thought. The world spun dizzily, sky, sea and beach whirling in her vision like a view glimpsed from the inside of a washing machine. She bumped against rocks, rolling madly over, completely out of control. She could hear her own voice screaming in her ears. Her shoulder struck a rocky spur, she saw the sand coming fast, watched it rush up to meet her as though the earth was bent on her obliteration, then a jarring light flashed in her eyes as the back of her skull cracked against some protuberance at the cliff bottom. She lay dazed, the wind knocked out of her lungs. She heard Farran clambering down from the rocks above.

"Myriam," he called frantically, "are you okay?"

She tried to sit up and a wave of dizziness almost made her faint. Farran staggered to her side and dragged her to her feet. Let me go, she thought, leave me alone, damn you. All she wanted was to pass out, drift into sleep. She didn't care about dying any more. The blow on her skull had wiped out even her sense of survival.

"Myriam," Farran gasped, "for Christ's sake try to move. We've got to get out of here."

He was holding her around the waist, her left arm hooked across his neck as they staggered toward the ocean. Myriam saw the beach tilting wildly, she saw bullets spurting into the sand from above. Her brain seemed curiously dulled, as though the blow had destroyed her sense of perception, making the world fragmented and grotesque. They stumbled across a hard flat surface, Farran holding her upright, falling sometimes, crawling a little, then rising and stumbling desperately on. There was a sharp tang in the air, salt and seaweed. She was moving by reflex now, allowing Farran to guide her as if she had lost her power of consent or denial. This is stupid, she thought. Why aren't we dead? We should have died ages ago.

Time seemed to lose itself, becoming distorted inside her skull. She remembered the beach, and the humming of bullets in the air, and the boat, a small coble moored on the sand, and Farran wallowing about at the ocean's edge, trying to push it out against the waves. Then she was lying in the bows and Farran was rowing, his face shiny with sweat. I'm very tired, she thought. So very very tired. She closed her eyes and tried to sleep, but sleep wouldn't come. Delirium came. Incoherence. She saw the shoreline bobbing gently on the peripheral of her vision. She did not understand what it was doing there, or how they had drifted so far from land, or what had happened to the men with the guns, or where Farran thought he was going.

Voices jabbered from above. Angels, she wondered? The coble struck something solid, another vessel. They were being hauled on board. Dreamily, Myriam felt hard hands lifting her over the deckrail. She smelled the pungent odour of fish, and heard the voices loud and excited in her ears. They were speaking in French. She wanted to laugh at that. French fishermen. She opened her mouth to laugh out loud, but no laugh came, only a curious rasping noise that seemed somehow disjointed, abstract. That can't be me, she thought. I don't sound like that. She closed her eyes and sank into oblivion.

THIRTEEN

It's hard to imagine that at a more peaceful time anyone would have viewed Colonel Richard Savage's takeover of the wildest, most uninhabited tract of countryside in England with anything but the wryest amusement. Savage himself had been the butt of assorted journalists in the past, all of whom, in their saner moments, would have rejoiced mightily at the prospect of this tin soldier with his half-squadron of Harrier aircraft challenging the retaliatory wrath of the entire Royal Air Force, and would undoubtedly have sat down with creative pulses twitching to compose their blackest comedy, their richest satire. As it was, in Britain that particular December, humour was at a premium, and the thought of any lunatic squatting on the Scottish Border, no matter how sparsely equipped or how flimsily supported was enough to create alarm and unrest from Land's End to John o' Groat's.

Savage's real strength lay in the Petrol Restriction Act, for few reporters were able to get anywhere near his emplacements, and those who did were turned back by the authorities who had effectively sealed off the occupied area. As a result, news reports on the colonel's resources were grossly exaggerated, based to a large degree on interviews conducted by telephone with Savage himself (a procedure which took place six or seven times a day and which, surprisingly, neither the GPO nor the government took any steps to prevent.)

In a strange way, the people almost welcomed the extraordinary development of armed insurgents carving out a portion of England's green and pleasant land for it became, in a sense, a culmination of all they had been through, a reason for their suffering. Coming so close, Savage's appearance must, they felt, be linked to the bombing of their cities, and their confusion was lost in the awareness that the misfortunes of the past were about to be resolved or exacerbated in the process of direct military action.

Meanwhile, although the army was moved into position with seemly haste, neither the Prime Minister nor the Defence Secretary seemed willing to give the order for hostilities to commence, a fact which staggered the media, unsettled the country and utterly confused Colonel Richard Savage. At Camp Fremont, he had been schooled in his campaign to the finest detail, going over the events of the first few days until he could repeat them backwards. But the one thing no one had considered was the fact that the government might not respond.

The Prime Minister was interviewed almost daily and insisted (in a monotone which made the noses of political historians twitch with suspicion) that what was happening on the Scottish Border was the work of only a very small group. Stories which began as rumours soon developed into hard fact until even *The Times* was crediting Savage with an army of several thousand and an arsenal of sophisticated weaponry which included tactical nuclear missiles.

On Friday, December 9th, Savage rose early and made his way to the office of the little country police station where his adjutant, Major Ian Forster, short, thick-set, thirty-two years old, sat directing operations on the field telephone. It was cold in the station at that time of the morning, and through the window the sky looked sharp and bright, casting shafts of wintry sunshine across the dour street.

Savage felt good, better than he had felt for nearly twenty years. He peered around the office with approval. It had been transformed into a War Operations Room, the walls hung with weather charts, Daily Routine Order Sheets, and complicated lists showing the availability of reserve vehicles and weaponry. To the left of the window was a large map of Northumbria, bristling with tiny flags. Two sergeants in shirt-sleeves pounded furiously at typewriters. A captain with a pencil tucked behind one ear came in from the other room, checked the wall charts and wandered out again.

Savage enjoyed the air of bustle and efficiency. His first memories were of the army. His father had been a soldier, and Savage remembered as a boy the smell of male sweat, dusty barracks, blancoed webbing and oiled leather. His nose had carried that smell all his life, and he could say with utter truthfulness that no memory was more dear to him than his days as a British officer, and no emotion deeper than his love of England. He'd always known he had been put here for a purpose. He was doing now what he had been born to do.

He strolled across the room to where Forster was still furiously at work on the field telephone. Despite the activity, Forster's face was calm and tranquil. Nothing ever seemed to bother him.

"How's it going, Major?" Savage asked.

"Quiet, sir."

Savage frowned. "Strange," he murmured.

Seven days had passed. Seven days and not a hint of hostile action. As far as Savage was concerned, they'd been the happiest seven days of his life, but there was still the worry of the battle to come.

The major looked at him. "Almost makes you think they're trying to wear us down," he said. "A war of nerves, sort of."

"You don't suppose the Prime Minister's lost his stomach for a fight?"

"Too much to hope for, sir. They'll be at us soon enough, we can count on that."

There was something about Major Forster that Savage did not like. It was nothing he could put a finger on, but Forster always seemed as though he knew more than he was telling. Polite and respectful, his voice nevertheless managed to convey the point that he did not consider himself inferior. It was his tone Savage objected to. It simply was not servile enough.

"Supposing they don't attack, sir?" Forster asked. "I mean, never. What then?"

Savage raised his eyebrows. The possibility was something he hadn't even considered. "I don't know," he admitted, "I'm not keen on starting a push to the west without some kind of military victory. We need that."

"So the ball's firmly in their court."

"It looks that way, Major," Savage said.

It was a damned nuisance really. He'd expected an immediate reaction. They all had, including Spengler. What was the government playing at, he wondered? If something didn't happen soon, he'd go crazy with frustration.

He took his coat from the line of wall pegs and pulled it on.

"I think I'll take a turn outside," he said. "See how our defences are shaping up."

He was about to step through the door when the field phone buzzed again. Forster reached for the receiver.

"Squirrel Five, this is Patsy One."

Savage stood where he was, watching Forster's face. Something held him, an inner sense, a premonition.

Forster listened in silence for a few moments, then he looked at Savage. His face was icily calm. "It's started, sir," he said. "Squadrons of Phantoms and Python V/STOLs have just passed over Alwinton, heading north."

Savage took a deep breath. He felt excitement throb inside his chest. At last, he thought.

"Get our planes airborne," he ordered crisply. "Alert all missile defence units. I want those fighters blasted out of the sky."

Charlie Curry heard the alarm bell even before the order came through. He was sitting in the crew-hut reading a tattered copy of *Playboy*. The sound was muffled, almost lost in the throb of Buller's radio.

"Sssshh," Curry hissed, tilting his head to one side.

Buller was busy cleaning his shoes. He spent hours a day brushing furiously as if nothing in the world mattered so much as seeing his reflection in the polished leather. He paused, one hand still clutching the soiled rag.

"Turn off the radio," Curry ordered.

Buller gave the knob a twist. The bell sounded louder, more insistent.

"Hear that?"

"Christ," said Buller. His face looked pale.

The door flung open and Terry Wainwright dashed in, gasping for breath. "We're under attack in three minutes," he shouted, his voice breaking with hysteria.

Without hesitation, they leapt to their feet and raced madly for the field outside where six Hawker Harrier jets stood in line ready for take-off. Already, their mechanics were warming up the engines. Curry glanced at the sky as he ran. Clear and sharp, and not a breath of wind. Perfect. A peach of a day. Win or lose, they couldn't ask for better.

For nearly fifteen years, Charlie Curry had been an officer in the RAF. He'd flown Lightning and Buccaneer long-range fighters, patrolling the northern half of the Air Defence Identification Zone, that invisible buffer area running the length of the East German border. He'd undergone a Harrier conversion course at the Advanced Flying School at Valley in Anglesey and had flown jump-jets as ground support for NATO forces all over Europe. At the age of thirty-one, he'd been switched from air crew to signals, and at his own request left the service on the eve of his thirty-second birthday. Like the other pilots, Curry had been carefully indoctrinated in Building 3. He felt no sense of guilt at what he was about to do, and no qualms at going into battle against the very men he'd once served with. Months of conditioning had convinced him beyond any doubt that the future of his country depended on destroying the forces in control. As he reached his aircraft and shuffled into the seat, he was filled with a genuine boyish enthusiasm for the encounter in hand. There was no machine in the world he'd rather go to war in than a Harrier, he told himself. They had two 30 mm cannon in the fuselage and four rocket-carrying wing pylons, and with a full weapon load could get off the ground in less than 350 yards. Even the Python couldn't manage that. Inside a Harrier, he could twist and turn, move sideways, stop dead in the air if he felt like it. Just let the bastards come, he thought.

The drone from the engine vibrated inside his skull. He got the green light from Control. Bottoms up, here we go. He opened the throttle and fuel cock, waiting for the exhilarating feel of the ten tons of engine thrust pushing him vertically into the sky. The adjustable nozzles were pointing downwards at the ground, but once aloft he would aim them backwards at the tail and watch the earth streak past his belly and the horizon drop swiftly out of sight until only the sky existed.

Nothing happened.

Curry frowned, his brain trying to assimilate this unexpected development. The green light flashed again. He rechecked his indicators, touching each dial with his fingertips. Sound as a bell. He glanced at the temperature gauge. Healthy. Once again, he opened the throttle, waiting for the moment of propulsion.

Nothing. What the hell?

He peered through the window. The six aircraft stood in line, their engines roaring in the crisp morning air. A flock of birds, terrified by the noise, left the cover of the nearby woods and wheeled skyward in perfect formation. His green light was flashing continually now. God Almighty, why didn't somebody move?

Curry felt his excitement turn to alarm. Three minutes was all they had, and that was an optimistic estimate. There was a click in his headset as a microphone switched on.

"Control to Kettle Hunter," a voice shouted. "Will you, for Christ's sake, get your arse into the sky."

"I can't," Curry bellowed. "My aircraft's malfunctioning."

"Check your indicators, Charlie," the voice yelled. "You must've forgotten something."

"All systems A-okay," Curry screamed back. "The damned thing's buggered, I can't move."

Another click, then a second voice came on, a pilot from one of the other aircraft. "Crimson Robin here. I'm stuck too. My throttles won't respond."

Curry felt his stomach contract. Oh my God, he thought, was it possible all the machines were defective? That was crazy. The mechanics had checked them from nose to tail. Something was happening, something strange and terrifying.

The voice came back on his headset close to hysteria now.

"Control to all aircraft. Somebody move, dammit. Anybody."

Curry tried again. Still no response. Feathery smoke drifted around the metal nose. Curry's clothes were drenched with sweat. He heard the thunder of the approaching squadron even above the roar of his own engine. A split second after, he saw them streak over the rolling horizon, flying in fighter formation. He made no attempt to get out of the cockpit. No point. Pythons moved with the speed of thought. They were done for.

He watched the aircraft tilt as they zoomed in to the attack, following their assault path admiringly with his eyes, seeing the twin streaks of flame as they let loose their rockets, hearing the sharp high-pitched whine and the *Vvvroooomph Vvrooomph* as the nearby farmhouse disintegrated, the walls swelling outwards in a spreading pumpkin of fire that burst the seams of the weatherworn timber and scattered blazing wreckage right across the open field.

Whooomph Whooomph Whooomph, the explosions came in rapid bursts, making the earth shudder with their impact, flinging trees and soil and buildings into the air like bits of flimsy confetti.

Curry watched the aircraft next to him burst apart like an egg. Direct hit. Screams of pain and terror echoed in his ears. He stared out at the shimmering inferno with a kind of numbed horror.

It didn't make sense. Nothing made sense. They'd been deceived. Hoodwinked with faulty equipment. But why?

Keeeerrrumph, another Harrier exploded, battering his eardrums, showering his windscreen with white-hot particles of steel and flesh.

"It's madness," he yelled, pounding the control panel with his fists. "Madness."

They were the last words he ever spoke. Glancing up, he spotted a Python streaking down from above. Scarlet flame jetted from its underbelly and Charlie Curry's aircraft erupted across the field, hurling glass, rubber, metal splinters and bits of Charlie Curry through the chill December air.

On the craggy sumit of Easter Tor, Captain Jock McKay

watched the Harriers going through their ritual of destruction. Jaw clenched, muscles taut with tension, he saw them pull back, wheel gracefully and come hurtling in from the north in tight formation.

"Fire dammit," he yelled. "Didn't you hear my order?"

The young sergeant operating the Grail surface-to-air missile tube stared at him with panic in his eyes. His cheeks were glistening. "Something's wrong, sir," he shouted. "It's not working."

"Christ Almighty," McKay snapped, feeling his control beginning to break. "Do I have to do every bloody thing myself?"

He pushed the sergeant out of the way and quickly checked the tube mounting. The fighter squadron had separated now, and the roar of the jets screamed in his ears as they pounced on targets along the ridges of the Cheviot Hills. The earth shuddered beneath his knees, and his facial skin twitched with alarm as pieces of shrapnel hummed and whirred through the air. The racket of the aerial bombardment was disorientating. Around the missile tube, his men flattened themselves to the ground, peering at him with tense sweaty faces. Bloody thing's turning into a fiasco, McKay thought grimly. They're picking us off like a bunch of pigeons.

"Okay," he snapped, slithering backwards. "Try again."

Shaking with fear, the sergeant raised the Grail to his shoulder. Above, the fighters were streaking low over the hilltops, picking out individual emplacements and blasting them out of existence. McKay could see mushrooms of dirt and flame as mortar crews and artillery units fell under the remorseless bombardment. What's happening here? he wondered. Why is nobody hitting back?

The sergeant chose a low-flying Python and began to track it through open sights. A red light appeared in his scanner, changing swiftly to green as the heat-seeking guide device locked on to the aircraft's exhaust fumes.

"Fire," McKay yelled with all the determination he could muster. The sergeant squeezed the trigger of the pistol grip. McKay could see the crew peering back at him, eyeballs bulging as they waited for the boost motor to propel the missile from the plastic tube. Nothing happened. Oh, Jesus.

The sergeant fumbled with the tubing, frantically dismantling the firing mechanism. His face was pale with panic.

"Captain," he shouted. "Take a look at this."

"What is it?"

"We've been sabotaged."

McKay felt his throat chill. "That's impossible," he snapped. "That missile launcher was checked less than twenty minutes ago."

"See for yourself, sir."

McKay slithered across the churned-up clay and peered at the rocket tube. Its wire-guided booster chamber was a clump of charred twisted metal, the entire interior scorched black. Some of the metal components had melted, giving the impression of stretched plasticine.

"Good God," McKay breathed.

"It's been done with some sort of explosive charge, sir," the sergeant croaked. "A small one, but big enough to be effective. It must have been wired to go off when I squeezed the trigger. We wouldn't hear the detonation because of the din."

McKay stared at him, his face muscles beginning to twitch. The thunder of the explosions seemed to shake his brain loose inside his skull. He had never heard such a nerve-stunning racket of noise

"Who's been near this thing?" he shouted.

"Nobody, sir. Not since the final check."

McKay hesitated. An unpleasant thought occurred to him. "That's when the charge must have been set."

"Seems likely, sir."

"Then it must have been done by one of our crew."

"Looks that way, sir."

"Jesus Christ."

McKay stared at the frightened mud-stained faces peering back through the smoke. They were white with terror, quivering with confusion. Was it possible one was a traitor? McKay scuttled to the field telephone. "Patsy One," he yelled into the receiver, "this is Hill 24."

Forster's voice, when it came on the line, sounded calm but muffled.

"Come in, Hill 24."

"Major," McKay shouted, "we've been sabotaged. Our damned missile unit won't function and the RAF are all over the place, blasting our emplacements one by one. It's like a fucking shooting gallery out here."

There was a faint crackling on the phone. Then Forster's voice said, "Control yourself, Captain, you're supposed to be in command. Give me a situation report."

McKay wanted to laugh hysterically. "I've just given it," he bellowed. "We've been sabotaged, can't you hear? They're shooting us to pieces, Major, and we've nothing to fight back with. Our booster chamber's blown to bits."

"Easy, Captain, easy. Are you satisfied you can't put it right?"

"Out of the question. We need a replacement and we need it fast. We're being hammered to hell."

"Well, keep at it, Captain," Forster said evenly. "I want that missile unit back in action and those squadrons neutralised by nightfall. Good luck."

With a click the line disconnected, and McKay stared at his men in disbelief. "He didn't listen," he said. "Did you hear that? He didn't listen to a word I said."

"What do we do now, sir?" the sergeant asked, flinching as earth and rubble cascaded over them.

"I don't know what the hell we *can* do except lie and pray," the captain admitted.

"But, sir, why's nobody firing back? Those aircraft are tearing us to shreds. Somebody should do something."

"Maybe they're screwed up just like us," a man suggested.

McKay felt a surge of terror. Was it possible? Were they lying here, white-eyed and sweating, without a weapon anywhere to defend themselves? The sergeant was right. Nobody *was* firing back. The Phantoms and Pythons were streaking backwards and forwards across the summits, choosing their targets with almost casual leisure.

Suddenly, chillingly, McKay realised it was true. Nothing

worked, nothing. The missile systems, the aircraft, the artillery, the tanks – like his own Grail SA-7, they had all been wrecked. Oh God, he thought. Sweet suffering Jesus, why? All these men out here, helpless, vulnerable, they would all die. The saboteurs too. Didn't they realise that? He could feel the bile rising in his chest. The sergeant was staring at him, white with fear.

"What do we do, sir? Tell us what to do."

McKay made up his mind in an instant. "Scatter and run," he yelled. "It's every man for himself."

But before he could move, a rocket hit their summit head-on. In the sickening explosion which followed, McKay's body was torn into four parts and distributed over the wreckage-strewn hilltop. Of the six-man missile crew, only the sergeant remained alive, watching the flames lick at the moor grass, his face, chest and arms sticky with the blood of those who had died around him.

"They're coming," said Corporal Wilson. His face looked pale and wretched. Lieutenant Straker squeezed his elbow reassuringly.

"Don't let them panic you. They're just as scared as we are," he said.

Nevertheless, he felt uneasy as he listened to the rumble of approaching enemy armour. It was a good spot he'd chosen, he thought. The hills crowded in around them, offering excellent cover for their Wombat anti-tank gun. They were protected on three sides. Amber streams swirled down slopes of snow-covered heather and gorse. Trees clung to jagged outcrops of rock. Before them lay a grassy water-meadow, its surface pockmarked by shell-craters where the fighter squadrons had tried to winkle them out of their sanctuary. Only their enclosed position had saved them. The rockets had ruined the hillsides but little more. Now the meadow looked like a dead man's land, shell-holes littering its surface like open sores.

Straker wondered how the units had fared. An attack like that was difficult to survive. What had happened to their own aircraft, and their surface-to-air missiles? As far as he'd been able to judge, the RAF had had a clear field. Something was wrong, Straker was certain, but he would worry about that later. For the moment he had to keep his mind on the job in hand.

The rumble of the approaching tanks grew louder. Straker studied the far rim of the meadow through his field glasses. White ribbons fluttered from the grass clumps, offering a focal point for their Wombat rangefinder. The first vehicle to cross those dancing tendrils would be pounded into shrapnel.

"Prepare to fire," Straker ordered curtly.

The rumbling intensified, almost deafening now. Drifting blankets of battle smoke obscured the sun, grim and oppressive. Straker spotted the first of the tanks lumbering over the tip of the water meadow, a massive Chieftain. It looked absurd and unwieldy, its turret even wider than its body. The lid was open, and he could see the commander's head perched above the metalwork like a tiny button. The barrel of the huge 120 mm gun gave the vehicle a slightly precarious air, as if it would topple forward at any second.

Straker held his breath. It was approaching the ribbons now. Easy, he thought. Don't rush. Wait until it's level. There.

"Fire," he shouted.

The explosion was sharp and dry on the December air, but it did not come from the gun's nozzle. Instead, a flash of flame and a puff of white acrid smoke belched from behind the firing button. The soldiers leapt back in alarm.

Straker blinked. "What happened?" he yelled.

The corporal looked back at him, his eyes bright with panic. "Something's wrong, sir," he shouted. "It's been got at."

"What d'you mean, got at?"

"Looks like sabotage. Somebody's stuck an explosive charge in there."

"Don't be an idiot. Nobody's been near that gun since we checked it ourselves less than an hour ago."

Corporal Wilson's face was pale and sweaty. "That's right, sir," he croaked, "which means it must have been done by one of us . . ."

"You're out of your mind."

"Whether I am or not, sir, makes no difference now. The bloody thing's completely buggered."

Straker turned back to the Chieftain. He saw the heavy 120 mm gun swivel into position. The range was questionable, but he didn't doubt it would be a direct hit. How could they miss? With hills on either side, all they had to do was send the shell straight up the funnel. Oh shit, he thought.

Peeeerrrdoooom, the gun went off with a thunderous roar, followed instantly by a mushroom of black smoke. Straker felt himself spinning backwards. Debris and mutilated bodies leapt into the air.

Straker lay in the heather, holding hard to his abdomen. Something was wrong there, something he could not quite distinguish. There was a gaping hole where his stomach should be. He tried to get up, but his body remained rooted to the earth. Not fair, he thought dully. Not fair at all. Damned gun spiked by one of our own team. Who'd have thought it? Just not fair.

He heard the scream of caterpillar treads as the tanks came through. Nothing to stop them now, nothing.

On the chilly hillside, with half his body blown clean away, Captain Straker laid his cheek against the snow-crusted heather and quietly died.

Savage felt the blood drain from his face. "What is going on out there?" he hissed. "What's happening?"

Major Forster didn't answer. He was too busy barking instructions into the field telephone. The little police station shook with the reverberations of distant explosions. Jet fighters screamed above their heads.

"They're running all over us, for God's sake," Savage shouted. "Why are we so helpless?"

Forster looked at him, still clutching the receiver. His face was cool. Sometimes Savage thought nothing could penetrate that icy self-control. It was almost as if Forster had expected this.

"Our equipment isn't working," Forster said calmly. "The

aircraft, the missile systems, the anti-tank guns, they've all been put out of action."

"What?" Savage couldn't believe his ears. *"What?"*

"We appear to be victims of a complex sabotage operation. Our men are unable to defend themselves. They're being shot to pieces."

"This is *insane*," Savage gasped. "That equipment was working perfectly when we left Camp Fremont. How many saboteurs are you talking about? Where have they come from?"

"It's quite impossible to say, sir. No one's had either the time or the means to identify them."

Savage felt a burning sensation drifting through his entire body, blunting his perception, blocking the signals from his brain. We've been betrayed, he thought. The din of battle hammered at his eardrums.

"What are your orders, sir?" Major Forster asked, peering up with that maddening complacency.

"Orders?" Savage echoed. His thoughts were losing definition. Stunned, he struggled to bring his brain into focus.

"Why, carry on, of course," he said vaguely. "We must carry on to the bitter end."

On the summit of Yeavering Bell, Corporal Monaghan studied his mortar crew anxiously. They looked a mess, two dead, two wounded. One of the wounded was dying fast. He'd been hit by shrapnel and was vomiting blood. They'd pulled up his shirt, displaying a skin as smooth and white as the snow around them, and above the pubic hair was a scarlet hole tinged with blue. His cheeks looked ghastly and his eyes were glazed. Monaghan knew he would never last the afternoon.

The air attack had been a nightmare. Nothing in Monaghan's life could compare with the whistling of those rockets, or the heavy whumph-whumph-whumph of their explosions.

Monaghan stared glumly at the distant summits. The back of his skull was streaked with blood where he'd banged it on a rock. He wondered how anything so meticulously planned could go so incredibly wrong. None of it made sense. There'd been no resistance, nothing at all. Their entire force had folded without a shot being fired.

Monaghan peered about him bleakly. The hill on which they sat had once housed an ancient fortress. Only the foundations remained, a small roughstone wall, completely covered with snow.

He heard a movement and lifted his head. A muffled cough rose on the thin cold air. People.

"Down," Monaghan screamed.

The sky above them erupted into life as a machine gun ripped into the silence. Bullets hissed around their ears, kicking up the snow in furious spurts.

"The mortar," Monaghan gasped. "Get it into position."

He began to belly through the soft yielding snow. It slid up his sleeves and inside his shirt. Above and around him, the air was a nightmare of noise and confusion. He tried not to think, to focus only on propping up the white 81 mm barrel. The snow kicked like an angry ocean as bullets peppered its surface.

"Now," he commanded Stevenson, "*now*."

The barrel hiccupped, but no shell emerged from its mouth. The two men looked at each other in amazement.

"Something's wrong," said Monaghan.

In the same instant, they saw a grenade trace a graceful arc in the sky and plunge into the snow barely four feet from where they were crouching. The summit exploded like a volcano. Flame belched outwards, leaping into the air in swirling columns of crimson and black. As Monaghan staggered over the top, his clothes ablaze, a single shot caught him in the chest. He spun wildly across the hillside, shuddered once and crashed motionless into the snow.

By four o'clock, it was all over. It had been a sorry muddle of a battle, made more unsavoury by the delays leading up to it, and more vicious by the cold-blooded manner in which Savage's men, defenceless, scattered in disarray, were hunted down and destroyed. No one could remember a war operation of such ruthlessness since the destruction of the Warsaw ghetto, and out of the original force of nearly four hundred, only a handful of bewildered prisoners survived. They were a sorry lot, most of them, young, dazed, fighting for something they could not even comprehend. Under guard, they shuffled with the tragic stoop of defeat past the ruins of shattered farmhouses, the blackened bodies of their comrades and the burnt-out shells of tanks and artillery which littered the snow-covered hills.

It's not easy to comprehend how any civilised government, even in the most sordid part of the greatest mess in its history would, in a rational way, conduct such savagery, but there is in the human animal a need quite separate from the physical calls of food, warmth and affection, and that is the need for vengeance. The punishment of crime is not merely to deter the offender, it also, if it is to be effective, must satisfy the victim's desire for revenge, a desire generally commensurable with the degree of the original outrage. Perhaps the Prime Minister, shrewd diplomat that he was, realised the people needed a bloodletting after their months of suffering, or perhaps the troops misinterpreted their orders, but the mopping-up after the fighting was over was brutal, mediaeval and merciless.

In his Operations Room, Colonel Savage received the news with stunned incredulity. For the first time in his life he was filled with a paralysing self-doubt as his resolution finally deserted him. He reached out, holding on to a chair for support. I'm cold, he thought. Cold.

Major Forster put down the field phone and looked at Savage with genuine compassion.

"We were set up, Forster," Savage whispered, his voice barely a croak.

Forster nodded. "I'm afraid so, sir."

"Tricked. Like a bunch of idiots.

"That's right, Colonel."

Savage's face became paler as the full import of his betrayal grew clear. "Spengler," he hissed. "Everything he said was a lie. He knew all along he was lying, but why? Why?"

211

Forster shrugged. "Who can understand the machinations of diplomacy, Colonel?" he said.

Savage looked at him sharply. For a moment his anguish was suspended. Peace of a kind eased through him, the peace that came with the ending of uncertainty, the realisation that whatever had to be faced could be faced now, measured in all its aspects.

"You knew, Forster," he whispered. It was a statement, not an accusation.

"Yes."

"All the time we were sitting here, waiting for the attack to come, you knew we were going to be betrayed."

"Yes."

"Who are you?"

"Lawrence Forster, sir."

"I mean who *are* you?"

Forster sighed. He got up and strolled to the window. His face held a look of strange sadness. "The name's genuine," he said, "but don't let the accent fool you. I'm an American citizen. I work for a department of the CIA called the Foreign Operations Co-Ordination Board."

"Spengler's man?"

"Yes, sir."

Savage ran his fingers through his hair. He felt hollow and drained, but not angry. "How was it done?" he murmured. "That equipment was in perfect working order this morning, I'm certain of it. We checked and re-checked every nut and bolt. How could those planes and missile units break down so completely? Where did the saboteurs come from?"

Foster hesitated. "It was no accident," he said. "What happened here today was set in motion weeks ago, in sensory-deprivation chambers of Building 3. Certain members of your army were conditioned to experience last-minute changes of heart on the battlefield. They destroyed their own weapons rather than face the prospect of killing fellow-countrymen. Of course each man believed he was acting independently, and had no idea he was part of a co-ordinated sabotage programme."

Savage shook his head in wonder. "Is this what we've come to?" he mused. "Have we reached the stage where we can even control the human mind?"

"Well, not completely," Forster admitted. "When it came to the test, fourteen subjects failed to respond to conditioning, but those fourteen weapons weren't sufficient to withstand the full might of the British army."

"But this whole thing," Savage said, "the build-up, the battle, our defeat, was engineered by the CIA?"

"Yes, sir."

"At least tell me why. Surely I have a right to know that."

Forster turned to look at him. "Sorry, Colonel, I can't tell you because I don't know myself. All I do know is that you've done more for your country than you'll ever realise. You haven't lost this war, sir, you've won. You saw yourself as the saviour of your people. Well, that concept is accurate." He hesitated, his face gentle, composed. "You've only one last function to fulfil," he added.

"What's that?"

Forster strode to his desk. He took out a key, unlocked the drawer and pulled it open. He reached inside, picked up a .25 calibre pistol and handed it silently to Savage. The colonel looked at the gun and looked at Forster. "I see," he whispered.

So it had come to this. Death in the grand tradition. Savage wanted to run, to hide, to lock himself away, only he knew in his heart it wouldn't work, just as he knew with penetrating certainty he would have to go through with it.

"I have no fear of dying," he said softly. "I've never feared it, never. But I hate to go . . . I like the truth, you see. I've always been fascinated by truth. It isn't easy . . . not knowing."

Major Forster didn't answer. He stared at Savage sympathetically. His eyes looked strangely moist. Savage walked to the window, still clutching the gun. He peered out at the afternoon sky, and the distant hummocks of the snow-clad Cheviots.

"My family have lived in these hills for generations, you know."

Forster was silent.

"It's wonderful country, Major," Savage said. "A shame you have to see it in such circumstances. It's immensely beautiful, rich in folklore. Did you know these hills have been the site of bloody battles and bloodier massacres since the beginning of time? They say at night you can hear the screams of the men who've died in the heather."

Savage paused. His shoulders seemed to stoop a little, and the arrogant head hung forward, lost in thought. Savage's vitality had always transcended the boundaries of age. Now, for the first time since they'd met, Forster saw him as an old man.

"Just north of here," Savage said softly, almost talking to himself, "there's a little hill with a cross on top. It's not much of a hill really, just a swell in the ground above the road that runs by Branxton Church. In summer, its slopes are clustered with mustard flowers. That's where the battle of Flodden was fought. Ten thousand fighting men were slaughtered that day. Do you know there was not a single Scottish family of importance that didn't lose someone at Flodden Field?"

He turned from the window, smiling thinly. "You see, Major, we couldn't have chosen a finer setting for our little tragedy. These hills were made for bloodshed. They absorb it, swallow it up. What happened today will soon be lost under a fresh covering of moor grass and heather. Man makes his paltry changes, but the hills always take back what is their own."

He walked over and stood in front of Forster. He was still smiling. "Give me your hand," he said.

The major hesitated.

"Come on," Savage chuckled, "you can't refuse a dying man."

They shook hands.

"Goodbye, Major Forster, whoever you are."

"Goodbye, sir," Forster said quietly.

He stood where he was as Savage left the room, listening to the footsteps scraping on the concrete stairs as the colonel made his way to the cells below. Forster stood like that for a very long time. When the shot came, it sounded muffled, like the snapping of a twig in the dark. Forster sighed. He closed the desk drawer and carefully locked it. Then he walked to the filing cabinet, took out a bottle of Scotch and poured himself a stiff drink.

FOURTEEN

Five months after Savage's death, on Wednesday May 24th, the British Prime Minister paid an official visit to Washington DC. He was met at the airport by the President, and after inspecting the guard of honour was driven first to Capitol Hill where he chatted to several congressmen, and later to the White House where he planted a tree on the South Lawn and conducted a press conference in the Oval Room on the second floor. The Prime Minister looked relaxed and happy, and parried all queries about the recent unrest in Britain with the resilience and sharp wit that had made him famous throughout the world.

It was several hours later, when they moved into the Lincoln Sitting Room, that the President and Prime Minister were alone together for the first time. The President looked tired.

"My God, how I hate these official circuses," he complained, crossing the deep pile carpet. "They give me a pain in the neck. Take the weight off your feet, Nigel. I don't know about you, but I feel I need a drink."

The British Prime Minister made no attempt to sit down immediately. Instead, he wandered around the room, peering with interest at the pictures on the wall.

"I'd love a whisky, Warren," he murmured.

"Scotch?"

"I thought I might try your special brew."

The President chuckled. "Consider yourself privileged," he said. "I keep that only for distinguished guests."

He opened the cocktail cabinet and filled two glasses, dropping in ice from the freezer compartment. The British Prime Minister settled himself in an elegant Penshurst armchair and

216

stretched his legs. He looked unmoved by the strain of the afternoon. The President handed him his drink.

"Well," he said, "how's it shaping up, Nigel? Life getting back to normal over there?"

"Splendidly, thank you. Your assessment of the British temperament was bang on target. Give them an adversary to fight and they pull together like a team of Oxford crewmen. The docks are back in operation, the power stations functioning normally, unemployment's down by twenty-four per cent. Strike has become a dirty word. There's a spirit in the people I haven't seen since the war. There are even signs that we're beginning to curb inflation."

"We'll arrange a loan to help alleviate that," the President said, settling himself on the Hawkhurst sofa. "Supplies getting through okay?"

"Perfectly, with our own merchant fleet back in action."

"Oil?"

"No problem. Since the collapse of the revolt in Oman, the Strait of Hormuz has reopened. Everything, from start to finish, went like clockwork, Warren."

The President sighed. "Well, I guess I should be thankful for that," he said.

The Prime Minister looked at him, his face softening into an expression of sympathy. It was a face that seldom changed to any vast degree. Emotions were registered by a twitch of the eyebrows, a crinkling of the lips. They were never involuntary. His facial muscles, and everything they conveyed were under the complete control of his conscious mind.

"Still blaming yourself, Warren?" he asked.

"Aren't you?"

The Prime Minister shrugged. "It was a dirty decision, I know, but that's what leadership's all about."

"Dirty?" the President exclaimed, "Dirty's hardly the word. All those people dead."

"Be reasonable, Warren, we kept casualties down to a minimum, and even then they were the drop-outs, the disaffected, the petty criminals, the kind of people any society can well do without. I'm not saying it was desirable but, good God,

Warren, what was the alternative? Utter disaster. The way things were going in Britain, it was becoming impossible for any government to establish order. It had to be done, Warren, for your sake as well as ours."

The President regarded him shrewdly. "I wish I had your faith, Nigel."

Somewhere outside, a plane buzzed by. Its engine sounded shrill and distorted, a vibration sensed inside the skull rather than the eardrums. The Prime Minister put down his glass and stood up. He walked to the fireplace and stood with his back against it, hands in pockets. There was no fire in the grate, only a log-and-ash structure lit by electricity to give the illusion of flames. The light cast orange patterns across the Prime Minister's legs.

"Poor Warren," he said, "you think we can rule nations the way the British play cricket? In the game of politics, people are eggs. Shuffle them around and some get cracked. It's messy and regrettable, but you can't avoid it."

The President looked at him coolly. "I've always believed society can only survive on the belief that human life is sacred."

The Prime Minister smiled. "It's impossible to survive without killing something, Warren. The earth's a living planet. Push a spade into the soil and you kill."

His smile, the President thought, was the most irritating thing about him, for he seemed to switch it on at will, aiming it around the room like a searchlight, picking out his target and homing in with the inexorability of a cruise missile.

"You musn't hold yourself responsible," the Prime Minister said. "The entire project, after all, was a British idea – my idea – though of course, only selected members of my Cabinet know that."

The President shook his head in wonder. "You're a cold man, Nigel. Sometimes your coldness chills even me."

"I don't mind your contrition, Warren, but you do realise it would be disastrous if even a hint of what actually happened ever leaked?"

"Don't worry. Joe Spengler's a meticulous man. He's

developed the compartmentation principle to a fine art. There's nobody alive, apart from a small chosen handful, who knows the real details."

"In which case," the Prime Minister said blandly, "I have drawn my country back from the brink, saved it from anarchy and humiliation, and at the cost of what? A few misfits and agitators? I'm not proud of what I've done, but I refuse to feel guilty about it." He smiled again, and despite himself the President shuddered.

"Recriminations are admirable among ordinary people, Warren. But in men who rule nations, they're a sign of weakness."

The boat was small. It was an ancient dinghy, fourteen feet long, no more, with an Evinrude outboard that had come off a cruiser, but she was all Marcel had and he nursed her into harbour as if she'd been the *Queen Mary*. The hot May sun shimmered off the sea. Along the shoreline the multi-storey hotels looked like tombstones. Yachts danced close to the beach.

Farran took the painter and went up to the bow. The little French harbour drew near, a fairytale harbour with a fairytale town climbing the hill behind it. The houses were small and neat and white, and they baked in the heat with their shutters closed.

They chugged between the piers and Marcel nudged the boat gently alongside the quay. Farran leapt ashore and made the painter fast to the metal bollard. A handful of tourists watched him curiously. Marcel tossed him a rope from the stern and he fixed that too. Marcel shouted something in French that Farran couldn't understand. He was laughing. They'd had a good catch, and he was in fine spirits.

They unloaded the fish and the tourists crowded round to watch. They cleaned and gutted them on the quayside, tossing the entrails into a bucket of salt water to be tipped back into the harbour.

The sky was dark by the time they'd finished, and they walked up through the town in the late evening, leaving the seafront hotels behind and entering the old walled city where the fishermen lived.

Marcel puffed at his pipe, his wind-and-sea-tanned face glowing in the evening light. He wore a navy-blue singlet, denim trousers and frayed rope sandals. His shoulders were wide and square, his arms strong as tree trunks. His white hair was bleached by the sun.

"Did you think on what I said last night?" he asked.

"No," Farran answered.

"You young men. Always the same. Never a thought to the future. When you get to my age, you realise the past is littered with missed opportunities."

"I don't think about the future much," Farran admitted.

They passed a café with tables laid on its terraces. There were red-checked tablecloths and scarlet candles stuck in wine bottles. The waiters stood in groups waiting for the first customers to arrive. The terrace was brightly lit and looked cheery in the cobbled square.

"I will soon be an old man," Marcel was saying patiently. "I cannot go on for ever. Once I was the best fisherman on the coast, the strongest too. But age is the great equaliser. Soon the boat may be too much for me alone. A boat is freedom, Jacques, a boat is security. A man with a boat will never starve. That is worth thinking about. You would be a full partner. A half-share in every catch. Perhaps we could make enough to buy a schooner. Expansion, Jacques, always expansion. Nothing in life can stand still."

The street steepened and narrowed, the houses high and white on either side. Women watched them from wrought-iron balconies. The choking heat of the afternoon had slipped away, and the cool of evening was like a salve on Farran's face and throat.

"How long have you been with us, Jacques? Six months?"

"Five."

"Aren't you happy here?"

"Happy enough," said Farran, "but you don't know anything about me. You don't know what I did before I came, or what I may be forced to do when I leave."

Marcel paused. He took the pipe from his mouth and tapped out its contents against the wall. He said, "You think I am a complete fool, Jacques? You think I do not know that you are in some kind of trouble? That night we found you, both of you, in the little boat, you were half-demented, half out of your mind. I have seen you sit at the window for hours, staring out to sea. I have seen you at the harbour, always watching the road out of town. Always watching, Jacques, and waiting. You are waiting for someone and you are afraid."

His wrinkled eyes looked shrewd and thoughtful. Farran walked on.

"There is nothing to fear here, Jacques," said Marcel. "We are your friends. We have never asked questions. We have accepted you both as you are, a couple with no past. A couple born five months ago, in a tiny boat, that is true?"

"It's true," said Farran.

"Then stop running. You are safe here. We want you to stay, we want you to make this your home."

Farran looked down the hill at the housetops descending in terraced confusion. The old town was a sanctuary. Tourists seldom entered. Inside these walls, he felt protected.

"I'll think about it," he promised. "Give me time."

The house Farran had rented stood at the top of the hill, just below the church. It was a fine house, tall and very clean, with red shutters and a sloping roof. There were flower boxes below each window. From the doorway, you could see boats dancing in the harbour below.

Myriam was cooking in the kitchen when he entered, stirring the contents of a huge pot. She came up smiling and kissed him on the lips. "How's the shoulder, darling?" she asked.

"Stiff today," he grunted, "but getting better."

"Go and bath. Dinner's almost ready."

Later, when they were eating, Farran murmured, "Marcel has offered me a partnership. A half share in the boat."

Myriam stared at him. "What did you say?"

"I said I'd think about it."

"Will you really? Or was that just a put-off?"

He looked at her, his eyes sullen. "I lied," he said. "I can't accept. My shoulder's practically healed, and your ribs are fine now. We've no right to be here, you know that."

She felt a shudder go through her body. It was the moment she'd been dreading. She'd watched it build inside him month by month like a slow-burning fuse ready to burst into flame. Without the cassette tapes to reactivate their response patterns, the effects of their indoctrination had worn off, but both Myriam and Farran had been left with a new and disquieting uncertainty. Huge gaps had opened up in their memory banks, and they were each filled with a sense of bewilderment and a fear of the outside world.

"Can't we stay here?" she whispered pitifully. "We're happy here, Jack. We're safe."

Farran threw down his fork. "How can you stand it," he snapped, "knowing what we know, knowing what those bastards did to us."

She bit her lips together, trying to stop the tears coming. She'd always known it would come to this. Sooner or later, Farran's fury had been bound to explode. She'd sensed it, felt its force transmitting itself to her own body.

"We know nothing, Jack," she cried, "nothing. What can we tell? What can we say without turning ourselves into laughing stocks?"

Farran looked dark and hostile. She'd never seen his face so haunted. He'd lost weight, and his eyes seemed lost and helpless, filled with a sullen fury as if he had a fire smouldering inside and couldn't rest until it had burned itself out.

"I'm going back, Myriam," he whispered. "I'm going back and I'm going to find out what happened, and why. Then I'm going to bawl it from the rooftops until the whole world knows the truth. It's the only thing that's kept me going. I can't settle, can't think about anything until it's done."

Myriam looked at him, her eyes troubled. Tears ran down her cheeks. She reached out and gently squeezed his hand.

"You're right, darling," she whispered. "I'm being selfish. We can't hide like squirrels for the rest of our lives. As soon as your shoulder's completely healed, we'll go back together.

We'll tell everything we know. We'll make somebody listen. Maybe then we'll find some peace."

Farran nodded. Satisfied, he picked up his fork and resumed eating. Myriam sat for a long time staring at her plate. Even when Farran finished and went into the kitchen to make coffee she remained where she was, motionless and silent. The bell in the church tower rang once at nine o'clock. The clang echoed across the village, fading slowly, drifting out to sea across the evening tide. Myriam raised her head, listening miserably. She thought it sounded like the knell of doom.

A selection of bestsellers from SPHERE

FICTION
UNHOLY CHILD   Catherine Breslin £1.75 ☐
THE GRAIL WAR   Richard Monaco £1.75 ☐
WARLORDS   Bob Langley £1.25 ☐
TO LOVE AGAIN   Danielle Steel £1.25 ☐
THE ELDORADO NETWORK   Derek Robinson £1.50 ☐

FILM AND TV TIE-INS
LLOYD GEORGE   David Benedictus £1.25 ☐
RAISE THE TITANIC!   Clive Cussler £1.50 ☐
BUCK ROGERS
IN THE 25TH CENTURY   Addison E. Steel   95p ☐
BUCK ROGERS 2:
THAT MAN ON BETA   Addison E. Steel   95p ☐
CLOSE ENCOUNTERS OF
THE THIRD KIND   Steven Spielberg   85p ☐

NON-FICTION
SUPERLEARNING   Sheila Ostrander &
                              Lynn Schroeder with
                               Nancy Ostrander £1.75 ☐
WHAT NEXT, DOCTOR?   Robert Clifford £1.00 ☐
MENACE: The Life and Death
of the Tirpitz   Ludovic Kennedy £1.25 ☐
THE BREAST BOOK   Anthony Harris £1.50 ☐
MANDY   Mandy Rice-Davies
                             with Shirley Flack £1.25 ☐
NAZI GOLD   Ian K. Sayer &
                             H. L. Seaman with
                             Frederick Nolan £1.50 ☐

*All Sphere books are available at your local bookshop or newsagent,
or can be ordered direct from the publisher. Just tick the titles you
want and fill in the form below.*

Name _____

Address _____

_____

Write to Sphere Books, Cash Sales Department, P.O. Box 11,
Falmouth, Cornwall TR10 9EN

Please enclose cheque or postal order to the value of the cover price
plus:

UK: 30p for the first book, 15p for the second and 12p per copy for
each additional book ordered to a maximum charge of £1.29

OVERSEAS: 50p for the first book and 15p for each additional
book

BFPO & EIRE: 30p for the first book, 15p for the second book plus
12p per copy for the next 7 books, thereafter 6p per book.

*Sphere Books reserve the right to show new retail prices on covers
which may differ from those previously advertised in the text or
elsewhere, and to increase postal rates in accordance with the PO.*